AN IDEAL PRESENT

by

SERENITY WOODS

ISBN-13: 978-1522908173
ISBN-10: 152290817X

DEDICATION

To Tony & Chris, my Kiwi boys.

CONTENTS

Chapter One

"I feel as if I've stepped into *Invasion of the Body Snatchers*," Ophelia said with a smile.

The doctor in the white coat paused in the process of paying for his muffin and looked over the top of his dark-framed glasses at her. His frown suggested confusion rather than amused interest, as she'd hoped.

In the background, someone was playing Eartha Kitt's *Santa Baby* in their office. She fought the urge to sing it to him, not sure it would help her situation, and tapped the paper bag in his hand. "Since when have you ever bought a savory muffin? You always pick sweet. Blueberry or chocolate usually. Clearly, you're a duplicate from an alien seed pod."

Okay, so maybe it wasn't the funniest joke in the world, but she'd expected a polite smile if nothing else. The frown remained in place, however. Either he thought her sense of humor severely lacking, or she'd weirded him out with her observation of his baked goods.

"Sorry," she mumbled, admitting defeat. Grimacing, she turned on her heel and walked back through the corridors to the wing of the hospital where she worked.

Once inside, she tossed her bagel onto her desk, flopped into her chair, and stared at the clock. Ten thirty. Far too early to admit the day was doomed and go home.

She blew out a long breath. Was she really surprised the cute doctor hadn't laughed at her joke? How long had they been meeting at the snack cart—nearly a year? And he'd barely said two words to her in all that time that didn't involve food or the weather. Clearly, he wasn't interested, and it was about time she took the hint.

1

She leaned forward and covered her face with her hands. It was irrelevant anyway. She was hardly in the right place to start seeing someone. She might have been separated from her husband since June, but it had proved surprisingly difficult to extricate herself from the emotional ties to her ex.

It didn't help that even though Dillon had moved out, he was always at the house. She felt as if she couldn't object—he was either seeing their daughter, which of course he had every right to do, or carrying out the occasional bit of building work to improve the house for when they put it up for sale. But she knew it was all a pretense, because he'd made it quite clear that although he was willing to let her have some time apart, he didn't want the marriage to end.

"You'll always be my girl," he'd said to her only a few weeks ago when he'd tried to persuade her to go out to dinner with him for his birthday. She'd declined, but she'd felt bad about it. When he'd moved out, she'd thought it would draw a line under their marriage, and her emotions might finally be able to level out after the rollercoaster ride she'd been on for well over a year. But six months later, she still felt torn in two every time she saw him. He represented comfort and security, which were not to be sniffed at. She knew every little thing about him and in many ways that was reassuring in a relationship. He was Summer's father, and of course Summer would prefer the two of them to stay together. And it wasn't as if he had some immense flaw that had forced them apart—he wasn't an alcoholic or a gambler, he was a good looking guy, and he was decent in bed.

And yet all the million-and-one tiny reasons that had driven her to tell him it was over were still there. The jealousy, the possessiveness, the superior way he had of talking to her occasionally as if she was stupid, the nasty, cruel side of him that only came through when they argued. She knew that if she asked him to move back home, the first time they had an argument and he twisted her words the way he always had, she would regret her decision, and it would be even harder to convince him to leave a second time.

Then she thought of Summer, who missed her daddy, and her throat tightened.

She swallowed hard. She'd made the right choice, and this was one of the very few cases where she felt she had to put herself first if she didn't want to spend another year feeling miserable and depressed.

Being on her own was scary, but she shouldn't let that be the reason she stayed with Dillon. It would be worse for Summer if her parents remained together but argued all the time.

She'd known him since they were in high school, and he'd been her first real boyfriend. For seven years, she'd compromised and negotiated her way through their marriage until she'd forgotten who she was and what she wanted. She needed time alone, a fresh start, to rediscover the Ophelia that hopefully still existed beneath the mum and wife. The last thing she needed was to start dating again.

Sighing, she lowered her hands, ready to start work. Then she inhaled sharply at the sight of the cute doctor leaning against the doorjamb, watching her.

"Oh." She stared at him, stunned into silence. He'd never once come to this part of the hospital. And it didn't look as if he was here on business. He didn't march up to her desk and give her any paperwork. He didn't speak. He didn't even smile. He just stood there, leaning, watching her.

"I'm sorry about the alien joke," she said, wondering if he'd come to tell her off. "It sounded funnier in my head."

"It *was* funny," he said. His deep, gravelly voice sent a shiver down her spine. "I just thought you were comparing me to the duplicates in the story."

She blinked. As far as she remembered, the alien duplicates had been devoid of all human emotion. "What do you mean? Why would I compare you to them?"

"It wouldn't be the first time."

She wasn't sure what to make of that. "Well, I wasn't. It was purely a muffin-based gag."

He nodded, although he still didn't smile. Then he raised the hand not holding the paper bag with his muffin. He touched the top button of his coat. Slowly, he popped it through the buttonhole, then continued down until all the buttons were undone. Once the white coat hung open, he flicked back the side of it and slid his hand into the pocket of his well-worn jeans.

Aware that her jaw had dropped at his pseudo-striptease, Ophelia closed her mouth and took the opportunity to admire him. She estimated he was maybe six-three or four, but it was the geeky scientist look he sported that tended to draw her attention rather than his height, with his dark-rimmed rectangular glasses, longish, slightly scruffy hair, and vacant look, as if he was constantly trying to calculate the value of pi to a thousand decimal places in his head.

He looked like the kind of guy who might have worn a faded T-shirt under his coat with the logo of some nerdy computer game, but to her surprise he wore one of the performance-fit All Blacks rugby tops, and it clung to an impressively flat abdomen and a broad, muscular chest. She hadn't expected that, either. He didn't look the type who spent hours at the gym, but there were definitely muscles showing through the clingy fabric.

His jeans were tight, too, emphasizing muscular thighs that could squeeze a girl to death. Well-worn Converses finished the look, giving him an air of casual indifference. He didn't care what he wore, but it didn't stop him wearing it well.

She lifted her gaze back up to his face. Now he looked slightly nonplussed, as if the reason for her lazy perusal eluded him. He had no idea how sexy he looked.

"What can I do for you?" she asked softly.

He pushed himself off the doorjamb and walked toward her desk. "I hear you're leaving."

He knew she was leaving?

Wait, he knew who she was?

Act cool, Ophelia. She leaned forward, intending to rest her chin on her hand, but her elbow missed the table and she almost fell off her chair. He raised an eyebrow.

Face burning, she leaned back and cleared her throat. "Yes. Second week in January."

To her surprise, he pushed the contents of the corner of her desk into the middle and sat on the edge. "Why?"

Ophelia tried not to stare at the jumble of spilled pens and paper clips that rested very near his muscular thigh. "I have a new part-time job nearer to my daughter's school. She has—"

"Cystic Fibrosis, yeah I know," he said. "How is she?"

Her jaw dropped. Until now, she'd assumed he hadn't even known she existed. How was he aware of her daughter's condition? "Um, she's had a few chest infections this year, so her doctor recommended I start upping her physiotherapy sessions to three times a day. It's just too far to travel from here to see her at lunch time."

"Fair enough." He looked at the ground for a moment. Then, to her surprise, he slid his glasses off, folded them, and slipped them into his top pocket before looking at her.

She inhaled slowly, entranced by his beautiful deep brown eyes. Wow, the guy was gorgeous. Yes, there was something slightly geeky about him, but after being married to a rough-and-ready builder for seven years she found his gentle manner and intelligence incredibly attractive.

He studied her face for a long moment, and she realized that whereas a blank expression on Dillon's face tended to indicate an absence of thought, in this guy it meant he was contemplating what to say.

"What are you doing this evening?" he asked eventually.

It was such a clumsy question that it took a few seconds for her to understand what was going on.

Slowly, her lips curved up in a smile. It was extremely unlikely she'd be busy on a Wednesday evening, unless he counted her and Summer watching *Frozen* for the umpteenth time before falling asleep in front of the TV. "I don't have anything planned."

"Okay. I wondered if you and your daughter would like to come out for a drink. Well, obviously, your daughter wouldn't like an alcoholic drink, but maybe we could go to, I don't know, McDonald's or something, and she could have one of those Happy Meal things. You know, with a toy."

He looked alarmed at his inability to express himself, as if he couldn't stop his mouth from moving, and the words were just tumbling out.

"Are you asking me on a date?" she said, trying not to chuckle.

He scratched the back of his neck. "Apparently it's difficult to tell."

That made her laugh. He was so sweet. She felt as if they were fifteen and he was trying to ask her to the school ball.

Briefly, an image of Dillon flashed in her mind, and she felt a flicker of guilt at how hurt he'd be if she dated anyone else. And hadn't she just told herself she needed some time alone?

But the cute doctor's gaze rested on her, warm and interested, and her resolve melted. She and Dillon were separated, and she'd made it quite clear she wanted their marriage to be over. It *was* over. Maybe going out with someone else would help her to move on.

"I didn't think you even knew who I was," she murmured.

He looked at the paper bag in his hand. "I don't like muffins."

"Sorry?"

"I don't eat them. Luckily, my colleagues in research do."

He was telling her that he went to the snack cart so he could see her. Every day, for a year! Warmth spread through her as if she'd drunk a large glass of Scotch.

She smiled. "I'd love to go out. I'm not sure I can get a babysitter at such short notice, though, so it might have to be McDonald's a little earlier, I'm afraid, if you want to make it today."

"That's great. I've always wanted to try a chicken nugget."

She raised her eyebrows. "You've never had chicken nuggets?"

"Nope. Never been to McDonald's. Or Burger King. Or Pizza Hut."

"Good Lord."

"I've been told I'm completely disconnected from modern civilization. I feel I should point this out now in case you'd rather back away while there's still time."

Was he being serious? *It wouldn't be the first time*, he'd said when referring to the alien duplicates, so clearly other people had struggled with his apparent lack of emotion. But his eyes were filled with warmth, and a gut feeling told her he just had an incredibly wry sense of humor that for whatever reason didn't reflect in his features. What a strange guy. And yet her life had been filled with worry and disappointment and sadness for so long that the thought of getting to know him better and injecting a little romance into her day brought a lightness to her heart.

"I'll risk it," she said.

Did she imagine it, or did his expression flicker briefly with relief? "Shall I pick you up from your house at, say, six? Or is that too late? I have no idea what time children go to bed."

"Six will be fine."

"Cool." He stood and attempted to help her rearrange the items he'd knocked over on her desk.

Their hands bumped, and her cheeks warmed. "It's okay, I'll do it," she said.

"Sure." He ran a hand through his hair and headed for the door.

"Hey," she called out, "I don't even know your name."

He stopped and turned around for a moment, shoving his hand back in his pocket. "Charlie," he said. "Charlie King. See you later." He walked away and disappeared around the corner.

Only then did she realize she hadn't told him where she lived. How would he know where to pick her up? It was really odd how he...

She blinked a few times. Wait a minute. Charlie King?

Her jaw dropped again. Brock, Charlie, and Matt King were three brothers who ran the company called Three Wise Men that designed medical equipment specifically for children.

Brock King was the consultant pediatrician specializing in respiratory diseases who'd first diagnosed her daughter with CF. Matt King had written a series of children's books called *The Toys from Ward Seven*, and the new medical equipment was decorated with his characters, with the hoping of making it less scary for kids.

Charlie King was the brains behind the design. Ophelia knew that throughout the hospital he was famous for having an IQ that was one point off Einstein's. With Brock's help, it had been his invention of a revolutionary new asthma inhaler that had catapulted the company into success. All hospitals in New Zealand and a few in Australia now contained Three Wise Men equipment, and there was talk of expanding the business to Europe and maybe even America.

But the fact that stunned her the most was connected to the charity called We Three Kings that the brothers ran. The charity funded research into respiratory diseases, and it paid for wishes to come true for terminally-ill children. It also had a website with chat rooms where parents of sick children could talk to each other, as well as ask advice of doctors out of hours. The site had grown from having a few hundred members to around fifty thousand, and many parents found it a comfort to keep in contact with others who were also struggling to cope with looking after sick kids.

The three brothers were known to go on there under pseudonyms, and Ophelia had spoken many times to Caspar—the name Charlie King used online. That's how he knew about her daughter. She hadn't mentioned leaving the hospital though, had she? So he must have asked around to discover that piece of information. He was quite flirty online—strange when he appeared to be so inept at it in real life!

She sat back in her chair, her mind whirling. A few months ago, the New Zealand Herald had published an article on the three King brothers, praising them for their ceaseless charity work, as the guys all visited hospitals dressed as Ward Seven characters to cheer up sick kids.

The article had also stated they were thought to be billionaires, and that all three of them were single. Since then, she was sure they'd been inundated with women hoping to snag a rich husband. They must get propositioned hundreds of times a day.

And yet Charlie had known who she was, and had come to ask her out.

Okay, McDonald's wasn't exactly the romantic destination she would have picked, but she was deeply touched that he hadn't assumed she'd just dump her daughter to go out with him. He'd included Summer in his plans, and that meant more to her than anything else he could have said or done.

Leaning on the table, she covered her mouth with her hands. She was going on a date with Charlie King, a gorgeous billionaire genius philanthropist who'd never eaten a chicken nugget in his life.

Oh my God. What was she going to wear?

Chapter Two

"You're taking her to McDonald's?" Brock grinned. "Nice one."

Charlie leaned back, balanced his laptop on his legs, and propped his feet on the chair opposite. "Never let it be said I don't know how to show a girl a good time."

Both his brothers laughed. It was early afternoon the same day, and the three of them were talking on Skype. They usually caught up a few times a week late at night once they all got home but, at the weekend, Brock had finally convinced Charlie to ask Ophelia out on a date. It had taken Charlie a few days to pluck up the courage, but regular phone calls from his brother routinely nagging him into it had helped. When Brock had discovered his socially inept brother had actually gone through with it, he'd patched Matt in on the call so they could celebrate together.

Brock was speaking from his office in the children's hospital in Auckland about half a mile away from Charlie. Matt worked from his spacious home in the Bay of Islands, several hours' drive away, and behind him Charlie could see the picturesque town of Russell and the Pacific Ocean sparkling blue.

Charlie's office lay at the back of the hospital building, a tiny cave without any windows and with books and papers strewn over the desk and floor. The hospital board—embarrassed by the amount of money the King brothers brought into the place and wanting to reward Charlie for his work—had offered him a huge, prominent office in the center of the laboratories, with leather furniture, a view over the grassy courtyard, and a secretary of his own. Charlie had refused. He loved his tiny retreat and spent most of his time in the lab anyway. Also, out of all three brothers he was the least interested in money and appearance. His iPod nano for listening to music and his iPad for reading were all he needed to keep him happy.

Well, almost all. Some regular sex wouldn't go amiss.

"When was the last time you went on a date?" Matt asked.

Charlie pushed his glasses along the bridge of his nose and thought about it. "What year is it?"

Brock laughed, and Matt rolled his eyes. "God help her, poor girl."

"Come on, that's not fair. I'm not completely useless."

As if they were a mirror image, they both raised an eyebrow.

Charlie sank his hands into his hair. "You're right. I am completely useless. One of you needs to come with me to tell me what to say."

Brock chuckled. "You'll be okay. Just be yourself."

"But not as geeky," Matt advised.

"Oh God. I'm doomed."

"Why are you so useless with women?" Brock asked. "I've never figured it out."

"No idea. I'd be fine if I could take them straight to the bedroom. It's the conversation stuff I can't do."

"Just keep asking her questions," Brock said. "Get her talking about herself."

"Good idea."

"Compliment her on her hair and shoes," Matt suggested.

"Why would she want me to compliment her on her shoes? Wouldn't she rather I tell her she had a nice arse or something?"

"Charlie," Brock warned, "please promise not to tell her she has a nice arse on the first date."

"I'm not promising anything of the sort. It's worked before."

"Yeah and look how well that ended," Matt said.

Charlie fell silent as he thought about Lisette. Tall, busty, and with legs all the way to the ground, she'd shot through his solar system like a comet, blazing so bright he'd had stars in his eyes. The two of them couldn't have been more mismatched, though. She'd talked incessantly about celebrities and fashion and other things about which he knew precisely nothing, and then she'd grown angry because he wouldn't talk to her about every little thing going on inside his head. That had completely puzzled him, because ninety-nine percent of the time he'd been thinking about issues like whether overuse of corticosteroid preventers increased the chance of osteoporosis, and why would he want to talk to her about that?

Usually, he had no complaints from his partners in bed, but for the first time in his life things had gone terribly wrong there, too. He didn't want to think about that now, though.

"Point taken," he said. "No comments about her butt."

Brock smiled. "I have a feeling you and Ophelia are going to hit it off. She's nice. Very genuine and down-to-earth."

"I'm going to miss her at the breakfast cart," Charlie said. "It was the highlight of my day."

"If things go well, maybe you'll still be seeing her every morning," Matt pointed out.

"I doubt I'll be able to convince her to stay. She's leaving because of Summer."

"No, you idiot. I meant maybe you'll be waking up with her every day."

"Oh. Ah. One step at a time, I think."

The guys laughed. "Well, good luck," Brock said. "Let us know how it goes."

"Will do."

They went on to talk about their visits to various hospitals the day before. Each of them had dressed up as one of the characters from Matt's Ward Seven books to cheer up the sick kids. Brock had swapped with Matt because he'd wanted to meet Erin, the mum of a boy who'd been admitted to Whangarei Hospital after an asthma attack. He'd been communicating with her online through the forums for some time and, by his smile, the meeting had gone very well.

Charlie was pleased for his brother. Brock's wife had died a few years ago from breast cancer, and he'd been so devastated that Charlie had wondered whether he'd ever be able to move on again, but it looked as if he might finally have taken a step back into the land of the living. Charlie looked up to his brothers where relationships were concerned, assuming they were both more skilled than him in the art of love.

However, Brock then admitted he'd offered to pay for a night away in a hotel for Erin's birthday the following week. He was waiting to see if she would say yes. Apparently she was concerned about accepting such an expensive gift from a man she hardly knew.

Charlie didn't see a problem with what Brock had done, but Matt called him a fucking idiot and said she was going to think he expected sex, and he should just have bought her flowers and chocolates. After a brief argument, Brock swore back at him and hung up.

"At least you're not the only one who's useless with women," Matt said after a short silence.

"That's scant consolation," Charlie replied. "How come you're not a romantic disaster like me and Brock?"

"Pure skill. Gotta go. Break a leg tonight."

"Sure. Catch you later." Charlie ended the call.

He lifted the laptop onto the table, leaned back in his chair, and stared at the ceiling.

Both he and Brock might have considered Matt the leading expert on women, but the truth was that Matt had never been in a long term relationship either. He always ended an affair after a few months, so he obviously had commitment issues.

Charlie sighed, wondering if the Kings were particularly useless, or if all guys had problems understanding women. He'd never lived with a girl, had never had to deal with all the complications of putting another person first. All his relationships had been short-lived casual friendships that had occasionally morphed into more before the girl had broken it off, stating, "I don't think this is going to work out," while promising, "but we can still be friends." Following which they'd run a mile and he'd never seen them again.

He just didn't understand women. Or, rather, they didn't understand him. They took his absent-mindedness as neglect and his thoughtfulness as reservation, and he'd been called cold, heartless, and infuriating, often all three by the same woman. And he wasn't any of those things—or at least, he didn't think he was. He wasn't cold or heartless, anyway. He understood how he might appear infuriating, but it certainly wasn't intentional. He just had a lot on his mind.

That didn't mean he didn't value the women in his life, but his brain resented thinking about more than one thing at a time. He knew he was smart, and if God had given him the ability to use his brain to help people, it seemed like a sin not to use it. But while he was working on a project—which was most of the time—he didn't want to mess with his mind by thinking about feelings and emotions. They confused and distracted him, so he tended to ignore them, and that's where the problems started.

Maybe it was time he gave up on the dating game. He couldn't think of a single thing he had to offer a woman, apart from his money, and he didn't want any woman who only wanted him for his cash anyway. Part of him longed for the sort of relationship he'd observed Brock have with Fleur, his late wife. He yearned for that casual intimacy, and he wanted the confidence and security that would come from understanding his partner and knowing they understood him. From trusting someone else, and knowing it didn't matter what he said—his partner wouldn't take it the wrong way because she would know how his brain worked.

Was there somebody out there like that? He thought of Ophelia, with her curvy figure, her gorgeous, tight butt, her long brown hair that looked as if it were made of melted chocolate, and her light green eyes that gave him goosebumps whenever they looked at him.

He'd liked her since the moment he'd laid eyes on her over a year ago, but when he'd asked around he'd discovered she was married, so he'd had to content himself with admiring her from afar. He'd found out she was separated the same day he'd found out she was leaving. Typical. But Brock had talked him into asking her out anyway ("Seize ye rosebuds, Charlie,") and after several days of pacing his office, Charlie had eventually plucked up the courage to do so.

Perhaps he should have accepted that her leaving the hospital was a sign he was supposed to be alone. Maybe God had given him an ultra-efficient brain on the proviso that he didn't burden the female race with his attempts at romance.

If that was the case, then He shouldn't have given Charlie working equipment. He only had to think about Ophelia's butt in her pencil skirt and his body went into overdrive. And as for her breasts… They were just the right size for a man's hands. They'd feel like soft, plump pillows in his palms, and he could imagine the way her nipples would harden when he ran his tongue over them…

He shifted in his seat and adjusted his jeans. He'd saved lives with his inventions—he was a real-life superhero. But he'd happily forego the cape and tights for some occasional hot sex.

Sighing, he lifted his feet from the desk and pulled his laptop toward him. See? This was what happened when he thought about women. His brain refused to concentrate on the important things, like which suspension of salbutamol sulphate per actuation would be best for a new nebulizer he was working on.

Concentrate. He pushed all thought of green eyes and curves to the back of his mind and focused on the notes in front of him.

*

That worked for about ten minutes, and then he spent the rest of the day in a very un-Charlie-like state of restlessness. By the time it got to five thirty, he felt relieved that the wait was over and left the hospital with a mixture of both nervousness and excitement at the prospect of seeing Ophelia.

Usually, he worked in the lab until his stomach drove him to find food, which meant he tended to leave when it was dark, so it made a refreshing change to drive home in the daylight.

Brock, who often entertained other consultants and their wives, lived in a large, impressive apartment on the waterfront, while Matt's home in Russell had high ceilings and lots of glass to provide light for his artwork.

Charlie spent so little time at home that he saw no point in spending money on a luxurious mansion he was only going to rattle around in whenever he did get home. Instead, he'd bought a house in Parnell, not far from the hospital, overlooking Hobson Bay. The main points he liked about it were the long deck that ran the length of the house and the large swimming pool it overlooked. The only thing he did other than swim or work in the lab was listen to music and, after a session in the pool, he liked to relax in the evening by popping his headphones in his ears, turning up the volume, and sitting on the deck with his feet up to study the stars with a beer.

This afternoon, though, he went straight into his bedroom and changed, then immediately left and headed across town to Newmarket, where Ophelia lived. He arrived a few minutes before six, drew up outside, turned off the engine, and sat there for a moment.

Panic threaded through his veins, and his heart raced.

There was still time to back out—she might not have seen him arrive. He could phone or text and say something had come up at work. He didn't have to put himself through this. Why didn't he just accept he was doomed to stay single for the rest of his life? Yeah, sex was great, but would it really kill him never to have sex again?

He thought about Ophelia's tight butt, leaned forward, and banged his head on the steering wheel.

Chapter Three

"Is that him, Mummy?"

Heart racing, Ophelia ran across the living room to join her daughter at the window.

She wasn't sure what she'd expected Charlie to arrive in. Nothing would have surprised her—a helicopter, a racing car, a Batmobile... Something wildly impractical no doubt. But she was pleasantly surprised at the sensible, sleek Mazda sedan parked in front of the house.

In the driver's seat, she could just see a man—what was he doing? It looked as if he was banging his head on the steering wheel. At that moment, however, the door opened, and he got out of the car and began walking toward them.

"That's Charlie." She allowed herself a couple more seconds to admire him. For the first time since she'd known him, he'd ditched the white coat. His All Blacks shirt clung deliciously to his muscular chest and bulging biceps. "Yum," she said.

Summer giggled. "He has floppy hair. He looks like Prince Charming from Shrek. With glasses."

Laughing to hide her nerves, she took Summer's hand and they went to open the front door.

Charlie stood outside, hands in his pockets. As usual, his expression didn't betray what he was thinking, but as the door opened he said, "Hi. Wow, you look nice."

"Thank you." Ophelia smoothed the pretty summer dress she'd borrowed from her sister.

"I was talking to Summer," he said. "Cool outfit."

Ophelia looked down at her daughter, not sure whether he was serious. Summer wasn't sure either, judging by her red cheeks. "I'm a princess," Summer told him, tugging at the well-worn long pink gown with sequins that she wore over her shorts and T-shirt. It had only cost Ophelia fifteen dollars at the Warehouse, but Summer practically lived in it.

"Excellent," Charlie said. "Guess that means you have lots of ceremonial duties like shaking hands with the public, so you'll be used to this." He held out his hand. Summer slid hers into it shyly, and he shook it firmly before releasing it. "So what are you, fourteen, fifteen years old?" he asked the little girl.

"I'm six," she said, her lips curving up as if she couldn't make out if he was being funny or just idiotic.

"Ah. Sorry. I don't know many young ladies." Behind the glasses, his warm brown eyes met Ophelia's. "You look okay too, by the way."

She laughed, still not sure whether he was genuinely useless at conversation or if his sense of humor was drier than the Sahara. "Thanks. I think." Picking up her handbag and Summer's car seat, she stepped out of the door.

"I've got one of those in the car," he said, gesturing at the seat.

"Oh." Ophelia put it back inside before locking the door. "Do you have friends with young children?"

"No. I bought it earlier." He led the way along the path. "I thought yours might be bolted into your car, and I read that young children needed to have a booster seat."

"Where did you read that?" she asked, amused and touched he'd bothered to do research.

"On   TakeAHotChicktoMcDonald'sWithHerSixYearOld-dot-com," he said, deadpan. Opening the car door, he held out a hand to help Summer climb in.

So, Ophelia thought, dry humor rather than useless, then.

As Summer clambered into the seat, he finally smiled, and it lit up his whole face.

A warm glow radiated through Ophelia. "I like you," she said.

His smile widened. "And I adore you for telling me so frankly. I should warn you, I'm terrible with signals and sub-text and picking up hints."

She remembered he'd cautioned her that he was disconnected from modern civilization. "You come with a lot of warnings," she observed.

He bent to clip Summer's belt in, then straightened and shut the car door. Finally, he turned to Ophelia and shoved his hands in his pockets. "As far as I can remember. It's been a while."

You come with a lot of warnings. Her cheeks warmed as she realized how he'd interpreted it. "You're going to be trouble, aren't you?" she said softly.

His gaze dropped to her mouth. "Not sure whether I should answer yes or no to that."

Her heart picked up speed, racing away at the sultry look in his eyes. Why had he said that some people criticized him for having no feelings? They might not show on his face, but his eyes were full of emotion. They told her he found her attractive, and he wanted to kiss her.

"Please say yes," she whispered. "I need a bit of excitement in my life."

He reached out and tucked a strand of her hair behind her ear, the brush of his fingers on her neck sending a tingle down her spine. "I can promise you I'll be trouble," he said. "It's up to you whether it's the good or bad kind."

"So you're not by nature a bad boy?"

He pulled gently on the strand of her hair so it slipped through his fingers. "I'm like electricity. Sure, it's a problem if it's misunderstood, but if used right it can also do amazing things."

Ophelia shivered at the thought of what amazing things this man could do to her. She couldn't take her eyes away from his. "I should get in the car," she said faintly, aware of Summer watching them from inside.

"Mmm." He pulled his fingers to the end of her hair and let the last inch slide through. "If you must."

Trying to catch her breath, she walked around the car and got in the passenger side. Clipping in her seatbelt, she glanced over her shoulder at her daughter. "You okay?"

"Yes." Summer was watching Charlie get in. She wasn't quite sure what to make of him, Ophelia could tell. She wasn't surprised. Charlie was the complete opposite of Dillon, Summer's dad.

Dillon ran a building firm, played rugby, went fishing, drank beer, liked sex hard and fast, and pretended to respect women, although she was sure that deep down he thought they were there for the amusement of men.

Charlie… well, she wasn't quite sure what Charlie thought of women, but she was pretty sure he had respect for them, and she already liked his calm, quiet manner, so refreshing after Dillon's touchy temperament.

"Okay," Charlie said, starting the engine. "Here we go. I'm expecting you two to educate me in the delights of fast food. I have no idea what to order." He set off, heading for the main road into town. "Should I have a Happy Meal?"

Summer giggled. "They're for kids."

"Oh. I thought the toys looked cool."

"You should have a Big Mac," Summer said. "You're so big and it will fill you up."

"Summer," Ophelia scolded, trying not to laugh. "That sounds a little rude."

"No, she's right." He signaled and turned the corner. "I have a large appetite."

Had he meant the double entendre? He glanced at her, amusement glimmering in his eyes behind his glasses—yes, he had. He *was* going to be trouble.

Ooh.

"I hope we're not dragging you away from something important at work," she said, trying to distract herself from thinking about what he would look like without his clothes.

"Are you a doctor?" Summer asked.

"Yep."

"Do you have a steffyscope?"

"A stethoscope? Yes, but I don't use it much. I work in the laboratory now."

"You made my inhaler," Summer said.

"Well, I helped to design it."

"Mummy said you are a jeen-yus."

Ophelia rolled her eyes, heat rising in her cheeks. Charlie chuckled. "Well that was very nice of her, but no, I'm not a genius, just an ordinary guy."

That made Ophelia scoff. "Yeah, right. You're just being self-effacing—which I happen to like, by the way, but I read that article on you in the Herald. You sounded like a right smart-arse."

Summer giggled.

"Oops. 'Scuse my French," Ophelia added.

He slowed the car as they approached traffic and took a quieter side road. "I paid them to write that."

Ophelia smiled. "You have a PhD, don't you?"

"Yeah."

"How old are you?"

"Twenty-nine."

"Jeez. I read that you were fast-tracked, but that's crazy."

"Having no social life or friends does have its benefits."

She laughed. "It's bizarre because I read all about you, and I've talked to you online, but I've never seen a photo of you. I didn't connect Caspar with the cute doctor at the muffin stall."

He glanced at her then, real surprise in his eyes. "Wait, you didn't know who I was?"

"Nope. I asked you your name, remember?"

"And you agreed to go out with me? Wow. I could have been a nutcase."

"You are a nutcase. But a nice one, it seems."

He turned the corner and signaled again for the McDonald's car park. "Your mother just called me a nutcase, Summer. Do you think she's right?"

"Yes," Summer said.

"Fair enough." He parked the car and switched off the engine. "Come on."

Loving the way he seemed to enjoy being teased, Ophelia got out, unbuckled Summer, and took her daughter's hand. They all went inside and walked up to the counter. "Shall I order?" Ophelia suggested.

"By all means," Charlie said.

She placed the order for the three of them and took out her purse, but Charlie pushed it away. "My treat," he said.

"Let me pay half at least."

He handed the guy behind the counter his credit card. "It's a first date. I think I can stretch to a takeout." He hesitated then and glanced at her. "If that's okay."

"It's fine, Charlie." Unable to help herself, lifted up onto her toes so she could whisper in his ear. "Are you really a billionaire?"

He slipped an arm around her waist, holding her there. "No idea," he murmured. "But feel free to do that again."

She placed a hand on his arm for balance, feeling warm, firm muscle beneath her fingers. "You really have no idea how much money you have?"

"Not a clue," he said cheerfully. "Brock tells me we're doing okay, and that's good enough for me."

"You're a very strange man."

"So I've been told." He looked as if he was about to kiss her, so she moved away, not wanting to do that in front of her daughter.

"Brock's my doctor," Summer said. "He's your brother."

"That's right."

"Mummy said your other brother writes the Ward Seven books." Her eyes were wide with wonder.

"Yep. Speaking of which, he gave me something for you." Charlie slid a hand into the back pocket of his jeans and extracted a small item. It was a keyring with a tiny Carmel the Cat hanging from it—one of the characters from Matt King's books.

Summer's mouth formed an O of wonder. "For me?"

He smiled and gave it to her. "Yep. I wasn't sure which your favorite was, but Carmel's mine so I chose her."

"Carmel's mine too!"

"We both have excellent taste, then."

"What do you say, Summer?" Ophelia prompted softly.

"Thank you, Charlie."

"You're very welcome." He gestured at the counter. "It looks as if our meals are ready. Wow. Now I see why they call it fast food."

They carried the trays to a table by the window, not far from the children's play area, because Ophelia knew that as soon as Summer had finished her last chicken nugget, she'd want to play.

Charlie took off his glasses, opened the box they gave him, and investigated its contents. "What's this?" He extricated a slice of something green from his burger.

"It's a pickle," Ophelia said, passing Summer the Creon tablets she had to take with every meal to help her digest fat.

Summer swallowed her tablets with a mouthful of orange juice, then stuck out her tongue. "Pickles are disgusting," she said before tucking into her chicken nuggets.

"I'm trying to teach my daughter that not everything green is disgusting," Ophelia said wryly.

He eyed the pickle with suspicion, crunched it cautiously, and pulled a face. "I think she's right on this occasion."

Summer dunked a nugget in ketchup. "Mummy says I have to have vegetables."

He took a huge bite out of his burger and chewed for a moment before replying. "Unfortunately, she's right. Vegetables are good for everyone, but they're especially good for someone with sixty-five roses."

Ophelia smiled. Sixty-five roses was what many children called Cystic Fibrosis because it was easier to say. "I like that name."

"I only use it for the pretty girls." He winked at Summer.

She blushed a pretty pink. "But vegetables taste horrible."

"Some do, but they're magic for your body. Like broccoli—it has all the major vitamins in it, especially the one you need, Vitamin K."

Ophelia paused in the process of eating her chicken wrap and stared at him. CF was a genetic disorder that mainly affected the lungs, although it commonly also affected other organs. Less common was the Vitamin K malabsorption that led to a coagulation problem with Summer's blood, which meant she bruised easily.

"Have you read her file?" Ophelia asked.

He met her gaze for a moment. "Yes. I also spoke to her doctor." He took another bite of his burger.

"Oh." Of course—she kept forgetting they were brothers. Brock was quite different—older, down-to-earth, more sure of himself. She'd yet to meet Matt.

She wasn't sure how she felt about Charlie talking about Summer behind her back. Sure, he was a doctor, but he wasn't her or Summer's doctor, Brock was. What about patient-doctor confidentiality? What other private details did Charlie know about them?

"I'm running a new research project on CF," he said. "Three Wise Men has just allocated it extra funding."

The news about the research pleased her, but selfishly her heart sank a little. "You want to use Summer as a test subject for your project? Is that why you asked me out—to find out more about my daughter's condition?"

He tipped his head to the side and studied her with those strange, intense eyes. "No. I'm running the project *for* her."

Words deserted her. She stared at him, jaw dropping, while he licked his fingers free of ketchup.

"I still don't like broccoli," Summer said.

"You just have to pour cheese sauce over it." Charlie pinched one of her chicken nuggets.

Ophelia wasn't surprised when Summer let him.

Chapter Four

Charlie ate the chicken nugget, which actually wasn't bad, then realized Ophelia was still staring at him with a sagging jaw. Alarm bells rang in his head. He was used to that kind of look from women, and they often followed it by giving him a torrent of abuse or walking out.

Shit.

"Mummy, can I go and play?" Summer had only eaten half of her meal, but the play area was beckoning to her.

"Go on, then," Ophelia said without taking her eyes from Charlie. "Be careful."

He watched the girl run off and noticed that she took the Carmel keyring with her. Bringing his gaze back to the woman who sat opposite him, he saw she was still staring at him, eyes wide.

He sighed. "I've said something stupid, haven't I?" He tried to think how he could have offended her. He shouldn't have mentioned the study. Maybe she found it upsetting that he'd brought up her daughter's illness.

A frown marred her brow. "I just... don't understand. What do you mean you're running the project *for* Summer?"

He sat back, puzzled that he'd upset her. What should he do? Make a joke of it? Change the subject? Be honest? This was why he needed Brock and Matt by his side to tell him what to say. He was half tempted to escape to the bathroom so he could phone them and ask for advice.

Ophelia shivered. "You have the strangest eyes of any guy I've met—I can almost see your brain whirring away behind them."

"I'm trying to decide how to answer. My instinct is always to tell the truth, but Matt has informed me it's not always the wisest action."

"I prefer the honest approach," she said.

"Okay." So did he, and what did he have to lose? "I've liked you since the day you started at the hospital. The first day I met you at the muffin cart, I told Brock about you and discovered you were his patient. He informed me that unfortunately you were married, so I knew a relationship was out of the question. He went on to tell me about Summer, though, and I thought that if I couldn't have you, I could at least try to help her with her CF, so I started planning a research project. I only found out you were separated recently, otherwise I would have asked you out before."

He stopped talking and waited for her to say something. She remained silent, however, and as he watched, her pale skin flushed a deep rose. Crap. He should have changed the subject.

"But…" She blinked several times. "What if we go on a few dates and it doesn't work out?"

He already knew that if it didn't work out, it wouldn't be from his side, but history suggested it was entirely possible she might decide she didn't want a relationship with him. "What do you mean?"

"Well, that's a huge announcement to make on a first date. How can I separate how I feel about you from how important this research project would be to me?"

"I don't understand."

"Charlie, if we don't work out, are you going to end the project?"

"Why would I end the project?"

"You said you're running it for me. That's fine all the time we're getting on, but what if it goes wrong, if I say something stupid and ruin things, or I'm not what you're looking for, will you just redirect the money into research for something else?"

"I said I was running it for Summer, not for you. The project has nothing to do with the fact that I like you, other than through you I found out about Summer's condition." He was still confused as to why Ophelia seemed distressed. "Three Wise Men has only been running a few years, and Brock and I have concentrated mainly on asthma. After I discovered Summer had CF, I realized how some of the research I was doing could help kids with CF too. Brock told me how many times she's been in hospital, and all the treatment she's had, and we wanted to help her. Even if you were to walk out of the door now and never talk to me again, it would have nothing to do with the project."

Ophelia's cheeks still bore a blush, and she wasn't smiling. "Are you for real?" she whispered.

He shifted in his chair. He really liked her, but somehow he'd screwed up, again. "I'm sorry if I offended you by talking about this on a first date. I'm so crap at this."

"Charlie," she whispered, "are you under the impression I'm mad at you?"

"I honestly have no idea." He hesitated for a moment, then took a deep breath. "When I was younger, my parents thought I might have Asperger's. Tests were inconclusive—if I do have it, it's at the high-functioning end of the spectrum. But I wasn't being coy earlier—I genuinely have trouble with non-verbal communication."

She pushed herself up, and for a brief moment he thought she was going to walk away. To his surprise, however, she said, "Let me make it clear for you, then."

She leaned forward until her lips were only half an inch from his. She waited, presumably to see if he'd pull away, and when he didn't move—when he didn't even breathe—she closed the gap and pressed her lips to his.

Completely baffled, Charlie closed his eyes. He tried to ignore the way his brain was attempting to analyze what had happened, and focused on Ophelia lips. They were soft and pink, and slightly sticky with lip gloss. When they peeled away from his, the erotic sensation made him hard in the space of seconds.

She kissed him once, twice, then a longer third time before she eventually sat back in her seat.

Her cheeks were still flushed, but now she was smiling. "Say something," she prompted.

"Cherry," he said, mentioning the first thing that came into his head. He sucked his bottom lip, tasting the gloss.

She laughed. "You fascinate me, Charlie King. I'm so glad you asked me out today."

"Me too." His head still reeled at the fact that she wasn't angry with him. No woman had ever found him fascinating before either. It gave him a little glow inside.

She reached out and squeezed his hand. "I'll be back in a minute." Rising, she walked across to the play area to check that Summer was okay.

Charlie watched her go, his gaze sliding down the pretty sundress that flowed over her curves. He watched Ophelia pause on the edge of the playground, making sure Summer was enjoying herself and playing safely. Physical exercise was important for kids with CF to clear the thick mucus that built up in the lungs, but he was aware it must be a constant worry having a child who bruised so easily. From the little he'd observed of them so far, though, Ophelia wasn't what Brock called a helicopter mother, constantly hovering around her daughter and fussing over her health. He liked her practical approach.

How strange that she was worried he'd stop the research if things didn't work out between them. That made no sense to him at all. Were there really guys out there who were so cold-hearted they'd use a position of authority to gain control over a woman? *Of course there are, you naive idiot.* He could almost hear Matt's voice in his head. It didn't help him understand, though.

Out of sight, he heard a child give a chesty cough, presumably Summer. Ophelia didn't say anything, though, just waited until she'd finished before walking back to him.

He knew exercises like blowing up balloons or blowing bubbles in paint helped teach younger children how to expel air from deep in their lungs to get the mucus moving. He thought about the Carmel keyring, contemplating a new idea as he watched Ophelia pause by another table, turn and bend to pick up a toy that a child had dropped, and return it to the child before coming over.

She sat opposite him, her eyes sparkling. "I love how you always look deep in thought. Are you considering some crazy scientific theory or something us lesser mortals would understand?"

"Unusually for me, both. Normally, I can only think of one thing at a time. But I was considering the prospect of developing a toy for CF sufferers, using the Ward Seven characters, where a child could blow along a pipe to get a character to move. Say for example if they blew long and hard enough, Dixon the Dog would score a rugby try or something. We could even try a digital version, where they had to blow to watch a cartoon on a screen."

"It's a great idea."

"It would have to be adjustable to take account of the individual child's peak flow. Actually, come to think of it, it would also work as a peak flow meter for asthma sufferers." He made a mental note to draw up some plans later and speak to Brock about it.

Ophelia picked at some of the fries Summer had left. "So what else were you thinking about?"

"Sorry?"

"I asked whether you were thinking of something scientific or something ordinary, and you said both."

"I didn't say ordinary." He thought about what he'd promised Brock he wouldn't say on the first date, and weighed that up against Ophelia's statement, *I prefer the honest approach.* He decided to compromise. "I was thinking how nice you looked in that dress. And it's far from ordinary, I assure you."

She laughed, a sound of pure pleasure that made him smile.

"I listen to you every day, by the way," he said.

That made her raise her eyebrows. "Really?"

"Yep. Ten until eleven. We have the radio on all the time in the labs."

Ophelia was in charge of Te Karere Hauora, the department that connected the hospital with the local community, including the volunteers who ran the hospital radio. She presented a program on the radio every morning, and he'd grown used to her sunny voice brightening up his day. He even planned meetings around her, making sure he was free when it was time for her feature.

"You're blushing again," he observed.

"Charlie! Stop it." She pressed her hands to her face. "Change the subject."

He liked having an effect on her, but he did as she asked. "Okay. Tell me about Summer's father."

Her smile faded, and she pushed away the leftover fries. "On a first date? You are a strange one."

"You don't have to talk about him if you don't want. I just say what's on my mind. I'm interested in you, and I want to know more about you. When did you break up?"

She scratched at a mark on the table. "Officially, June."

"Was it amicable?"

She gave a short laugh, but there was no humor in it. "Not really, no." She lifted her gaze to his. "You really want to talk about it?"

"I wouldn't have asked if I didn't."

Her lips curved a little. "No, I'm sure you wouldn't have." She sighed. "His name's Dillon. He runs his own building firm. I knew him at high school, but we didn't get together until I was eighteen. When he asked me to marry him, I said yes because, well, it's what you do, and there had never been anyone else." She shrugged. "He's not a bad guy, and he's a good father to Summer."

Charlie tried to fill in the gaps, and failed. "So why did you break up?"

She looked out of the window at the traffic, giving him the opportunity to study her profile—her pert nose, and her lips that always seemed to have a tiny smile on them, even when she was frowning. "I loved him in the beginning, or thought I did anyway. It was like loving the sun. He has a huge personality, and I think I was blinded, you know? But as time went by, I felt... overshadowed. He's incredibly possessive, but he's manipulative too. He wouldn't say 'I don't want you to see your friends,' but if I went out with them, when I got home he'd be resentful and jealous and make me feel guilty. He was always twisting my words and making me upset. I just got tired of it—it's not what I want from a relationship. He makes me angry, and I'm not an angry person. Does that make sense?"

"Yes." Charlie thought of how Lisette had made him feel—frustrated and irritable, which wasn't him at all. "I think there are people with whom you are the worst possible version of yourself."

Her eyes lit up at his understanding. "That's it exactly. And I was tired of feeling like that. So just after Christmas last year, I told him I wanted a divorce."

"What did he say?"

"He said no. He yelled. Screamed at me. Threw things and broke the TV. Walked out. Came back drunk. Yelled some more. Then he cried. Told me he'd change. That he loved me. Kept going on about Summer and how it wasn't fair to her, until I was so mixed up I didn't know what to do. So I let him stay, because I didn't want to be the sort of person who just gives up on a relationship. I know they take work, and I don't expect it to be paradise all the time. Plus he's Summer's dad, and I felt I owed it to her to give it another chance."

"But things didn't improve?"

"For a while he tried to be better, but I guess you can't change what you're like deep down—it's like painting over a black undercoat with white paint. Eventually it shows through."

"So you called it a day?"

"Yes, in June. I told him it was over. After a huge argument, he agreed to move out, although he told me it was only for a while, until I'd 'cooled off.'" She stopped and swallowed. "He keeps pushing to come back. It's been hard. He's been good in that he's not played us off against each other with Summer—he could have said 'Mummy's making me leave', but he hasn't done that. And that makes it worse, somehow." Her eyes glistened, and she rubbed her nose.

Charlie could only imagine how hard it had been for her. "Are you getting a divorce?"

"I applied for a separation order in June. We have to have lived apart for two years, though. It feels like forever. I can't believe it's only been six months."

"Can he contest it?"

"He can make it difficult."

"Will he?"

"He told me he's determined to get me back. He keeps playing on my emotions, reminding me of the good times, telling me it would be better for Summer if we stay together, that sort of thing."

"You think it's over, though?"

Her green eyes glistened. She was so beautiful, she took his breath away. "Yes, it's over. But I'm a mess, Charlie. I try to pretend I'm not, but I am. I feel guilty for Summer because she really needs us both, and it would definitely be easier if I had Dillon around all the time. I feel as if I'm being selfish putting myself first, but I'm sick of being miserable. I'm getting there, and I want to move on, and I really, really like you, but I wouldn't blame you at all if you said you'd rather give me a wide berth. I have a lot of baggage, and you're a gorgeous guy who deserves better. If you want to just take me home now and say goodbye, I'd rather you be honest and say so now rather than later."

*

Ophelia finished her little speech and sat back, waiting for him to reply. Her mind and emotions were so mixed up that she couldn't separate one from the other.

If only she was closer to getting her divorce and Dillon had accepted they were over. Soft-hearted Charlie didn't look like the kind of guy who'd be able to stand up to Dillon and his notorious temper. It wasn't fair for Charlie to have to deal with her bolshy ex and her confused state of mind.

She should tell him it wasn't going to work. First she had to get Dillon out of her life completely—then, and only then, would she be free to move on and open herself to love again.

But Charlie sat there with that intense look in his brown eyes that suggested he was using Pythagoras' theorem to help him decide the best way to get her clothes off, and her mouth refused to form the words.

The silence stretched out between them. Then, just as she was about to beg him to say something, he pushed his chair back and got to his feet.

He was about to walk away. Panic filled her, and she inhaled and opened her mouth to say *Please don't go.*

But he came around the table, leaned one hand on the back of her chair, and with the other hand slid a knuckle under her chin and lifted it. He bent and paused with his lips a fraction of an inch from hers, the same way she had earlier, and then, when she didn't move, he closed the gap and kissed her.

Relief and exultation flooded her, and she gave a long sigh as she closed her eyes and lifted a hand to slip her fingers into his hair.

Last time, she'd done the kissing. This time, it was his turn to press his lips to hers. For a guy who appeared to have trouble communicating with women, he certainly left her in no doubt as to his decision.

Eventually, he moved back to look at her with amusement in his eyes.

"Come on," he said. "Go get Summer, and I'll take you home."

Chapter Five

"So did he ask you out again?"

Ophelia scratched at a mark on the kitchen counter, not meeting her sister's eyes. It was late Friday afternoon, and Kate had called in on the way home from work to catch up with the gossip about Ophelia's date with Charlie on Wednesday.

"No," Ophelia said. "He drove me home, and I got out, and that was it."

"He hasn't phoned you?"

"Not yet. He sent me a couple of texts, and I've seen him both mornings at the breakfast cart, but he hasn't mentioned going out again."

"Did he kiss you?"

Ophelia looked over her shoulder at where Summer sat out on the deck with Kate's daughter, Megan. The two of them were busy coloring in pictures of Disney princesses, talking away, and were hopefully out of earshot.

She looked back at Kate, whose eyes were gleaming. "Yes."

Kate gawped. "Whereabouts?"

"Right in the middle of the restaurant."

Kate rolled her eyes. "I meant where on your body? Was it a polite peck on the cheek or a real snog?"

Ophelia's face grew hot. "A brief-ish kiss. On the mouth." She omitted to say she'd kissed him first.

"Cool. I like him already."

Ophelia laughed and stood to pour water from the just-boiled kettle into the plunger. "He's lovely. Super cute, and incredibly sexy in an understated, mad scientist kind of way."

"Do you think he'll ring?"

"I hope so. I think." She topped the cups up with milk and pushed Kate's over to her.

"You think?" Kate sipped her coffee. "You're not sure about him?"

"Oh… I have no doubt that Charlie King would bring a whole box of delights to my life if I let him. I just don't know whether I should or not."

"Because of Dillon?" Kate gestured to the tin of biscuits. Ophelia pushed it over to her.

"Yeah. When Charlie asked me to go out with him, he caught me by surprise and I said yes without really thinking about it. But I was lying awake last night, and when I thought of how Dillon would feel if he knew I was going out with someone else…"

Kate put down her mug and frowned. "Sweetie, you're separated. You're getting divorced. How many times have we been through this? It's been six months. I thought that by now both of you would have moved on."

"We've been married seven years, Kate. It's not a small amount of time. And he was never bad to me. We have a lot of things in common, and he understands me, you know?"

"Jesus, you have a short memory." Exasperation filled Kate's voice. "Do I have to list all the times you rang me in tears to tell me about another argument you'd had?"

Ophelia stared into her mug. "No. And I'm not saying it was all roses around the door. Of course I'm not."

"Honey, please tell me you're not having second thoughts about this separation."

"I'm not. I just feel guilty every time Summer asks me when she's seeing her daddy again. I feel terrible. Because the separation is all down to me. I split the family up. It's my fault. I keep thinking about what Mum said, about how in her day if they broke a vase they mended it, they didn't throw it away, and I feel like a quitter, like maybe I should have tried harder."

Kate reached out and put a hand over her sister's. "It's not your fault. You've been a fucking angel. I would have murdered that bastard years ago."

Ophelia's lips twisted in a wry smile. Kate and Dillon had never gotten on. "Yeah, I know."

"Mum means well, but life has changed, and it's a good thing, not a bad one. Remember nanna and gramps, how they spent their whole lives in separate rooms because they couldn't stand the sight of each other? Well I don't know about you, but I wouldn't want to waste my life like that. I work hard at my marriage, but if we were both unhappy, I wouldn't stay."

"Not even for Megan?"

"What's the point? Of course Summer misses her dad, but do you think she loved seeing you in tears and listening to Dillon yell at you?"

Ophelia's throat tightened. "No. It's okay, Kate, you don't have to go over it all again." They'd talked this subject to death, and she was tired of it. "I'm not saying I want to get back with him. Just that it's hard."

"I know." Kate met her gaze and gave a sympathetic smile. "Come on, let's not talk about that arsehole. Tell me more about Charlie."

Ophelia sipped her coffee, relieved the topic of conversation had changed. "What do you want to know?"

"Is he really a billionaire?"

"Apparently he has no idea." Ophelia chuckled. "But his brother seems to think so."

"I can't imagine not knowing how much money was in my bank account. I know what my balance is almost to the cent. How can he not know?"

"I get the feeling he buys what he needs and doesn't worry about it. He doesn't appear to be very materialistic."

"But he is gorgeous?" Kate's eyes twinkled.

"Oh yeah," Ophelia said enthusiastically. "He swims every day, and he's six foot four and all muscle. Honestly, you'd think he was an All Black if it wasn't for his Einstein hair. Except it's not white. But he's clever—I mean, *really* clever. I like that he's smarter than me." She stopped talking as a smile spread across Kate's face. "I'm waffling, aren't I?"

"It's lovely. You really seem to like him."

"He's nice, and I don't mean that in a bland way. He's a gentleman. I'd love to see him in a suit. I bet he looks like an artsy version of James Bond. And he's running a research project for CF because of Summer. How lovely is that?"

"Good Lord. He must like you."

"It does appear that way." Her cheeks grew warm as she thought of the look in his eyes. It gave her goosebumps.

"So you do want to see him again?"

Ophelia nodded slowly. "I do. He made me feel good, and that hasn't happened for a while."

On cue, as if the universe was waiting for her to come to that realization, her phone rang. She took it out of her pocket and looked at the screen. "It's him."

"Go on, then. Answer it!"

Her heart racing, she swiped the screen and held it to her ear. "Hello?"

"Hey, Ophelia. It's Charlie."

Her face burned at the sound of his deep voice and she knew she must have gone scarlet. Kate looked most amused. Ophelia turned away and walked over to the open window, hoping to blow cool air onto her skin. "Oh, hi. Lovely to hear from you."

"How's your day going?"

"Good, thank you. Long, but I'm home now. My sister is here having coffee. And biscuits." *Jeez Ophelia, stop waffling!*

"That's nice. I've just spoken to Brock. He said I should ring you."

"Oh."

"That came out wrong. Shit, I'm terrible at this."

She laughed and pushed a crayon that had fallen onto the kitchen floor with her toe. "I think we both are."

"I was going to ring Wednesday night, and then again last night, and then I worried I'd frighten you off by being overeager. Then Brock said you were probably thinking I didn't want to see you again, which is absolutely the last thing I'd want you to think, so here I am."

"I'm glad you rang," she said. "I had a nice time on Wednesday."

"Me too. I was wondering if you were free tomorrow?"

"It's my turn to have Summer this weekend," she admitted, "although Kate would probably look after her if I asked nicely..." She shot a look at her sister, who gave her the thumbs up.

"Well actually, I wondered whether you and Summer would both like to go out for the day. I've heard that Rainbow's End is a fun place to go."

Ophelia raised her eyebrows. Summer had never been to the amusement park. "Apparently so. But... is it your sort of thing? I can't imagine you on a roller coaster somehow."

"I happen to be a thrill seeker," he said amiably. "I've bungee-jumped."

"Charlie, seriously?"

"Yep. And I've dived off the Sky Tower."

"I bet it was some sort of scientific experiment about weight to speed ratios," she teased. "Did the results find their way into your research?"

"Might have." She could hear the smile in his voice. "But this wouldn't be for us. Apparently there's a place there called Kidz Kingdom for children under eight years old, and they can meet Princess Sapphire and have their photo taken with her. I thought Summer might like that."

Ophelia put her hand over her heart, touched he'd given it so much thought. "She would, Charlie, thank you."

"Does she have a friend she'd like to bring? We could make a day of it. Have lunch out. I have a taste for chicken nuggets now."

She laughed. "Yes, I'm sure Kate's daughter would love to come too. They're the same age. Are you sure you're ready for two six-year-olds though?"

"It's okay—I'll just stick a bottle of whisky in my back pocket to numb the pain."

"For you or them?"

He chuckled. "What time shall I pick you up? It opens at ten."

"Nine thirty then?" Ophelia knew the girls would be up early, but they'd be tired by mid-afternoon and wouldn't last the whole day.

"Sounds good."

"Thank you," she said, looking outside at where her daughter was coloring, still dressed in her favorite princess dress. "For thinking of Summer." He could have assumed she'd get a babysitter, but instead he'd made an effort to include her daughter again, and that meant a lot to her.

"Of course," he said, sounding surprised that she would have expected anything less. "See you tomorrow, then."

"Yeah. See ya." She hung up.

For a moment she stared at the phone. Then she turned and looked at Kate.

"I like this one," Kate said.

"Me too." She put the phone down and picked up her coffee.

"You're still blushing."

"He has a nice voice."

"Do I get to meet him tomorrow?"

"I suppose. Look, why doesn't Megan stay the night here so she's ready for the morning, and we'll drop her off tomorrow so you can meet him?"

"Sounds good." Kate finished off her drink. "Are you going to tell Dillon where you're going?"

Ophelia hesitated. Usually, if she was out for the day she would have let Dillon know. She took the cups over to the sink. "I'll tell him once there's something to tell him about. I might go out with Charlie on Saturday and then we'll decide that's it. There's no point starting off an apocalypse with Dillon until I'm sure."

"Why do you think that will be it after Saturday?"

"I don't know. Maybe he'll think I'm not smart enough for him. Or he'll decide he doesn't fancy me." She thought of the way he'd kissed her, and felt a little melty inside. He seemed to fancy her. And she fancied him too. So that boded well.

"You're thinking about kissing Charlie, aren't you?" Kate grinned, and Ophelia blushed again. "It's so nice to see you like this."

"It's nice to feel like this. It's been a while." She scratched her nose. "It feels a bit odd, the thought of dating someone other than Dillon." Kate knew that Dillon was the only guy she'd ever gone out with.

"Exciting though, eh?"

"Yeah." It was. She had a feeling in her stomach as if she was on one of the roller coasters that would be at the park. It had been such a long time since she'd felt excited about life like this. That had to be a good thing.

"Come on, let's tell the girls," Kate said.

They revealed the news, laughing as the two girls squealed and jumped up and down with excitement.

"Who's Charlie?" Megan said when they'd finally both calmed down.

"Mummy's friend," Summer said. She looked up at Ophelia. "Is Daddy coming?"

Ophelia swallowed, not looking at Kate, who'd glanced over at her.

When Dillon had first moved out, Ophelia had explained to Summer that Dillon wasn't going to live with them anymore. She'd purposely not mentioned the word divorce, not sure that Summer knew what it meant anyway, and hoping to lessen the pain a little by easing her daughter into the idea of her and Dillon's separation.

Since then, they hadn't talked about it much. Before Charlie had taken them to McDonald's, Ophelia had explained that a friend from work was taking them out, but she hadn't yet had the conversation with Summer about dating someone else. Perhaps she should have talked to her about it first. But it had all happened so suddenly, and again, she didn't want to make a big deal out of it if it didn't work out.

"No, sweetie," she said. "Daddy won't be coming."

Summer nodded. "Okay." She looked down at her clothing. "Can I wear my dress?"

Ophelia blew out a silent breath. "Of course, but I'll have to wash it first. Why don't you give it to me now?"

Taking it from Summer, she went inside to put the dress in the machine while Kate explained to Megan that she'd be staying the night. After pressing the start button, she leaned on the machine, suddenly shaky.

One step at a time, she told herself. If things went well with Charlie on Saturday, she'd consider telling both Summer and Dillon about the new relationship. But until then, she'd play it cool, and let things unfold at their own pace.

Chapter Six

"Are you sure you aren't regretting this yet?" Ophelia teased.

Charlie watched the two six-year-olds tear off to the next ride. "I don't know where they get the energy. They could fuel a small city."

"You wait," she said, "we'll have lunch and then about two o'clock they'll be dead on their feet."

"I'm having trouble believing they'll ever sit down again. No wonder parents look so tired all the time."

Ophelia smiled. Then he saw her glance down to where he held her hand. Only half an hour into their visit they'd been walking between the rides when she'd slipped her hand into his. He suspected she'd done it automatically, because she hadn't said anything, but she'd sucked on her bottom lip and looked away as if embarrassed at her gesture. He'd tightened his fingers on hers, though, and since then he'd hardly let go.

He'd wondered whether Summer would notice and say something, but so far the girls had been too excited to pay attention to anything but the rides and the characters in costume who wandered around having their photographs taken with the visitors.

"They're having a fantastic time," Ophelia said as if reading his mind. "Thank you so much."

"It's a pleasure," he said, meaning it. The girls were no trouble at all, and he found their excitement contagious. All morning he'd felt as if it was Christmas Eve, buoyed up by just being with Ophelia.

Part of him had expected her to turn him down when he'd rung to ask her out again, and he'd been thrilled when she'd agreed. Brock had suggested he ask her if someone could look after Summer so he could take her out to dinner, but Charlie didn't want Ophelia to feel as if she had to choose between him and her daughter. He wanted to get to know Summer, because he knew that if he and Ophelia were to have any kind of future, it would have to include the girl, and it was important to him that Summer saw him as a friend and not as a rival of her father's. He was glad he'd made the suggestion about the amusement park, because Ophelia seemed touched that he'd included Summer in their plans.

Luckily, it was a beautiful day, the sun holding its usual New Zealand December heat. All four of them wore hats and sun lotion, and Ophelia carried several water bottles and made sure they drank regularly.

The girls had been heading toward the next ride, but they came to a halt as they saw Princess Sapphire ahead of them, resplendent in a blue satin gown sewn with white roses, and carrying a parasol to keep the sun off her pale skin.

"Mummy!" Summer clapped her hands over her mouth for a second, so excited she looked about to explode. "Can I have my photo taken with her?"

Ophelia laughed. "Of course. Come on."

They made their way to the small queue waiting to meet the princess. The two girls were very patient, Charlie thought, considering how excited they were. When it was their turn, they approached the area where the princess stood under a pohutukawa tree, and the photographer smiled and got them to stand either side of the princess while he took their photo.

Then the photographer looked across at Ophelia and Charlie standing to the side. "How about one with mum and dad?" he asked, beckoning them forward.

"Charlie's not my dad," Summer said, the smile sliding from her face.

Ophelia froze. The photographer flicked his gaze over to her and then back to Charlie, clearly mortified at his faux pas.

"I'm just a family friend," Charlie said with a smile. "Go on," he told Ophelia, "have yours taken—four princesses all together. I'll hold your rucksack."

To his relief, Summer seemed pleased with that, and they all posed with Princess Sapphire for a photo, which the photographer promised would be available from the main office after one o'clock.

"I'm sorry," the photographer murmured to him as Summer showed Princess Sapphire her own dress, and the princess told her how beautiful she looked. "I shouldn't jump to conclusions—I apologize for any embarrassment I've caused."

"No harm done," Charlie said, hoping that was the case. He watched Summer wistfully fingering the silk flowers on the princess's voluminous skirt. The last thing he wanted was to upset Ophelia or her daughter.

Ophelia ushered the girls away so the next visitors could have their photo taken, and the girls ran away toward the next ride.

He and Ophelia followed along slowly. To their right, one of the bigger roller coasters swooped down past them with a rattle of iron and an array of screams, then vanished just as quickly, leaving them in peace. To their left, families were eating lunch in a small park, the central green surrounded by flowerbeds filled with bright flowers. The aromas of candy floss and hot dogs wafted around them, the smells of summer, and he tilted his face up to the sun, liking the warmth on his skin.

"I'm so sorry," she said. "For embarrassing you."

He looked down at her. They both wore sunglasses so he couldn't see her eyes, but her face had paled and she wasn't smiling.

"It didn't embarrass me," he said. "I'm sorry if it upset Summer."

Ophelia looked down, hiding her face beneath the brim of her sunhat. "That's kind of you, but I still apologize. I haven't spoken to her about us, because there isn't an 'us' yet, not really, and I didn't want to make it seem more than it was. But I wish I had now. I could have died back there. I really am sorry."

"Ophelia, it's okay." He stopped and turned her to face him, only then realizing she was near to tears.

"Everything's just so messy." She sniffed, her chest heaving, clearly trying not to cry. "A new relationship should be all romantic and sexy. And our first date was in McDonald's and on our second date you have to put up with a stroppy six-year-old and her messed up single mum."

He ran a hand through his hair. "Brock said I should have taken you out to dinner on your own. I just didn't want you to think I wasn't interested in getting to know Summer."

"Oh Charlie, that's not what I'm saying at all. You've been wonderful, and I really appreciate you including Summer—I can't tell you how much it means to me. But you deserve so much more. You're so lovely—you should be with a simple, uncomplicated girl who's wearing a little black number and high heels and carrying a designer handbag, not an old frump wearing a faded dress and carrying a backpack."

He glanced over to see that the two girls were settling in a carriage of a smaller ride, facing away from them.

Moving closer to Ophelia, he carefully removed her sunglasses and did the same with his. Holding both pairs in his left hand, he cupped her chin with his right and lifted it so he could see beneath the brim of her hat into her eyes.

"You're not a frump," he said. "You're the polar opposite. You have a fantastic figure, and you're the sexiest woman I've ever known. You're gorgeous."

She blinked rapidly. "Oh."

"You're the most beautiful woman in the entire park. Princess Sapphire included."

She gave a little bashful laugh. "Stop flattering me."

"Why?"

That took the wind out of her sails. "Because... I don't know."

"I want to flatter you." He brushed her cheek with his thumb. "I want to give you compliments that make your cheeks turn pink."

"Charlie..."

"Life is messy," he said. "It would be a lot easier if we could put each chapter of our life into a box and tie it up neatly before opening the next, but it doesn't work like that. You're separated, and it's going to be hard at times, while everyone gets used to the new situation. There will be ups and downs while your ex comes to terms with losing you, and while Summer learns that her mum and dad will want to meet new people and make new lives apart from each other. It's sad for you all, but it's life, and it doesn't scare me. Emotion doesn't frighten me. It fascinates me, like electricity, and I'm expecting it to be like one of those roller coasters, so don't worry about me. I'm here, and I'm not going anywhere. I'll wait at the bottom of the roller coaster until you're ready to get off."

She swallowed and blew out a shaky breath. "You're very sweet."

He stroked his thumb across her bottom lip. "And I want to kiss you. May I kiss you?"

She looked over her shoulder, saw the carriage with the girls disappearing around the corner, and looked back up at him with a shy smile. "Okay."

Sliding his hand into her hair, he moved a little closer and lowered his lips. But he didn't kiss her immediately. He let his lips just touch hers, and then waited, enjoying the notion that he was finally dating this beautiful woman, reveling in the anticipation of being about to kiss her. A small part of his brain noted the way her chest rose and fell rapidly, and he felt an answering increase in his heartbeat as his blood raced around his body. Her pupils had dilated, and he knew his would be doing the same, their bodies responding to invisible pheromones in an age-old instinctive seduction. Her lips parted, her sweet breath entwining with his, and she closed her eyes. Charlie kept his open for a moment though, observing the flush in her cheeks and how soft her lips looked, before he lowered his mouth the final fraction of an inch, and kissed her.

He closed his eyes. He was barely moving, just pressing his lips to hers in the slowest, softest kiss, and yet his senses were awakening, blooming like a flower. A tiny part of him was conscious of the laughter of children in the distance, the rumble of the roller coasters through the ground beneath his feet, the brush of the summer breeze across the back of his neck, the silkiness of her hair slipping through his fingers, the smell of sun lotion on her skin. But the majority of his consciousness focused on her lips, and how it felt to touch his to them.

Why did the kiss feel so erotic when the only place he was touching was her lips and her hair? They were in public, and hardly anyone gave a passing glance at their innocent smooch.

But it was sexy and intimate to be so close to her after having worshipped her from afar for so long. To have his mouth on hers, and then, when he touched his tongue to her lip, to have her tongue slide against his, warm, slick, and sensual. He could taste the chocolate mints they'd bought earlier and eaten together, and he shivered when her hand rose to cup his cheek, her light touch bringing goose bumps out on his skin in spite of the warmth of the day.

But it was the way she returned the kiss, as if she was enjoying it, as if she wanted to kiss him back more than anything in the world, that fired him up and meant he had to fight with every ounce of willpower he possessed not to slip his arms around her and pull her to him so he could feel all of her soft body.

He lifted his head and gazed at her through a haze of sexual longing.

"Oh..." she whispered, looking up at him. "Don't look at me like that."

"Like what?" He didn't kiss her again, conscious of people passing by as his senses reawakened to the world, but he didn't move back either, not wanting the delicious moment to end.

"Like I'm a melting ice cream cone," she said.

His lips curved up. "What a great description. And yes, that's exactly what I'm thinking."

She moistened her lips with the tip of her tongue. "We should… the girls…"

"Yes," he said reluctantly. With supreme effort, he moved back and took her hand. "Put that thought on hold for later."

Chapter Seven

Charlie's words rang in Ophelia's ears for the rest of the day. *Put that thought on hold for later...* What had he meant? Was he thinking about kissing her again? She hoped so. It had been wonderful to be kissed so reverently, as if he couldn't believe she was allowing him to touch his lips to hers.

It must have been that way with Dillon once, she thought, when they were first together, but she couldn't remember him ever kissing her like that. "Kissing's overrated," he'd once said to her. "All guys would rather skip the teaser trailer and get onto the main movie."

And yet Charlie had kissed her as if there was nothing in the world he'd rather do than spend hours just caressing her lips with his.

She mused on that while they had lunch in the park while watching one of the shows, and continued to think about it through the afternoon. It seemed the memory of that kiss was determined to linger like the smell of Charlie's aftershave on her hand where she'd touched his cheek.

She'd predicted that the two girls would start flagging by mid-afternoon, but there was so much to do and see that they remained full of energy. They had a wonderful day and tried out every ride in the Kidz Kingdom and several of the bigger ones as well. They also spent ages trying to win some plush toys in the booths by fishing out ducks and throwing hoops around blocks, to little avail, until Charlie took over. Ophelia watched with amusement while he made his way through the booths winning them both an armful of toys each in the process.

"You seem to have discovered a hidden talent," she said as the girls skipped away to sit on a bench and choose their favorites.

"It's my glasses," he told her. "The lenses are fitted with a targeting mechanism."

"I said to Kate that you were like an artsy version of James Bond."

He grinned. "I can live with that."

He had such a sexy smile when it did eventually appear that her stomach did a strange flip-flop. She was tempted to kiss him again, but restrained herself as the girls came back over to stuff some of the toys in her backpack. Interestingly, she noted that although Summer tucked a plush toy tiger under her arm, the little Carmel the Cat keyring that Charlie had given her remained in her hand as her current most treasured possession.

Around three p.m., worried that Charlie might be getting bored, Ophelia tentatively suggested they make a move.

"Mum!" Summer looked distraught. "Please don't make us go!"

Charlie grinned when Ophelia glanced at him. "I'm in no hurry— I'm having a great time."

Pleased he didn't appear to be hating every minute, she gave in, and the girls ran off with delighted screams to try the next ride.

In the end, they made it all the way through until the park shut at five p.m. They headed back to the car park, and by the time they'd followed the slow train of cars leaving the park, both girls had fallen asleep.

"What a fantastic day." Ophelia took off her hat, grimaced at her reflection in the mirror on the sun visor, and ran her hands through her flat hair. "Thank you so much. You've been so patient today. They've had a wonderful time."

"That's good. Summer's a lovely girl and she deserves it."

Ophelia smiled as he negotiated the roundabout and headed toward the city. "I had a great time too."

"I'm glad. You deserve it, too. I know parents are happy when their kids are happy. Still, maybe next time we'll go somewhere a bit more upmarket. Fast food isn't as bad as everyone says, but I feel the need to treat you to a real dinner for once."

She laughed. "Fair enough." So there was to be a third date, then? Yee-hah!

She gave him directions to Kate's house, and when he'd pulled up outside and turned off the engine, the girls both roused and yawned.

"Come on," Ophelia said to Charlie as they unclipped their belts. "Kate wants to meet you."

Kate had already opened the door by the time they got there. She gave Megan a hug, but her gaze fell on the man standing next to Summer.

"Kate, this is Charlie," Ophelia said, a little nervously.

"Ah, so you're the brave man who's put up with my daughter and niece for an entire day." Kate smiled and held out her hand. "Nice to meet you."

"Likewise." Charlie shook it. "You're both a credit to your daughters. They're exceptionally polite and well-behaved."

Kate gave a mock frown at a grinning Megan. "Are you sure he's not getting you mixed up with someone else?" She winked at Charlie. "Thank you. They look worn out, so they've obviously had a great time." She stepped back and gestured inside. "Do you want to come in for a coffee?"

"No, we won't if that's okay," Ophelia said. "Summer's knackered and I think I'll get her home, have tea, and then get her to bed."

"Sure. I'll catch you later. Lovely to meet you, Charlie."

"Yes, nice to meet you too."

Kate went in and closed the door, and the three of them went back to the car.

"I'm shattered," Ophelia said as they got in and Charlie set off for her house. "Funny how fresh air can wear you out."

"I know what you mean. I spend all day in the lab so I'm not used to sunlight."

"Like a vampire," Summer said.

"I've even got the teeth." He bared them at her briefly, showing her his prominent canines. She squealed, and they all laughed.

"Daddy tries to bite my neck," Summer said. "I don't mind, but his bristles can be scratchy."

"Tell him he can only bite you if he has a shave," Charlie said. "That sounds fair to me."

Summer giggled. Ophelia smiled, but looked out of the window. Summer's words had brought her down to earth with a bump. Dillon still didn't know they'd been out for the day with Charlie. He would hate to think how much fun they'd had without him. Guilt rose inside her at the betrayal. Summer was Dillon's daughter, and he was naturally protective of her. She'd have to make sure she handled telling him right, or this could all turn very unpleasant, and that would be a shame when it seemed to be going so well.

She didn't say anything more, tired and a little dispirited, until they pulled up at her house.

Charlie left the engine running and said, "Well, thanks for coming out with me."

Ophelia unclipped her belt and turned in the seat to face him. It was time to give Summer a bath and then get her ready for bed. But she'd had such a lovely day, and she didn't want it to end.

"Do you, um, want to come in for a drink?" she asked.

Adjusting his glasses, he studied her face, and she knew he was trying to work out if there were any undertones to the sentence. She reminded herself that he struggled to read between the lines—she had to be clear with him, and tell him what was going through her mind.

"I've had a nice time," she elaborated. "But I don't want you to go yet. I have to give Summer a bath, so I'll understand if you want to shoot off, but if you'd like to come in and just have a coffee out on the deck with me when Summer's in bed, I'd like that."

He turned off the engine. "Sure. That would be nice."

So they went inside, Summer skipping along the path beside him, waving the Carmel keyring and talking to Charlie about which Ward Seven book was his favorite.

"I'll let you into a secret," Charlie said as Ophelia opened the door. "There's going to be a new Ward Seven character soon— Squish the Possum."

Summer gave a squeal of laughter. "Mummy! A new book!"

"I'll make sure you get one of the first copies," Charlie said, gesturing for Ophelia to enter the house before him.

She did so, liking the old-fashioned gesture, a little nervous as to what he would think of the inside of her house. Judging by his car and the clothes he wore, and the fact that he'd told her he had no idea how much money he had, she didn't think he'd pass judgement on her small home, but even so she waited anxiously for his reaction as he walked into the living room.

Small and neat, the house had an open-plan living room and kitchen, two bedrooms, and a smallish deck with an average-sized lawn. It was all she and Dillon had been able to afford when they first married, but she loved it even though it was small. She knew she was going to have to sell it, though, because Dillon deserved to have half the proceeds. Where she and Summer would live after that, she had no idea as yet.

One step at a time, Ophelia.

"Nice place," Charlie said, toeing off his Converses and leaving them by the door. "I like the cushions."

Pushing the panic away, she smiled at him. "I made them."

"Really?" He picked up one in the shape of a chocolate eclair. The top was made of brown silk, the bottom of fawn felt, and the folds of cream silk looked like cream oozing out of the sides. "I could not make something like this in a hundred years. Wow."

She glanced around at the other cushions. One was made from yellow, pink, and white felt and looked like a piece of angel cake, one looked like a muffin, and one resembled a doughnut with pink ice and beads for sprinkles. "I like cake," she said.

"So I see. You are obviously a woman of many talents."

"I like to think so." She smiled and then studied the kitchen thoughtfully. They'd eaten so much that day she didn't think Summer would want more than a biscuit and a glass of milk before she went to bed. "Have a seat—I'm going to run Summer a bath. Summer, talk to Charlie for a minute will you?"

She ran the bath, listening to Summer chatting away to Charlie in the living room and his deep voice answering back, still discussing Ward Seven.

She turned off the taps and swooshed the bubbles around in the water, then stopped as she heard Summer say, "I saw you kiss Mummy in the park."

Ophelia's heart shuddered to a stop. *Shit.* She hadn't realized the girls had spotted them. How was Charlie going to deal with that question?

"Yep," he said. "Very nice it was too."

Ophelia covered her mouth with a hand.

"Are you going to be Mummy's new boyfriend?"

Closing her eyes, Ophelia wished the ground would open and swallow her up. She should interrupt and tell Summer not to ask questions, but her feet were frozen to the floor.

"I'd like to be," Charlie said. "Depends, though. Do you think your Dad will hit me when he finds out?"

"Maybe," Summer replied thoughtfully. "If he hit you, would you hit him back?"

"I'm not the punching sort really," Charlie said, "so probably not."

Ophelia stifled a slightly hysterical laugh. She really should intervene, but they were clearly having a moment, and he appeared to be handling it surprisingly well.

"He wants to stay with Mummy." Summer's voice held a touch of defensiveness.

"Understandably so," Charlie said. "She's gorgeous, and he doesn't want to lose her. Do you think she should stay with him if she isn't happy, though?"

"Why isn't she happy with him?" Summer wanted to know. "She was happy when she married him."

"People change. They like different things when they get older."

"I didn't use to like strawberries, but I do now."

"There you go. The main thing you have to understand is that whatever happens between your mum and dad, it's nothing to do with you."

Summer was quiet for a moment. Then she said, "Mummy said Daddy didn't leave because of me."

"Of course he didn't. I'm sure he loves you very much."

"I'm not like other girls though."

"Nope. You're much prettier."

Ophelia leaned on the doorjamb and wiped away the tear that trickled down her cheek.

"Charlie," Summer scolded.

"What? Summer, your CF has nothing to do with why your dad moved out. Your lungs don't work properly. You know what? My eyes don't work properly. My mum had to pay for glasses and she was always taking me to the opticians. Nobody's perfect. Perfect's boring. Your CF makes you interesting. I'll tell you a secret—I'm in charge of a whole team of research scientists, and we talk about you all day."

"Really?"

"Really. Everyone in the lab knows who Summer Clark is. I'll take you in to meet them one day if you like."

"Okay."

Ophelia took a deep breath and walked into the living room. "Bath's ready."

"Okay, Mummy." Summer skipped toward her. "Can Charlie come?"

He got to his feet, holding one of the Ward Seven books that he must have picked out of the bookcase. "I tell you what—I'll sit outside and read to you. How's that?"

So Charlie sat outside the bathroom with his back to the wall and read to them from one of Dixon the Dog's adventures while Summer splashed around in the bath and giggled at the voices he used.

Afterward, when she was in her pajamas and Ophelia took her into her bedroom to do her physiotherapy, he asked if he could join them. Ophelia was surprised when Summer agreed, as she usually hated anyone watching.

"Have you ever used essential oils to massage her?" Charlie asked while Ophelia carried out the chest percussion on Summer to loosen the mucus in her lungs.

"Sounds a bit New-Age-y," Ophelia teased.

"Actually, tests have shown them to be surprisingly effective, especially the resins like frankincense and myrrh."

"Like the Three Wise Men brought the baby Jesus?" Summer asked.

"That's right," he said. "Lavender, tea-tree, and sandalwood too, or some sort of combination in a blend. Aerosol diffusers have also proved effective for respiratory problems."

"I'll look into it," Ophelia said. She held out a hand to her daughter. "Come on. Your eyelids are drooping. Medicines, then bed."

She took Summer into the kitchen and gave her the evening dose of pills, then put her on her nebulizer while Charlie watched and asked Summer questions about the machine. Finally, it was time for a glass of milk and a biscuit with a short story before Summer did her teeth and went to bed.

Ophelia came into the living room and pulled the door almost closed with a tired sigh. Then her eyes widened. Charlie was in the kitchen, and he'd just finished making a plunger of coffee.

"Hope you don't mind," he said. "I thought you deserved it."

"That's lovely," she said gratefully, accepting a cup from him. "Thank you so much."

"On the deck?"

"Sure."

After retrieving a small box of chocolates from the fridge, she followed him outside, and they sat together on the swing seat. The jacaranda tree in the garden had covered the lawn in lilac-colored petals. The sun hung over the horizon, the sky a beautiful mixture of blue and orange. The air was warm and sultry, a gorgeous early summer evening. Standing briefly, she collected the box of matches from the nook above the swing seat and lit the two citronella candles on either side of the deck to ward off any insects, then sat back next to him.

Sipping her coffee, she let the peace and quiet of the evening wash over her, watching the flames dance in the evening breeze. Opening the lid of the chocolates, she offered them to him, and he took a truffle.

"Thanks." He popped it in his mouth. "Summer looked tired," he observed as he took off his glasses and placed them on the table next to him.

Ophelia chose a truffle too. "She was. She'll be asleep in seconds, I guarantee."

"In that case..." He lifted his arm.

Ophelia hesitated, feeling suddenly shy, but the notion of a comforting hug from a sexy guy on a warm December evening was too strong a draw.

Moving up to him, she curled her legs underneath her and rested her head on his shoulder, sucking on the chocolate.

"Nice," he said, and kissed her hair.

Chapter Eight

Charlie closed his eyes, reveling in the moment. The air smelled of jasmine and coffee, his mouth was sweet with chocolate, and it was relatively quiet, the light sounds of traffic in the distance almost overridden by the chattering fantails in the tree. Ophelia was soft against him—her breast pressing against his ribcage, her silky upper arm under his hand. Her hair smelled of mint.

"I heard you talking to Summer," she said, and lifted her head from his shoulder.

He opened his eyes and looked down at her. "Oh?"

Her green eyes inspected his face. "You're such a nice guy."

"I'm glad you think so. You're not annoyed with me?"

Her eyes widened. "Why would I be annoyed with you?"

"For talking about your husband with her."

"Ex-husband. And I don't mind—actually it was nice to hear her talking about it. Summer's not really said much about Dillon moving out. When I told her, she listened, and she didn't make a fuss, but she didn't say anything, and she hasn't really talked about it since."

"When I don't know what to say, I keep quiet too."

"I guess." Her lips curved up at the corners. "I'm glad she spoke to you. And I like what you said to her."

He shrugged, noticing a tiny blob of chocolate on her lip. "It must be hard."

"Yes, poor girl, not only does she have a life-threatening illness, but her parents have broken up."

"I meant for you." He lifted a strand of her hair and slid it through his fingers. "Dealing with a break-up on top of Summer's condition. I can only imagine how difficult that's been."

"Don't be nice to me. I'll cry."

"I don't mind."

"Charlie…" A tear slid down her cheek. "A girl's not supposed to cry on a second date."

He reached across to place his coffee cup on the wrought-iron table next to his glasses, then leaned back. He slid a hand against her cheek and brushed the tear away with his thumb.

He touched his wet thumb to her lip, wiping away the tiny spot of chocolate there, brought his thumb to his mouth, and licked it clean. Ophelia looked up at him longingly, her lips parting a little, and gave a tiny whimper.

Hoping he'd read the signs right, he lowered his lips to hers.

He could kiss her all day every day for a year and never get bored. The thought went through his head as she gave a long sigh and relaxed against him. Her lips were plump and warm, and when he touched the tip of his tongue to them, she opened her mouth with a tiny moan. He slid his tongue inside, and knew he'd always associate the taste of chocolate with this moment, with the evening sun on his limbs, the smell of jasmine in the air, the feel of Ophelia in his arms, soft and yielding.

He tightened his arm around her, wanting to pull her onto his lap and hold her, but she placed a hand on his chest and pushed, so he lifted his head.

"I'm sorry," she whispered. "I'm so sorry." Fresh tears flowed down her face, and she got up and walked into the house.

A fantail fluttered down and landed on the table. Charlie studied it for a moment, noting the angle of its twelve splayed tail feathers, five white, two black, five white, more regular and exact than anything he could draw with a protractor. Then he got up and went inside.

Ophelia was nowhere to be seen, so he leaned against the doorjamb and waited, hands in his pockets.

After a minute or so, she came out of the doorway leading to the bedrooms, walking slowly. She stopped when she saw him. Her eyes were red, and as her gaze fell on him, her bottom lip trembled. She walked up to him and brushed past him, then stopped outside and leaned miserably on the balustrade around the deck.

"I'm sorry," she whispered again. "It's not you, it's me."

"Do you want me to go?"

Her lip trembled again but, to his surprise, she said, "No."

He waited for her to elaborate, but she didn't say anything. He was out of his depth in situations like this, unsure of the right thing to do. Brock would tell him to talk to her; Matt would tell him to try to kiss her again. He watched her wipe her face. Her shoulders sagged, and she looked defeated.

Moving forward, he took his hands out of his pockets and pulled her into his arms.

Ophelia leaned her forehead on his chest for a moment, and then turned her face to rest her cheek there. He stroked her back and kissed the top of her head, hoping the warmth of his body and the human touch would comfort her.

"I'm sorry," she whispered again. Her arms slid around him, pulling him close.

"It's all right. You're going through a tough time. I just hope I haven't made it more difficult."

"Of course not," she said, although he was sure he had. "I just want to be happy," she continued. "I'm tired of being miserable. I'm not a miserable person, and it feels wrong."

"Life's short. You have to go with your heart."

"I agree, but then I think of Summer... Her life's difficult enough as it is without me making it harder for her."

"I understand, but I'm sure she'd rather you be happy."

"I suppose. I don't know. We're all pretty selfish when it comes down to it."

He supposed she was right. If he wasn't selfish, he would walk away from her now and encourage her to try to give it another go with her ex. He'd tell her Summer should come first and the family environment would no doubt be easier on the girl. He would lie and say, "I have no feelings for you," and make it easy for her.

He didn't want to do that, though. She was too beautiful, and he wanted her. Her body was so soft beneath his fingers. He wanted to strip their clothes off and feel her skin against his. Did that make him a terrible person?

To his surprise, he felt Ophelia give a short laugh against his chest. He tipped his head to look at her. "What?"

"Nothing."

He slid a finger beneath her chin and lifted it. Her eyes were still red, but they were touched with warmth now.

"Are you laughing at me?" he asked suspiciously.

She chewed her bottom lip for a moment. Then she gave a surreptitious rock of her hips. "I can feel your erection, that's all."

"Ah. Sorry about that. It has a mind of its own."

"It's okay. It's kind of flattering."

He decided to be honest, because she'd said she liked that. "You're beautiful, Ophelia, and I want you—you can obviously see that."

Her eyes shone. "I want you too, Charlie. It's just... Dillon was my first. Being with another man makes me feel guilty, and that makes me angry. Does that sound stupid?"

"Not at all. There's no rush. I'll wait for you."

"I don't deserve it. I don't deserve you."

"It's not about what either of us deserves. I just want to make you happy." Only after he'd said it did he realize it was true. He'd never felt such a strong urge to put someone else's happiness before his own.

Jeez, he had it bad.

An idea came into his head. No doubt both his brothers would say it was a terrible idea, but he had the feeling that following his instincts with this girl was the right thing to do.

"It's not long until Christmas," he pointed out.

Her gaze caressed his face. "No. Only a few weeks."

He lifted his hands to cup her face. "How about I give you an early present?"

She blinked a few times, puzzled, but before she could answer, he lowered his lips to hers.

He kissed her for a while, enjoying the soft sweetness of her mouth, taking his time to tease her lips and tongue until she murmured and gave little moans of pleasure.

Then he lifted his head. He placed his hands on her shoulders and gently turned her around, keeping close behind her. Taking her hands in his, he lifted them above her head to hold the edge of the canopy over the swing seat.

Leaving her hands there, he began to trail his fingers lightly down her arms.

She shivered. "Charlie..."

He kissed her shoulder. "I just want to make you feel good. Nothing more. You deserve it."

She shivered as he circled his fingers around her elbows, then stroked the sensitive skin of her inner arm. "I don't deserve it. I'm a terrible person."

He continued to run his fingers down. "You're really not."

She twitched as he stroked under her arms, and she lowered her hands. "That tickles."

"Sorry." He lifted her hands up again, then went back to stroking her.

Her eyelids drifted shut. "What are you doing...?"

"Touching you. Enjoying myself." And he was. Her skin felt like cool velvet, silky soft. He was pretty sure she wasn't wearing a bra beneath the dress, and when he ran his fingers across her shoulders and down her back, he discovered he was right.

She shivered again and tipped her head back to rest on his shoulder. "Is this early present for me or for you?"

"I can't deny I might be receiving some pleasure from it." He stroked down to her hips, held them, and pressed against her so she could feel his erection against her butt. "But that's not the point. This isn't about me." He moved his hands up her ribcage, around to the front, and slid them beneath her breasts, stifling a groan at the feel of them sitting in his palms like plump peaches.

Lightly, he brushed his thumbs over her nipples.

Ophelia moaned.

"I want to give you pleasure," he whispered in her ear as he took her nipples between his finger and thumb and squeezed ever-so-gently. "I want to make you feel good. Is that so bad?"

She sucked her bottom lip and sighed. "No..."

While he continued to stroke her nipples, he kissed up her shoulder to her neck, touching his tongue to where her pulse beat beneath the skin. Covering it with his mouth, he sucked a little.

"Oh..." She arched her back, pushing her breasts into his hands.

"Soon," he said huskily, "when you're ready, I'll take you to bed and make love to you. I want to cover every inch of you in kisses, slide inside you, and take my pleasure too from your soft body."

With a groan, she tipped her head to the side, and he kissed up to her ear and sucked the lobe. "But for now," he murmured, "I'll content myself with tasting you and making you come with my mouth."

Her eyes flew open. "Charlie!"

He took her hands down and turned her in his arms, slid his hands into her silky hair, and kissed her. He was fired up now, and he plunged his tongue into her mouth, taking rather than requesting, encouraged by her answering moan and the way she pressed herself against him. Her hands slid up his back beneath his shirt, her nails scraping against his skin, and his breath hissed between his teeth.

Moving back, he dropped to his haunches, kissing down her body as he did so.

"Oh God." She gripped hold of the balustrade, trembling.

He placed his hands on her knees and slid his fingers up her thighs, taking her dress with them. Her skin was a warm brown, paling to a creamy white at the top. She wore a pair of tiny blue panties, and he admired them for a second before catching his thumbs in the elastic at the sides and drawing them down her legs.

She stepped out of them, still trembling. He tucked them in the pocket of his jeans and then returned his hands to her thighs, pushing her dress back up. He tipped forward onto his knees. Breathing quickly, she let him push her legs apart, and he thought he heard her mutter *Oh fuck* as he leaned forward and slid his tongue into her.

She groaned aloud. Charlie closed his eyes and concentrated on the smell and taste of her, the slick slide of his tongue through her already swollen, slippery folds. The balustrade had a railing lower down, and he lifted her foot onto it to give himself better access, then began to explore inside her with his fingers.

Her hand slipped into his hair as he slid two fingers deep into her and stroked firmly. Focusing on the swelling on the front wall of her vagina, he closed his mouth over her clit and swirled his tongue over it.

"Fuck." This time it wasn't a mumble, and her fingers tightened in his hair.

Taking that as encouragement he was doing it right, he slowed his movements and lost himself in the blissful task of bringing her to orgasm, teasing her slowly toward the finishing line with every touch and lick. He rested one hand on the tight muscle of her bare bottom, while his other hand grew wet with her moisture. It took all the willpower he possessed not to clamber to his feet, unzip his jeans, plunge into her, and ride her the rest of the way.

But he stayed on his knees, pleasure filling him as her sighs became longer, her breathing ragged.

"Fuck! Charlie!" She came then, hard and fast, clenching a hand in his hair as her muscles tightened in strong pulses around his fingers. "Oh, oh, oh!"

He sucked until she gasped for him to stop, then licked her gently a few times while she gave deep, long, calming breaths, before finally pushing himself to his feet to stand before her.

Tucking a finger under her chin, he lifted her face to his and kissed her.

"Oh my God," she said when he eventually drew back. Her cheeks were flushed, her eyes slightly unfocused. "I did not expect that."

He kissed her nose. "I hope that when—"

He didn't get the chance to finish the sentence though, because at that moment there was the distinct sound of a key sliding into the front door, a rattle as someone turned it, and the door opened.

Chapter Nine

Ophelia spun around in shock as the front door swung open. Charlie immediately took a few steps back, then stopped as a dark-haired man walked into the small living room.

"Dillon!" She said his name in horror as he shut the door behind him. He turned to face her with a smile, which vanished when he saw Charlie standing there.

For a brief second, silence fell. Ophelia's brain felt like scrambled eggs, her body still flooded with pleasure hormones that were rapidly being replaced by panic.

She strode into the living room, knowing her cheeks must be flushed, conscious of her own wetness on her thighs. "What are you doing?" she snapped, deciding attack was the best form of defense. "You can't just let yourself in like that."

"I always let myself in." Puzzled, Dillon held up the keys he'd owned since they bought the house. He gestured with his head toward Charlie. "Who's this?"

Ophelia couldn't think what to say. What should she call him? They weren't lovers yet, and he wasn't her boyfriend, not really.

"I'm Charlie," Charlie said, and he walked forward and held out a hand. "I'm Ophelia's friend from the hospital. You must be Dillon."

Dillon looked down at Charlie's hand, then back up at him without shaking it. "What's going on?" he demanded, his voice low and icy cold.

Charlie lowered his hand, surprisingly cool considering the circumstances. "We've just had a cup of coffee. Would you like one?"

Slowly, Dillon walked forward until he was only a few inches away from the other man. Ophelia's heart pounded, and she felt sick as she watched her ex glare at the guy who'd just given her such pleasure. Guilt mixed with resentment inside her. Dillon had no right to act the jealous husband—they were separated, and she didn't have to be faithful to him now.

Charlie topped Dillon by about four inches, and he looked down at her ex with the lack of expression that she was beginning to learn meant he was thinking furiously, presumably about how to handle this.

"Are you fucking her?" Dillon said.

"Dillon!" She gasped, appalled, her hand rising to her mouth. If they'd been alone, she would have yelled at him, but she felt humiliated and embarrassed with Charlie there.

Charlie blinked. "Not yet."

Warmth rushed into her cheeks at his intimation that it was only a matter of time. Dillon's gaze slid insolently down the other man as if assessing his worth. She knew he'd receive no clue as to Charlie's wealth, apart maybe from his expensive watch, which she suspected Brock had bought him as she was certain that, if left to his own devices, Charlie would have picked an All Blacks one for fifty bucks.

Dillon went still, and both she and Charlie followed his gaze down to where Dillon was staring at the other man's jeans. Her blue panties hung from Charlie's right pocket. They were only tucked in there by a corner, and from the lace and shape it was quite obvious what they were.

Lifting his gaze again to meet her ex's, Charlie gave a tiny shrug. Raising his hand, keeping his eyes fixed on Dillon's, he sucked the tip of his middle finger as if licking it clean.

Ophelia inhaled sharply and her face burned. Before she could say anything, Dillon pushed Charlie back against the wall with an arm pressed across his throat.

"Dillon!" she screamed.

He ignored her and snarled into Charlie's face. "I'm going to fucking kill you."

What happened next occurred so quickly that Ophelia couldn't be sure how Charlie had done it, but one minute Dillon was standing, the next he was on his back on the floor. Charlie must have taken his legs away, although he'd hardly seemed to move.

With the breath knocked out of him, Dillon's mouth formed an O of surprise. He didn't try to rise.

Charlie stood over him. When he spoke, there was no anger in his voice, but it carried a warning nevertheless. "Ophelia says you're a good guy, so I'm going to pretend that was out of character. I get why you're angry—she's gorgeous, and she was yours, and you clearly love her. But you lost her, and she's not your property. Act like a man, and deal with it."

Silence fell again.

Ophelia took Charlie's hand and let him away toward the front door. "I need to talk to Dillon," she said. "Is that okay?"

Charlie's brown-eyed gaze caressed her face. "You're sure?"

"I want to sort this out."

"All right." He hesitated, took out his wallet, and extracted a business card. "Will you call me later? I'd like to talk to you."

"Of course. Thank you for a lovely day." She looked into his eyes and gave a small smile, thinking of how it had ended.

His lips curved up a tiny bit. "You're welcome."

"Bye then."

He retrieved his glasses from the table outside, gave a quick glance back at Dillon, and left.

Ophelia shut the door behind him. She waited a moment, gathering her wits and her courage, then turned and walked across to the kitchen. "I'll make us a coffee."

Dillon, who'd gotten to his feet, walked outside and sat on the swing seat, right where Charlie had been sitting earlier. She emptied the plunger and rinsed it, then spooned coffee into it, using the time to calm herself and to try to decide what to say.

He wasn't a bad man, and he did love her, she knew that. *She was yours, and you clearly love her. But you lost her, and she's not your property.* How come Charlie had summarized in one sentence what she'd been trying to tell Dillon for a year?

The kettle clicked off, so she poured the hot water into the plunger, made the coffee, poured it into two cups with milk, added two spoons of sugar to Dillon's, and carried them outside.

"Here." She gave him the cup, and was struck with a wave of sadness as she sat. She knew this man so well—his likes and dislikes, every inch of his body and mind. She'd loved him once, but her love had spoiled like meat left outside in the sun. She wished it hadn't, but she couldn't un-spoil it, no matter how hard she tried. And she had tried. At least she could comfort herself with that.

"Dillon, I'd like you to give me your key to the house."

He sipped his coffee. "No. This is my house too."

She gritted her teeth. "Technically, yes, but you can't just walk in whenever you want."

He said nothing, looking across the lawn. Frustration boiled in her stomach. He wasn't going to give it to her. She should have asked him for it when he first moved out, but at the time he'd called in occasionally while she was at work to pick up his stuff, and it hadn't felt as important then.

"He works at the hospital?" Dillon asked, obviously referring to Charlie.

"Yes. You remember Summer's doctor there?"

"King?"

"Yes. Charlie is his brother."

Dillon turned his cool gray eyes on her and gave a wry laugh. "You're fucking kidding me. You're dating a billionaire?"

She didn't say anything. There was no point in denying the fact, and he wouldn't believe she hadn't known who Charlie was before she agreed to go out with him.

The humor disappeared from his face and a spark of jealousy darkened his eyes. "I don't want him flashing his money around in front of my daughter."

"He won't," Ophelia said. She couldn't imagine Charlie flashing his money around anywhere. Ten-to-one he had no idea how to use a cash machine.

Dillon looked back out across the lawn, then slammed his hand down on the seat, making her jump. "I fucking hate this. I don't want another man around my daughter. She's my girl."

Ophelia went cold at the thought that because he was finally coming to accept he'd lost her, he was going to turn his jealousy onto his daughter. She wanted to scream at him, but history had taught her that he flourished on high emotions. He was manipulative, but she'd learned to be more so.

"Of course she is," she said smoothly. "And there's no question of anyone replacing you where Summer's concerned. She adores her Daddy. She's really looking forward to staying with you next weekend."

He glared at her. "And I suppose you'll be off with Mr. Fancy Pants while I'm looking after our daughter?"

"I have no idea whether I'll see Charlie again after your little stunt," she replied hotly, irritated that her attempt at pacification hadn't worked. "But if I do, it's none of your damn business. We're done, Dillon. Over. And we can deal with this like grown-ups, or it can be horrid and unpleasant and make our and Summer's lives a misery. Is that what you want?"

"I want you," he said. His face was hard, uncompromising.

"Don't." She closed her eyes.

"We loved each other, didn't we? We were happy, once. I don't see why we can't be again."

"I'm tired, Dillon. Tired of fighting. Neither of us is innocent in this. I know I've not made it easy either. But you have to accept that we're done."

"I can't accept it. I've let things slide, I know that. I should have bought you flowers more, and taken you out every week. I work hard for the money I make, and I get tired, that's all. It happens in every relationship." His voice held a touch of resentment. "I know I can't be exciting for you anymore. But the excitement always wears off."

She knew what he was trying to say. Their sex life had been great in the beginning, but after Summer had been born they'd both been tired and worried after she was diagnosed. Lovemaking had become something they'd fitted in around the rest of their life, rather than it taking the pride of place it had when they were first together.

She didn't know what to say to that. She knew it was bound to happen in all relationships, especially when kids came along. It would happen with Charlie, probably, if they stayed together long enough. But it didn't bother her, because comfort and security in a trusted relationship replaced the spark of excitement of a new one, and those things were to be treasured, not sniffed at.

A lackluster love life wasn't the reason she'd wanted to break up. His jealousy and possessiveness were the cause. With him, she'd felt like a bonsai tree, restricted by her environment, encouraged to grow as far as Dillon was comfortable with and no further. He was intimidated by education and resentful of privilege, and he'd always made fun of her if she'd talked about taking courses or training for a job superior to her present one.

Unfortunately, it had taken her seven years and having Summer for her to realize it. But she couldn't bring herself to wish she'd never met him, because they'd made their beautiful daughter. Summer was the light of her life, and for that she had to be grateful to him.

"I'm glad I met you," she said, "and glad we have Summer. But it's over. We're not going to get back together."

"I don't believe that." Now he seemed calm. "Our daughter's sick. You can't tell me it wouldn't be better for her if we were together."

"Don't bring her into this. This isn't about Summer."

"Of course it is."

"It's not! It's about being happy, and I'm not happy with you."

"I know, but I can make you happy again."

"Dillon…" Despair threatened to make her cry again. "Please just accept it's over. We haven't slept together for nearly a year." They'd tried a reconciliatory session after she'd first told him she wanted a divorce back in January and he'd asked her to give him another chance. He'd been rough, and smug that he'd talked her into it, completely the opposite of what she'd hoped. She'd cried afterward, and they hadn't slept together since. "You should start dating again," she told him.

"I'm not cheating on you."

"It's not cheating when you're not together!"

"We will be," he said stubbornly. "We're just on a break. I love you. I don't care that you've met this guy. You're my wife, and I'm not going to give you up." He put his cup down. "I'd better go. I guess Summer's asleep?"

"Yes," she said miserably.

"I'll check in on her if that's okay." Without waiting for an answer, he went indoors.

She stood and leaned on the doorjamb while he went into Summer's room. When he came out, he crossed over to her and kissed her cheek.

Seconds away from bursting into tears, Ophelia didn't stop him.

"See you soon," Dillon said. "I love you."

He walked away, out the front door, and closed it behind him.

She shouldn't have asked Charlie to go. All of a sudden, she longed for him, for the comforting way he'd hugged her and kissed her hair.

Collapsing onto the sofa, she finally gave in to the tears.

Chapter Ten

"You did what?"

Charlie sighed. It was around nine p.m., and he was sitting on his deck having a beer, watching the sun go down. The cicadas were out in force, filling the air with a chorus of tiny violins. The pool was like a sheet of beaten copper in the rays of the setting sun. He'd have a swim before he went to bed, he decided, work off some of his angst.

"I knocked him over," he repeated. "I told Summer I wouldn't hit him, so I just took his legs out."

Brock and Matt stared at him through the screen of his laptop.

"Holy shit," Matt said. "He must have felt as if he'd been flattened by Pooh Bear."

"Hey, I've trained in the ring," Charlie protested.

"When you were eight," Brock reminded him. "And you were so bad at it that the trainer refused to put you in because you never hit your opponent back."

"What can I say? I had my aggression removed at birth."

Brock rolled his eyes. "Why did he hit you, anyway? You must have provoked him."

"Ah… I'd rather not say."

"Charlie," Matt said. "What did you do?"

He thought of the pair of panties that had protruded from his pocket, and how he'd licked his fingers. He couldn't believe he'd done it. Poor Ophelia—she'd turned scarlet. But Dillon had annoyed him with his possessiveness and the way he'd spoken about her as if she were an item of furniture. "I implied Ophelia and I had been intimate," he said.

Their eyebrows rose as one. "Had you?" Matt asked.

"That's irrelevant."

"Wow," Matt said, "you move even faster than me."

"Shit, don't say that." He sat forward and sank his hands into his hair. "I can't believe I've screwed this up already."

"Hey. You haven't screwed it up," Brock told him. "They're separated, aren't they?"

"Well, he's moved out, but he clearly wants her back."

"What did Ophelia say about him?" Matt asked. "Is she certain it's over?"

"She insists it is. She told him she wanted to break up at the beginning of the year, but he talked her into staying for a few more months. So she's tried to make it work. I know she feels guilty about it, though. Obviously, she feels she has to put Summer first, and that conflict of interests is hard for her." He flopped back into his chair. "What do I do? Surely, if there's a chance she can make it work with her husband, I should encourage that, shouldn't I?"

"I think you should be guided by what Ophelia wants," Brock said. "All relationships are about power play. In a good relationship, the exchange of power is equal—both parties give and take. But more often than not, the balance is off. I've watched Ophelia and Dillon together, remember, when they've come in with Summer. Ophelia's lovely, gentle and genuine, and there's no doubt he knows how to play on that. Kudos to her for recognizing it and trying to do something about it."

"Isn't it best for Summer, though, if her parents stay together?" Charlie asked.

"Not necessarily," Brock said. "Of course it's upsetting for a child when his or her parents break up. But it must be worse if the parents aren't getting on. It's distressing for the kid if her parents are arguing, or her mum's in tears. Staying together for the children is a noble aim, but if one or both of them are unhappy, what's the point?"

"We only have one life," Matt said. "Seems a shame to waste it in a destructive, unhappy relationship."

"I suppose." Charlie felt completely out of his depth with all this. "I just want to do the right thing. And if it means getting the girl, even better."

"Like I said, be guided by Ophelia," Brock said. "If at any point she intimates her marriage isn't over, then back off. But if not... Maybe you're just what she needs to help her through this. You have to remember that they weren't living together when this happened. She'd already made the break."

"I should have stuck to science," Charlie said gloomily. "There's little room for doubt in science."

"Speaking of which," Brock said, "how's the CF research coming along?"

"Ah. I had an idea." Charlie proceeded to tell them about his plans for the new peak flow meter.

"I love it," Brock said.

"Which character were you thinking of using?" Matt asked.

"Not sure yet. I suppose it depends on whether we make it a physical piece of equipment or digital. If it's physical, it'll have to be something simple like… the kid has to blow to get Dixon into his kennel or something."

"I could always come up with a new character," Matt said. "A rabbit they have to get into a warren, or a bird into a tree or something. I'll have a think."

"A physical piece of equipment would be more practical for home use," Brock said, "but we could always have a digital alternative at the hospital."

"Of course, yes. I—" Charlie stopped as his phone rang on the table. "Sorry, that's my phone. Got to go."

"Okay, see ya," Matt said.

"Good luck." Brock smiled. The guys rang off.

Charlie took a deep breath, picked up his phone, and swiped the screen. "Hello?"

"Charlie? It's Ophelia."

"Hey. I'm glad you rang. How are you doing?"

"I'm all right." Her voice was subdued.

He ran a hand through his hair. "I want to apologize."

"What for?"

"Jeez, how long have you got? For embarrassing you. For knocking Dillon over."

"It's okay," she said quietly.

"It's not. It was your house and whatever goes on between you and your husband is none of my business—I had no right to throw my weight around like that."

"Ex-husband," she corrected. "And I am embarrassed, but not for the reason you think. I can't believe he just walked in like that. I should have taken his key off him ages ago, but I didn't think. I'm so sorry." She stopped, and he thought he heard the sound of a tissue being pulled from a box.

He leaned his head on the back of the chair and looked up at the rose-colored sky. "Hey, come on," he said. "You weren't to know. It was just unfortunate, that's all. And I really am sorry for embarrassing you. I don't know what came over me—I'm not normally like that. I just didn't like the way he spoke to you."

"Neither did I," she said hoarsely. "Thank you for standing up for me. It meant a lot to me."

"Oh." That surprised him. "Well. I'm glad you're not angry. I'm sure the last thing you need at the moment is another surge of testosterone around the place."

That made her laugh. "The look on his face when you licked your finger was priceless."

"I can't believe I did that."

She started to giggle. "Neither can I. You're full of surprises."

He sipped his beer, the knot in his stomach starting to loosen. "I'm glad you can see the funny side."

"It's the only funny thing about this whole situation." She gave a long sigh. "I don't know what to say. My life is such a mess, and I feel terrible to think you got caught up in it."

"I don't mind."

"That's lovely of you to say, but it's not really the point. I shouldn't have gone out with you tonight."

His heart sank. "I see."

"It's just not fair on you. I have to get my life sorted first—it's the only way. Dillon's refusing to accept it's over, and I know he's going to make my life a misery until the divorce is through."

He thought about Brock's advice—to be guided by her. "Ophelia, I've not been married, I don't have kids, and I've never had to deal with someone who's on the receiving end of being dumped. I wouldn't presume to know what you're going through at the moment. I'll just say this. If you've decided you don't want to see me because you haven't made your mind up whether your marriage is over, I'll back away. If that's the case, and you want to try to make things work, I don't want to make things harder for you."

Or for me, he thought. He wasn't sure how he'd deal with her being torn in two as to whether to stay with Dillon or not. In all the relationships he'd had, and there hadn't been many, he'd been the one who'd been dumped, but he could honestly say none of them had broken his heart.

Next to him, on a table, was a piece of paper. He picked it up—it was the photo of Ophelia and the girls they'd had taken with Princess Sapphire. He'd bought it at the end of the day while she'd taken the girls for a final trip to the Ladies' before going home. He ran a thumb across Ophelia's image, thinking of how he'd kissed her, how she'd felt in his arms.

Even though he'd only been out with her twice, he already knew that if he continued to see her and then she decided she was going to stay with Dillon, his heart would not remain untouched.

He took a deep breath. "But if you're saying you don't want to see me again because you're worried things will get messy, well, you should know I'm not scared of that. I'd like to get to know you better, and if that means dealing with Dillon's anger and resentment at losing you, I'm happy to do that. I can cope with him and with your guilt over ending the relationship."

He sat up and leaned forward, his elbows on his knees. "I'm sorry if it seems cruel to force you to make this decision now," he said. "But you know I'm rubbish at reading between the lines. You have to tell me what you're thinking. Do you have doubt that it's over with Dillon?"

"Hold on." She must have put the phone down, because he heard her blowing her nose. After a short while, he heard her sigh, and then a rustle as she picked up the phone again. "Sorry."

"Are you okay?"

"I'm fine. I just can't believe you're being so sweet."

"I'm not being sweet. I'm being cruel. I'm practically Attila the Hun."

She laughed. "No you're not. And I understand why you want me to be clear. So here it is. It's over between me and Dillon. When we're apart, and ninety-nine percent of the time we're together, I'm certain it's done. I can't say it doesn't make me sad to think it's over, but I think that's natural, and I know that will pass over time."

She sighed. "That last one percent is just guilt. He's smart, and he knows me—he knows how to play on my emotions. He's not a bad guy, but he is manipulative. He knows exactly what to say to make me feel bad, and the worst thing is that he isn't afraid to use that skill to his advantage. And that's the one thing that washes away the last percent of doubt. Does that make sense? Even during those moments when I do feel guilt, part of me is aware I'm being manipulated, and that makes me resentful."

"It makes perfect sense."

"I loved him, but I don't love him anymore. He destroyed that love with his jealousy and possessiveness, and I know that if we were to get back together, within weeks, days even, I'd curse myself for being so weak. And I'm not weak—I don't think I am anyway, not normally. But I am good natured, and he uses that. It makes me angry just to think about it."

"I don't think you're weak at all. It takes courage to admit a marriage is over, and to do something about it, especially when you feel the odds are against you."

"Thank you," she said, and he could hear the smile in her voice. "I do want to see you again—very much. I've spent the last six months trying desperately to talk to you in the mornings, but I thought you never saw me."

"Oh... I saw you."

"I did catch you checking my butt out in the window once."

"Yeah. That sounds about right." He sighed. "So you do want to see me again?"

"I'd like to. As long as you're sure you can put up with my madness."

"I'll do my best. So... what are you and Summer up to at the weekend?"

"Well, Dillon and I have Summer alternate weekends, and it's his turn, so I'm free."

His heart soared. "Would you like to go away somewhere?"

"Oh! Where?"

"My parents have a bach in the Bay of Islands. Nice place near Paihia, right on the beach."

"It sounds wonderful."

"There are several bedrooms, so Summer's very welcome too. I don't want you or her to think I don't understand you come as a package. She's a lovely girl, and I want to get to know her better too."

"Thank you, Charlie, I do appreciate that. And it will be nice to do something all three of us again. But this weekend, I'd love to spend some time with you alone."

"As I said, there are lots of bedrooms, so please don't feel any pressure to... you know." He scratched his cheek.

She laughed. "I won't, but I do have a favor I need to return." Her voice sounded full of smiles.

Heat flooded his body as he realized what she was referring to. "Oh. Yes. Well. You don't need to... I'm sure that..."

She laughed again. "Thank you for today. It was... wonderful."

He closed his eyes and thought about the taste of her, and how it had felt when she'd come on his tongue. "Oh, you're so welcome."

"I'll see you Monday morning by the breakfast cart?"

"I guarantee it."

"Okay. Bye then."

He ended the call, and then lay back and looked up at the sky. The sun had nearly set, and the sky was a beautiful palette of pinks, purples, and oranges. He wasn't into art, but his heart swelled at the beauty of it, so much so that it even brought tears to his eyes.

You're only tearful because there's a chance you might get laid, he told himself, taking a swig of his beer and swallowing hard.

But his lips remained touched with a smile for a long while, as the color faded slowly from the sky.

Chapter Eleven

"You have your own plane?" Ophelia stared at Charlie, open-mouthed.

It was just after six on the following Friday, and a man called Lee, who Charlie had told her was Brock's assistant, had picked them both up and dropped them off at the airport. Charlie hadn't mentioned anything about the plane on the way, and she'd assumed they were flying Air New Zealand along with thirty-or-so other bodies.

Charlie tipped his head from side to side. He wore his prescription shades and she couldn't see his eyes, making it more difficult for her to read what he was thinking. "Technically, it's Brock's, but all three of us use it." He took her hand. "Come on. It's a beautiful evening. We'll have a great view over the bay."

Ophelia's heart raced as his warm fingers closed around hers, and they exited the cool lounge to cross the tarmac. The late sun beat down on them, glinting off the plane's windows and making her glad she wore sunglasses.

A slender woman called Pat in a smart navy suit had already taken Ophelia's bag, so she only had her handbag to worry about as she climbed the steps of the tiny plane. Her stomach bubbled with excitement, not just because of the plane flight and the holiday, but because she was going to spend time with Charlie.

He might not be interested in money, she thought as she reached the top of the steps and stepped into the plane's interior, but she had no doubt he was used to having it. He'd not batted an eyelid at being chauffeured to the airport, and she could tell from the way he led her into the plane and greeted Pat that this wasn't the first time he'd flown on it.

The cabin was small but beautifully decorated, much of the interior made from what looked like rimu wood polished to a high shine. He took her to the set of four leather seats facing each other across a polished table, and gestured for her to take the one by the window, while he sat next to her. He placed his sunglasses on the table, and she lifted hers onto the top of her head. The seats were nothing like the ones in economy—these were more like first class. What a treat!

"All ready, Mr. King?" Pat asked with a smile, checking to make sure they were fastened in.

"Good to go," he said, and Pat nodded and went to take her seat by the cockpit.

Ophelia grinned at the excitement in his eyes. "You like flying?"

"Love it. Something magnificent about defying gravity."

"Trust you to have a scientific reason for it." Ophelia held his gaze for a moment, her heart rate picking up again as he tipped his head to the side, his eyes turning interested. It was lovely to think they'd have two days to get to know one another, but it was even more exciting to think they'd have two nights. Alone. With no children, no ex, nobody to distract them from paying each other very close attention.

She still couldn't believe he'd gone down on her on her deck, out in the warm sunshine, giving her pleasure with no thought of his own. He'd been so gentle, and yet his touch had been sure and skilled—he wasn't quite the boyish innocent he appeared. What other delights did he know in the bedroom? She was quickly beginning to realize that his lack of expression and self-confessed difficulty in social matters masked a deep-thinking, passionate man. That dichotomy fascinated her, and she wanted to understand him better.

"You're sure you still want to come?" Charlie murmured. "The plane's not going that fast if you want to leap off."

"I still want to come," she whispered. She glanced at Pat to make sure she couldn't hear her. "And I'm aware of the double meaning in that."

Charlie's brown eyes studied her, and she could almost see his brain working furiously behind them.

She gave a mischievous smile. "You're using the theory of relativity to work out how fast you can get me into bed, aren't you?"

"Well, now I am."

Giggling, she looked out of the window as the plane stopped, revved up its engines, and then sped along the tarmac. Her stomach lurched as it lifted, and Charlie leaned forward to look out of the window before the plane climbed higher, heading for the bright blue sky.

It wasn't long before they could unclip their seatbelts, and Pat came up to them with a smile. "Can I get you anything to eat or drink?"

"Oh, the sun's over the yardarm, I reckon," Charlie said. "Must be time for something alcoholic, do you think?"

"I'd love a glass of white wine," Ophelia said.

"Of course," Pat said. "Sauvignon, Chardonnay, or Pinot Gris, or would you prefer sparkling?"

"Oh, Sauvignon would be lovely, thank you."

"Same for me please, Pat, and maybe just some nibbles," Charlie said. "I'm starving."

Pat smiled and nodded, then disappeared around the corner.

Charlie sat back and stretched out his legs, his thigh brushing against Ophelia's under the table. She felt happier than she had been in a long time, even though she missed having Summer around.

"Are you a big rugby fan?" She gestured at his All Blacks shirt. She hadn't seen him in anything else.

He looked down at it. "Sometimes I go to Brock's apartment to watch the internationals."

"You can't watch them at your house?"

"I don't have a TV."

"That's funny! I can't imagine not having a TV. So why do you wear All Blacks shirts if you're not into rugby?"

He scratched his cheek. "I don't want to tell you." For maybe the first time since she'd met him, he looked vaguely embarrassed.

She turned in her seat to face him, interested. "Come on, spill the beans."

"Unfortunately, there are no parachutes on board if you decide you want to leave."

"Now I'm intrigued."

He sighed. "My wardrobe consists of a rack of identical rugby shirts."

She stared at him. "You only have All Blacks tops in your wardrobe?"

"Well, there are a couple of white shirts and suits for formal occasions, but basically yeah. I just put a different one on every day."

"Why?"

"I can't be bothered to take time deciding what to wear."

"You really are a reincarnation of Einstein aren't you?"

He ran a hand through his hair and leaned forward to look out of the window again. "I know I'm weird. I never cared much before now."

He thought she'd be freaked out by his strange ways. It made her soften inside like a chocolate button left out in the sun.

"You're adorable," she said. She lifted a hand to his face and brushed a thumb against the smoothness of his freshly-shaved cheek. When he turned his head to look at her, she leaned forward and pressed her lips to his. He didn't object, and so she closed her eyes and just enjoyed the feel of being close to him.

The chink of a wine glass being placed on the table made her pull away. Her cheeks warmed. "Sorry," she said as Pat straightened after putting the second glass down.

"Not at all, and I'm sorry to have interrupted." Pat smiled. "It's lovely to see Mr. King so happy."

Charlie watched her walk away and picked up his glass. "She's obviously used to me looking miserable. See how good you are for me?"

"Have you been swimming?" Ophelia tried to distract his attention from her red cheeks. "You smell a little of chlorine."

"Ah, sorry. I did shower afterward but it lingers in the hair."

"No, I like it. It's a nice clean smell. You swim a lot?"

"Every day."

"You have your own pool?"

"Yes."

"Nice." It wasn't particularly unusual for Kiwis to have a pool, but she bet his was bigger than average.

"It's the only exercise I enjoy."

She couldn't help herself. "The *only* exercise?"

He sipped his wine, his eyes filled with lazy amusement. "We'll find out soon, won't we?"

She shivered at the thought of him going down on her again, of his lips on her skin, his firm body beneath her fingertips, him moving inside her. "I can't wait."

He opened his mouth to reply, but at that moment Pat returned with a plate of nibbles—slices of crisp peppers and carrots, tiny rice crackers, a variety of tempting dips, sushi with smoked salmon, and other little bits and pieces meant to tempt the taste buds.

"Wow, thank you. I feel like royalty." Ophelia chose a piece of the sushi and sat back to eat it with her glass of wine. Charlie picked a cream cheese puff and sat back. As he ate it, he winked at her.

She smiled. "I feel like I'm fifteen again."

"Is that a good thing? I hated being that age."

"No, it's nice. I was nervous about dating again. It's been a while."

"Dillon was really your first?"

"Yes. I thought I'd be with him forever. Well, I suppose nobody goes into marriage assuming they'll get divorced."

"I guess not." He dipped a slice of pepper in some hummus. "Was he okay tonight when he came to pick Summer up?"

Ophelia thought of how Dillon had glowered at her, snapped at Summer because she hadn't finished packing her bag, and generally made a nuisance of himself until she'd yelled at him to go. "Not really." She hesitated, feeling that she shouldn't bad mouth him, even though she was cross with him.

"If you'd rather not talk about it, that's okay," Charlie said.

She realized her spine had stiffened, and forced herself to relax. Taking his free hand in hers, she brushed his palm with her thumb. "No, I don't mind. I'm not normally a gossip and it feels mean to slag him off behind his back, but the truth is that he knew I was going away with you, and he was determined to make things difficult. I hate that about him—that he can't just accept it's over between us."

He watched her thumb moving across his skin. "He must love you."

"I don't know. Maybe he does. But it feels more like dog in the manger, you know? I'm not sure he really wants me—he just doesn't want anyone else to have me."

He turned his hand over and did the same to her, brushing his thumb over her skin. "Has he dated anyone since he moved out?"

"He says he hasn't."

"Do you believe him?"

"If he has, he's being incredibly hypocritical. I'm not sure which I'd prefer." She sighed dreamily at the sensation of being touched. Why was it so erotic? It felt as if every hair on her body had risen. "Let's not talk about him. I want to escape with you. I've thought about nothing else all week."

"Me too. It's been very distracting."

"Sorry."

"It's nice," he said. "Being unfocused. I've quite enjoyed it."

"My gift to you."

He met her gaze for a moment. Then he turned a little in his seat to face her. Cupping her cheek, he leaned forward and kissed her.

She closed her eyes, no longer caring if Pat was watching, not caring about anything except the pleasure it gave her to be kissing this man. He tasted of sweet wine, his lips firm and cool, and when she opened her mouth to him, he didn't lose the opportunity to slip his tongue against hers. The slick slide of it was erotic and sensual, and she felt her nipples peaking in her bra, and an answering twinge deep inside her.

"Mmm," she murmured as his lips left hers to kiss her cheek, her nose, her eyelids. "Tell me we can do this all weekend."

"Absolutely." He kissed around to her ear, nuzzled it, then touched his tongue to the sensitive skin behind the lobe. "I want to spend hours just kissing you. Getting to know every inch of your body."

"Ooh."

He kissed down her neck, his mouth hot and wet on her skin. "I want to draw you to the edge and keep you there as long as we can bear it, hovering on the edge of orgasm until every brush of our lips, every touch of our fingers, is almost unbearable."

Ophelia felt as if she was already there, her body aching for him. "Oh, Charlie."

His hand tightened in her hair, and he returned to her lips to kiss her hungrily. "I want you," he said, his voice surprisingly fierce, his eyes ablaze with passion as she looked up at him, her chest heaving. "I want to make you come so many times you forget everything else except that feeling deep inside you, until all you can think about is me, kissing you, touching you, moving inside you."

"Oh…" She let her lips brush his. "And I want to take you in my mouth and taste you, and then feel your body moving in mine, to feel your muscles tightening as you come inside me."

His lips paused over hers, their hot breath mingling. Then he groaned and leaned back in his seat. "Jesus."

She laughed. "Maybe we should wait with the dirty talk until we're properly alone."

"Yeah. That's probably a good idea or I'm going to severely embarrass myself."

Chapter Twelve

A hire car was waiting for them at the Bay of Islands airport. While Ophelia got in, Charlie put their bags in the back, and then said goodbye to Pat. She kissed him on the cheek.

"I've never seen you look this happy," she said with a smile. "She's lovely."

"She is," Charlie agreed. "I'm thinking of locking her in the bach and keeping her there."

"Okay, that's slightly scary so I wouldn't tell her that."

"Thanks for the tip," he said wryly. "See you Sunday."

"Have a great time."

He slid on his sunglasses, got into the car, started the engine, and pulled away. Next to him, Ophelia gave a happy sigh.

"This is like heaven," she said. "Sun, child-free, and off for a naughty weekend by the sea."

"It does sound a bit like paradise." He turned left toward the small but bustling town of Kerikeri. "Do you come up to the Bay much?"

"I've only been once, actually. Do your parents live up here?"

"No, in Auckland. Mum and Dad are both lawyers, and they run a firm together there."

"Do you have any other siblings apart from Brock and Matt?"

Charlie adjusted his rear view mirror. "I did. Pippa was two years younger than Matt, but she died when I was twelve."

Ophelia stared at him in shock. "Oh Charlie, I didn't know, I'm so sorry. How did she die? Do you mind me asking?"

"Of course not. She had an asthma attack. Matt and I were at a football game with Mum and Dad—Brock was at home with her. She pretty much died in his arms. It's the main reason he became a doctor."

"And why you're all so involved with respiratory diseases," she said softly. "How awful for you all."

"It was traumatic at the time. We all reacted differently to it, I think. Brock decided he was going to make sure no other family had to go through what he went through. He was a bit of a tearaway before that, but afterward he knuckled down and started to ace all his exams. Matt went off the rails, became a rebel, nearly got himself expelled, but managed to pull it together enough to go to Art College, and settled down after that."

"And what about you?"

He thought about it for a moment, slowing the car at the roundabout and indicating to take the state highway south. "I probably changed the least. I'd never been a rebel and had always worked hard at school, and I just continued doing what I was doing. I threw myself into my work. I felt… numb, I suppose. Still do, in a way, and part of me is ashamed by that. I loved Pippa, and when she died I felt there should have been earthquakes and stars falling from the sky, but I can remember getting up the next day and the sun was shining, and I was shocked that the world was still spinning. That sense of unreality has never really gone away."

Charlie rarely said more than one sentence in a conversation, preferring to listen rather than speak because of his tendency to misunderstand or misinterpret what others said, so it felt odd to give such a speech.

"Are you religious?" Ophelia asked. "Do you feel that everything happens for a reason?"

"I can't believe that any god worth his or her salt would take a person away from their loved ones to prove a point. But who knows? Maybe there is a bigger plan. Science will always come first for me, but that doesn't mean I don't see extraordinary beauty in everyday things." He glanced at her and winked.

Her cheeks flushed a pretty pink. "You're such a flirt."

"I honestly don't think anyone's ever called me that before. Somewhere in Auckland, Matt's laughing his head off."

She smiled. "You're very self-deprecating. I like that in a man. But I don't believe everything you say. You're gorgeous, Charlie, and warm and funny. I don't understand why you're single."

"I think that says more about you than me. Girls don't normally find me warm and funny."

"Really?" She looked genuinely bewildered.

"My last girlfriend called me cold and unfeeling."

Ophelia frowned. "Obviously she didn't understand you at all."

"That's nice of you to say, but she was only echoing what others have said in the past."

"That puzzles me. Your eyes are very expressive, even if you don't always say what you're thinking."

A seed of warmth grew in his stomach and spread throughout him. "I used to be more outspoken, but I put my foot in it so many times that I learned to keep my thoughts to myself until I was sure I'd gotten it right."

"What happened with your last girlfriend?" Ophelia asked.

"I met Lisette at the local swimming baths, before I bought my current house. We went for a coffee afterward and we dated for a couple of months after that. But we weren't really compatible. We didn't 'get' each other at all."

"She wasn't into science?"

He took the turn-off for Paihia, heading east toward the coast. "I don't expect the women I date to be science freaks."

"Like you." She grinned.

He gave her a wry look. "Yes, like me. But we were poles apart. All she talked about was clothes and celebrities and something called Shortland Street."

Ophelia laughed. "You've never watched Shortland Street?"

"I don't have a TV," he reminded her.

"It's a Kiwi soap opera."

"Oh. Well, she loved it anyway, and it frustrated her that I didn't know about the things she liked and, more importantly I suppose, that I didn't care. She'd talk for hours about the latest handbag she'd bought, and I'd just zone out and think about the pediatric dose of Prednisone for asthma. Apparently that made me a bad boyfriend."

"I can't think of any man who would want to listen to a discussion about handbags for an hour," Ophelia said, unable to contain her laughter.

Charlie's lips curved up reluctantly. "Maybe. I guess that wasn't all of it. She constantly wanted me to tell her how I was feeling and what I was thinking. In the end I had to make up stuff because being honest just got me into deeper water."

"I don't mean to be... well, mean, but to be honest she sounds a bit dim. Ask most ordinary men what they're thinking and they'll answer sport, food, or sex. Men don't analyze their feelings like women do, in my experience anyway."

"True." There was more to the story with Lisette, but he wasn't about to confide that yet.

Smiling, he reached out to hold her hand. "I'm glad you can see through me. That bodes well at this early stage."

She curled her fingers around his, but said, "Hey, don't think I'm lumping you in with ordinary men. I know for a fact that if I were to ask you what you were thinking, it would involve something brainy and scientific."

"Not necessarily. I'm currently thinking about what color underwear you're wearing." He glanced across and pulled an *eek* face when he saw her eyebrows rise above the top of her sunglasses. "Oops. Too honest?"

"Not at all. You're very welcome to tell me what's on your mind if you're thinking things like that."

He lifted her hand to kiss her fingers, loving that she wasn't easily offended. That also boded well. "I keep meaning to ask you, what job are you going to do when you leave the hospital?"

"I have a part-time post working as a liaison for the local health board. I'll miss working with radio, but it means I'll be able to meet Summer at lunchtime for her physio."

"Has her CF gotten worse lately?"

"She's had a run of chest infections so she's had a lot of time off school. Brock suggested upping her physio to three times a day, and he's changed her medication, so we'll have to see if that makes a difference." She looked out of the window.

Charlie didn't want to press her now—this was supposed to be an escape for her, a time for them to get to know each other. But he made a mental note to talk to her about it later. More than ever, he wanted his latest research project on gene therapy to be successful, but it was still in the early stages, and he needed more data, which hopefully parents like Ophelia could provide him with.

He changed the subject, and they chatted about music—one of his favorite non-scientific topics—for the rest of the journey until they reached the turn off for Paihia and took the coast road.

"Oh wow." Ophelia stared at the glittering Pacific Ocean. "Why is it that just seeing the sea is somehow healing?"

"I don't know, but it is," he agreed. The low sun had turned the water a deep pinky-gold. At the central pier, he could see his friend Niall's boat in the process of docking, bearing a group of tourists who'd been out to see the dolphins. Charlie had spoken to Niall the night before and had arranged for them to go out the next day to the Hole in the Rock, a spectacular cruise to Cape Brett with its Grand Cathedral Cave. It would be a lovely treat, but he had to admit he couldn't think past that evening, past being alone with Ophelia, finally removing her clothes, and taking her to bed.

Was it terrible that he had a one-track mind? Brock was taking Erin away this weekend too, and Matt had teased him for assuming Erin would sleep with him. Wasn't Charlie doing exactly the same thing? Maybe Ophelia was expecting them to sleep in separate bedrooms. She'd hardly pushed him away when he'd gotten carried away at her house, and when he'd just mentioned thinking about her underwear her reply had certainly suggested she wanted to go to bed with him, but she could always change her mind.

He sighed silently, wishing he understood the myriad small facial gestures and unspoken signals that other people apparently gave and received. The dating game was hard enough without feeling as if he was doing it blindfolded. He'd just have to do his best and try not to make an idiot of himself.

Wouldn't be the first time, he thought somewhat glumly. He'd had precisely three women slap him in his lifetime, and another one had made a scene at a party because he'd mistakenly thought her flirtatious comments had meant she'd wanted him to kiss her. Things had only been better the last couple of years because he'd made an effort to wait until the girl was practically jumping up and down in front of him waving her arms and yelling, "For God's sake, kiss me," before he made a move. The actions he'd taken on the deck with Ophelia had been completely out of character, and he'd been immensely relieved it had gone well.

"So serious," Ophelia scolded, reaching out to brush the back of her fingers against his cheek. "Still thinking about my underwear? Or are you back to Prednisone now?" Her voice was gentle, teasing. Or at least he thought it was.

Panic swelled briefly inside him, and all the self-assurance he'd felt the previous weekend fled. *Don't fuck this up, Charlie. If you do, you might as well call it a day.*

"Hey." Her smile faded as she obviously saw his concern. "What is it? Come on, tell me."

"I just… I want this to go well," he admitted. He concentrated on the road through the town center, which was busy with tourists heading out for the evening to bars, restaurants, and clubs.

"And why are you worried it won't?" she asked. "We're getting on okay, aren't we?"

"Yeah. It's great. But I'd like to say now, if I say the wrong thing, or do something stupid, just tell me, okay? Don't hold it against me."

"Charlie," she scolded, "firstly, you're not going to do anything wrong, and secondly, of course I wouldn't hold anything against you. You're a sweetheart, and you're not going to offend me."

He glanced across as they passed the *Between the Sheets* cocktail bar, which glowed with light, the outside areas already filled with customers, some couples cuddling up in the hammocks to one side. That was what he wanted—to get past the newness of a relationship where he felt constantly on edge. To get to the point where his partner knew him, where he could relax and be himself without worrying all the time.

"I've looked forward to tonight all week," Ophelia said. "Do you know why?"

"I'm assuming you're referring to the great seafood around here."

She chuckled. "No. I've been looking forward to getting to know you better. To learning about you and the things you like, and how your marvelous brain works." She rested her hand on his leg, and drew a figure of eight with a finger. "And to getting you into bed."

He swallowed and then looked across at her. Her lips had curved in a sexy smile. "Oh," was all he could manage.

"It's been a long time since I've been to bed with a guy," she continued, "and an ice age since I dated anyone like this, so I'm a bit nervous, but please don't mistake that for uncertainty. I've barely been able to think about anything else except sliding my hands under your shirt and feeling your skin. So don't worry about misreading the signs. Because you're not. I want you. And I'm going to have you tonight, at least once, but preferably more than that. Because I have a sneaky feeling that once isn't going to be enough."

Chapter Thirteen

Charlie stared at Ophelia for so long, she worried he might drive into a ditch. She couldn't see his eyes behind his sunglasses though, and had no idea what he was thinking. Eventually, he turned his attention back to the road, although he didn't say anything.

Shit. Had she gone too far? Maybe he hadn't been thinking about sex after all. She'd been certain he was nervous, and his words had suggested he was concerned about taking things further than she'd anticipated. Had she completely misread him? His face had taken on the blank expression that told her he was thinking about what she'd said and considering how to reply, so she waited, but he still remained silent.

He slowed the car and turned onto a long drive that wound toward the beach, finally drawing up outside a huge house. Her jaw dropped. When he'd said his parents owned a bach, she'd pictured a typical Kiwi beach house, ramshackle and held together with old pieces of wood and bits of string, with its floors covered with sand and the windows stained from kids' fingers sticky from sun lotion.

The truth was very different, and as Charlie turned off the engine, she got out of the car, lifted her sunglasses up, and stared wide-eyed at the low, wide house with its huge windows facing the ocean.

Charlie took off his glasses too and walked around the car to stand beside her, and she opened her mouth to say how impressed she was. She didn't get the chance, though, because in one easy movement he spun her to face him, and then he was pressing her up against the car, and his mouth was on hers.

Instinctively, she murmured her surprise, then lifted her arms around his neck so he'd know she didn't object to the kiss. And what a kiss it turned out to be. His body was hard against hers, and his mouth was hungry, demanding, the slick slide of his tongue immediately firing her up on all cylinders.

She moaned and tightened her fingers in his hair, welcoming the invasion, enjoying the firm muscles of his shoulder and arm beneath the fingertips of her other hand.

Charlie lifted his head so his mouth was half an inch from hers, his breath hot on her lips, and scanned her face as if checking for himself that she was enjoying this and he wasn't making a mistake. Letting her lips curve a tiny bit, she rocked her hips against the firm erection pressed against her mound.

"Nice," she whispered.

His lips mirrored hers, curving a little before he moved closer again. This time, his kiss was gentler, and he took his time to kiss from one corner of her mouth to the other before teasing her lips with his tongue, tasting her, while he slipped his hands into her hair, apparently enjoying the feel of the strands on his fingers.

"Mmm," she murmured, knowing she was going to have to be vocal with this man and leave him in no doubt as to how she was feeling. "That feels good."

"*You* feel good," he said huskily.

She moved her hands down his chest to the bottom of his shirt and then beneath, onto his warm, bare skin. Slowly, she slid them up, tracing over his flat stomach, his ribs, and around to his back. Lightly, she ran her nails across his skin.

He rested his forehead against hers and closed his eyes.

"Is that nice?" she whispered, drawing circles on his back, exploring the muscles and just enjoying touching him.

"Yes…" he whispered, clearly caught up in the moment, also enjoying the sensation of being touched.

She moved her hands up under his shirt to his shoulder blades, fanning out her fingers to cover as much skin as possible, and brushed her lips across his, teasing him with soft kisses. "I can't wait until we're naked together," she murmured, "and I can feel you against me, all hot and hard."

"This is like slow torture." He shuddered as she scraped her nails down. "You're driving me crazy—do you know that?"

"Mm hmm."

He gave a wry smile, finally opening his eyes to look into hers.

She kissed his nose. "Come on. Show me around the house. Then we can get to the interesting stuff."

It was even more impressive close up. Painted white and with almost all its front walls made of glass, the house was large and airy, but lived in enough so that it didn't feel like a show home.

"My parents spend most weekends here." Charlie climbed the steps to the deck, unlocked the sliding glass doors to the living room, and opened them wide. A comfortable suite was covered with a large blue throw, and mobiles made from driftwood and shells hung in front of the windows, turning slowly in the sea breeze. A simple Christmas tree stood by the door, glittering with tinsel and decorations, and he bent and flicked on its lights.

There was a large kitchen, and when she investigated the cupboards, she found them well stocked with food, including fresh salad, meat, and vegetables in the fridge, and a full wine rack.

There was a rumpus room with a pool table and a darts board, and also surf boards, Frisbees, cricket sets, and other items for the beach.

There were three bedrooms, and Charlie chose one facing the sea, looking cool with its light blue bedding and several large photographs on the walls of surfers caught mid-wave on the sparkling sea.

"These are great," Ophelia said, admiring them.

"Yeah, a friend of a friend took them. I'll take you to *Between the Sheets* tomorrow night—it's a cocktail bar, and there are similar photos on the walls there. Mum saw them and decided she wanted something similar for the bach."

"What a lovely view." She stood by the window to watch the boats sailing out to Russell. Large clouds peppered the horizon, white edged with gray. It would rain later, she thought, but she didn't care what the weather did as long as they were together.

"I could look at it all day," he said.

She turned to see him lying on the bed, arms behind his head, watching her with a smile.

"I was talking about the ocean." She climbed onto the mattress, crawled up to him, and snuggled by his side.

He put his arm around her and kissed the top of her head. "So was I."

"Yeah, right." She lifted her face, and he kissed her, a long lingering kiss starting a fire in her toes that spread right through her.

"Mmm." Still kissing her, he rolled, pinning her to the bed with his weight. She sank her hands into his hair, shivering as he placed a hand on her knee and then slid it up the outside of her thigh beneath her sundress.

She gave a long sigh, and he lifted his head to look at her.

"You're right," she said. "This is slow torture."

"Nice, though." Watching her, he stroked down to her knee, then up the inside of her thigh. Ophelia parted her legs, and he continued his fingers all the way up, finishing with a light brush between her legs over her panties.

She closed her eyes. "Oh..."

He did it again, just gentle strokes against her folds, teasingly light, lifting his fingers when her hips automatically pushed up to increase the pressure.

"Tease," she said, a little sulkily.

He chuckled and kissed her. "I told you, I want to draw you to the edge and keep you there until we can't bear it any longer."

She shivered, entranced by how confident he seemed once he was certain she wanted him. "I do want you," she whispered. "So much."

His smile faded, and his brown eyes were dark and intense. "I want you too. And I know that later, I'm going to have you, and the anticipation is almost killing me." Then his lips curved up. "But I like feeling like this."

"Mmm, me too. It's like we're about to have a wonderful meal, and it's already in the oven, and the delicious cooking smells are wafting through the house, and you're starving and your stomach's rumbling, but you don't want to eat anything because you know you'll spoil your dinner."

His eyebrows rose. "That's exactly what it's like." He kissed her nose and sat up. "I wish I could think of metaphors, but that ability has always escaped me."

She rose from the bed and stretched her arms up, loving how the skim of her dress over her bare nipples made her feel sensual and sexy. "You don't think you're creative?"

"I'm not creative at all." He rose too, and held out a hand. "Shall we go for a walk along the beach?"

"Ooh yes. That would be lovely."

He closed the sliding doors behind them, and they walked down the grassy bank onto the sand. She stood there for a moment, lifting her face to the last rays of the sun. It was so beautiful, the sea sparkling gold, the cry of seagulls in the air, and the smell of the sea mingling with jasmine from the flowers growing around the house.

Keeping hold of her hand, he led her to the water's edge, and they both replaced their sunglasses. She slipped off her sandals, and he took off his Converses and rolled up the bottom of his jeans.

"You say you're not creative," she said as they cooled their feet in the water. "I don't believe that, though. I think everybody is creative in different ways."

"Not me." He took her hand again, and they began to walk slowly along the beach. "I can't draw or paint to save my life—Matt definitely took all the talent when that was given out. I can't write stories because I have trouble imagining scenarios in my head. I don't even read much fiction for the same reason."

"So how do you relax? What do you do in your spare time, when you get home from work?"

"I go for a swim every day. Then I read through the latest scientific journals on my iPad. After that, I mostly listen to music." He pulled a face. "That makes me sound really dull."

"Not at all. I love that you're so passionate about science. What's your favorite thing about it?"

"I have to pick one thing?"

She laughed. "Yes. One thing."

"Its beauty."

She raised her eyebrows. "That's not a word I'd associate with science. Do you mean beauty in terms of its purity? Its absolutes? The way that with literature or history everything's open to debate and analysis, but with science, like mathematics, there are absolute answers? Or do you mean beauty in the physical things of the world, in the symmetry of petals on a flower or the crystals of a mineral?"

He stopped, pulled her toward him, and kissed her, a soft, gentle press of his lips on hers.

"What was that for?" she asked, a little flustered, as he moved away.

He shrugged. "For your insight." He started walking again. "Yes, that's partly what I meant, but there's also a beauty in invention. I like trying to find ways to make or do things better. The moment when there's a breakthrough is like... struggling through a forest, and then suddenly the trees open up and there's a glade, full of sunshine."

"I thought you didn't use metaphors," she said, smiling.

"You inspired me." He smiled back.

"Well to me, being creative isn't just about painting a picture. It's about appreciating beauty and trying to recreate it in whatever medium you prefer, and I don't see why what you're doing is any different. You're constantly trying to recreate the big bang, aren't you? That moment of creation, the scientific equivalent of Adam and Eve—you're trying to remake it in every experiment and piece of research you do."

He stopped again and stared at her. "You're just… exceptional."

She laughed. "I'm really not."

"You are. You make me feel ten feet tall and like I'm king of the world."

"Well, one of the Kings of New Zealand, anyway," she teased, trying to make him laugh.

But he remained serious. "I mean it." He cupped her face in his hands. "You make me feel special, and that's no small gift to give a person."

"You are special, Charlie. You're ten times smarter than I am, and you have the biggest heart of anyone I know."

"That doesn't seem to matter when it comes to relationships," he said, his voice husky with emotion.

"It matters to me. I promise I'll never jump to conclusions in our conversations. If I'm worried about something, I'll say so. Communication is key to a good relationship, and I'm tired of power games and manipulation and every conversation having an undercurrent so I have to go swimming around trying to find the real meaning. I'd much rather us be plain with each other, and both say what's on our minds."

"That's the nicest thing anyone's ever said to me." He wrapped his arms around her, pulling her closely to him.

Glowing inside, she pressed her cheek to his chest and hugged him back, the water washing over her feet, warmed by the summer sun.

Chapter Fourteen

They walked to the end of the beach where there was a fish and chip shop, and bought themselves some hot chips and a piece of hoki to eat on the way back. It was the nicest takeaway Charlie had ever had, walking through the water, the hoki burning his fingers, Ophelia sometimes talking, sometimes content to eat quietly.

Her words had touched him in a way he'd not thought possible. He'd always considered he must appear dull to those who weren't interested in science. He'd been okay with that, happy to leave the smooth talking to Brock and the sweet talking to Matt, content to find comfort in his books and research. But although he'd been with enough girls to know he wasn't terrible in bed, he'd always felt he was missing an indefinable something that girls looked for in a man.

Sometimes, when he really thought about it—which he tried not to do too often because it depressed him—he'd wondered if it was something to do with his soul. As someone who wasn't creative, he saw any talent for music or art as a gift, the expression of the soul, and that made him wonder whether maybe he didn't have one.

So for Ophelia to say she saw creativity in his work warmed him from the inside out. He'd never been with someone before who saw the real him that was struggling to get out.

He couldn't think how to express his feelings to her, but she appeared to understand, her fingers threading through his once they'd finished eating, and her eyes full of heat. She'd made it quite clear that she wanted him, and he was glad he didn't have to fumble through a complicated dance of body language to establish that.

The sun had nearly set, and purple-and-gray clouds clustered above the sea, heralding the arrival of a storm. Lightning flashed over the water, and after a pause, a rumble of thunder echoed in the distance.

Ophelia shivered, and he couldn't help but notice her nipples peaking against her thin dress.

"Are you scared of storms?" he asked.

"No, not at all. It's as if I can feel the electricity in the air. I feel as if my hair's full of static, and if I touch you, I'll get a shock. I don't know if it's the storm or what's happening between us."

She looked up at him. The light had dimmed and she'd removed her sunglasses. Her pupils had dilated, darkening her green eyes. Her brown hair shone in the last rays of the sun, like glossy melted chocolate where it flowed over one shoulder. He watched her moisten her lips with the tip of her tongue.

What's happening between us. She could feel it too, then. He knew it was a complicated scientific process, their bodies reacting to the age-old urge to attract a mate, producing pheromones and sending signals neither of them were aware of. And yet it was more than that. He couldn't explain it, but he had a sense of something greater happening here tonight, something more than physical attraction, and it gave him goosebumps, because he didn't understand it, and it excited him.

He'd swapped his sunglasses for his regular ones, but now he slid them off and turned her to face him. Cupping her cheek, he bent his head to touch his lips to hers.

Ophelia immediately lifted her arms around his neck and raised up on tiptoes to mold herself to him. He was still carrying the newspaper from their takeaway in his other hand, but he wrapped his arm around her. His body responded to her obvious passion, fired up by her enthusiasm, the softness of her breasts, and the way she rocked against his erection.

She opened her mouth to his, and he dipped his tongue inside, the erotic slide of her tongue almost too much to bear. But he kept the kiss slow, enjoying the feel of the warm sea breeze on his skin, the occasional light drop of rain, and the rising desire that spiraled through him.

He could have carried on kissing her like that all night, but the drops on his skin started to feel more frequent, and he lifted his head to see rain bouncing on the surface of the sea.

"Eek!" She grabbed his hand. "It's going to bucket down in a minute. Quick!"

They ran down the beach, but they weren't quick enough. The heavens opened with real New Zealand sub-tropical rain, and by the time they crossed the grassy bank and reached the sliding doors to the house, they were soaked.

Charlie unlocked the doors, let them in, and slid the doors shut behind them. They stood there for a moment, dripping on the floorboards and laughing.

"Hold on, I'll get some towels." He dropped his shoes by the door, dumped the soggy wrapping from their takeaway in the trash, and headed for the bathroom.

After taking two thick towels out of the airing cupboard, he came back into the kitchen, blowing out a breath as his glasses misted up. He slipped them off and left them on the kitchen counter. Drying his hair, he discovered that Ophelia had opened a bottle of wine and was pouring it into two glasses. He stopped to stare at her, entranced by the wet version of the perfect girl. Her hair stuck to her head, and her dress was almost transparent, clinging to her like a second skin. She looked amazing.

She glanced up and saw him, and her lips curved in a shy smile as she walked around the counter to accept a towel. "That came down quickly." She dried her hair and patted down her arms, then turned and gave him his glass of wine.

He took a mouthful, watching Ophelia sip hers, noting the way her throat muscles constricted as she swallowed. Fuck, that was sexy. Or maybe everything would be sexy to him at that moment, with the rain starting to hammer on the windows, the air turning hot and sultry.

"Do you want me to put on the aircon?" he asked her, not sure if it was rain or sweat running down his back.

She sipped her wine again, then, to his surprise, gave a little shake of her head. "You look hot hot," she said, and gave him an impish grin.

"You too." Actually, she looked hot wet. Clearly, she wasn't wearing a bra, as the dress clung to her breasts, her nipples standing out like buttons through the fabric.

Reaching across the counter, she pulled a box of chocolates toward her that she must have retrieved from the fridge. They were from *Treats to Tempt You*, the popular chocolate shop in Doubtless Bay. He vaguely recalled that the wife of the guy who'd taken the beautiful photographs ran the shop.

Ophelia popped open the lid and selected a truffle, bit it in half, then offered the rest of it to him. He closed his mouth over her thumb and finger to take it, then held her wrist while he sucked the small circle of chocolate off her thumb.

"Oh," she said, her eyes meeting his, wide and dark. "You're making me melt, Charlie."

Not quite sure why, he went to kiss her but, taking his hand, still carrying her wine, she led him around to the sofa facing the windows. Outside, the sea had turned iron gray and the wind had picked up, sending white horses galloping up the beach. It felt as if they were the only two people in the world, isolated in a haven while the storm raged on around them. Charlie shivered, wanting to prolong the moment, but desperate to get his hands on her.

Luckily, she didn't seem to want to wait either. Standing in front of the sofa, she swallowed another mouthful of wine, took his glass and placed them both on the nearby coffee table, and turned her attention to unbuttoning the few small buttons at the top of his rugby shirt. He let her, enjoying her taking charge. He liked the way she undid each button almost reverently, as if excited by the anticipation of finally seeing him naked.

The buttons undone, she caught the shirt by the bottom, peeled it off his wet skin, over his head, and dropped it onto the polished wooden floor.

"Wow." She placed her hands on his chest, her eyes hot with admiration. "You're all shiny."

He felt as if he was swimming through the humid air. Sweat was pinging out in beads all over him, but it only seemed to turn Ophelia on. She ran her fingers over the muscles of his chest, then down to his stomach. Her fingers lingered there, apparently captivated by the line of hair that disappeared beneath the waistband of his jeans.

"My turn?" he asked hopefully.

Smiling, she pushed him, and he sat heavily on the sofa, disappointment turning to desire as she reached up beneath her dress, caught the elastic of her panties in her fingers, and slipped them down. When she stepped out of them and dropped them on top of his discarded shirt, Charlie blew out a breath.

"Do you have a condom?" she asked, her voice husky.

Hoping his hands weren't shaking, he reached into his back pocket, took out his wallet, and extracted one before throwing the wallet on the table.

Keeping her eyes fixed on his, she straddled him, sliding down his thighs until she pressed close to him. Then, clasping the bottom of her dress, she peeled it up her wet skin and over her head before letting it drop to the floor.

Charlie inhaled sharply, captivated by the sight of her creamy, glistening skin and her generous breasts. The light pink nipples were large and swollen, crying out to have a mouth close over them and suck.

He restrained himself, though, placed his hands on her thighs, and smoothed them up over her hips and into the dip of her waist. She was curvy without being plump, soft and yielding. He stroked his thumbs across some silvery lines on her tummy.

"Charlie." Her cheeks reddened. "I was hoping you'd focus on something other than my stretch marks." She was embarrassed, but she appeared to be teasing him rather than upset.

"Sorry. But they're beautiful."

"Now I know you're mocking me."

"I'm not." He cradled her breasts. "You've grown a whole new life inside of you and given birth. Your body's a scientific marvel."

A smile touched her lips. "You're a strange man," she whispered, and leaned forward to kiss him.

Charlie relaxed into the sofa, content to let her lips move across his and her tongue delve into his mouth. He slid his hands around her back and up to her shoulders, his fingers skating across her damp skin, then returned his hands to her breasts, enjoying the weight of them in his palms.

Ophelia sat back, and he leaned forward to close his mouth over a nipple. She sank her hands into his hair and sighed, arching her back and pushing her breasts toward him. He took the hint and sucked, then teased the tip with his lips and the end of his tongue before sucking again.

"Mmm…" she murmured, rocking her hips and grinding against his erection through his jeans. "Charlie, you're driving me crazy."

He swapped to the other nipple and did the same, teasing it to a peak before sucking gently. By the time he lifted his head to kiss her again, her breathing had become ragged. When her mouth covered his, the kiss turned hot and hard, her fingers tightening in his hair as her tongue danced with his, warm and erotic.

It wasn't long before she lifted her head and shifted back a little on his thighs. Her fingers fumbled at the button of his jeans, so he helped her out, undoing the top and sliding down the zip.

His erection almost sprang out, eager to please, and the breath hissed through her teeth as she stroked him through his cotton boxer-briefs.

"Wow," she whispered. "Charlie King, talk about hiding your light under a bushel."

"I've no idea what that means, but thank you."

She giggled against his lips as she kissed him. "It means you are extremely impressive." She leaned back again and carefully pulled the elastic of his underwear over his erection. Closing her hand around him, she stroked up and down, watching with fascination as she revealed the tip, then closed the skin over it again. "Jesus, I can barely get my fingers to meet around you."

Charlie groaned and closed his eyes, swelling in her hands until it was almost painful. He wanted to throw her onto her back, slide into her, and carry them both off to that netherworld of dark bliss, but he reined in his passion, wanting to wait for her to guide him.

Eventually, though, he could bear her touch no longer, and opened his eyes to find her watching him, a sexy smile on her face. "I wondered how long you could take that," she said, amused. She reached for the condom and tore off the wrapper, tested it was the right way up, then rolled it carefully onto him.

Finally, she leaned forward and kissed him. "Ready, honey? Because I can't wait any longer. I want you so much, I'm almost self-combusting."

In a sexual haze, Charlie could only nod, and he held her hips as she lifted herself up, let the tip of his erection part her folds, then lowered herself on top of him.

Chapter Fifteen

Ophelia closed her eyes and just reveled in the sensation of Charlie sliding inside her.

She hadn't given him false flattery—the guy was very generously proportioned, and as she lowered down she could feel herself stretching to accommodate him. She rocked her hips a few times to make sure he was coated with her moisture, then finally pushed down all the way.

Jesus, he felt good. When she tightened her internal muscles, she felt incredible, full to the brim. Dillon had been her first, so she'd had little to compare him to, but there was no doubt that Charlie was way more impressive than her ex.

Opening her eyes, she focused hazily on his face, surprised to see his eyes open, fixed on her. The heat in his gaze sent tingles all the way down her spine.

He'd been quiet since they came back to the house. His eyes had barely left her, and he was clearly turned on, but she suspected he was nervous about saying or doing the wrong thing and spoiling the moment.

She'd thought she'd be the one who would have been nervous, but oddly, from the moment he'd walked into the kitchen and stopped to stare at her in the wet dress, she'd known that she needed to lead, for a while at least, until he felt confident enough to take charge himself.

"That feels good," she whispered, starting to move properly on top of him. "Doesn't it?"

He nodded, and his lips curved up a little, but he still didn't say anything, although his hands tightened on her hips, holding her firmly while he thrust up into her. His eyes had taken on that look that suggested he was calculating thrust-to-weight ratios, which made her smile.

"Relax," she murmured, kissing him, then leaning back to enjoy the different angle as he slid inside her.

He covered her breasts with his hands and rolled her nipples between his fingers, so gentle, and so far removed from Dillon's hard-and-fast style that it made her want to cry. Hard-and-fast could be good sometimes, but there was something beautiful about Charlie's overawed touch and the way he was obviously trying to control his passion for her.

For a while, she just rode him slowly, enjoying the crash of the rain against the windows, the warm air around them so sultry that sweat ran down between her shoulder blades. Charlie's skin glowed from the heat, the muscles of his arms and chest looking like honed and polished wood in the dim light. She bent and touched her tongue to the hollow of his throat, then kissed up his neck to his ear.

"You taste salty," she whispered, and sucked his earlobe. "Hot and sweaty. You know how that turns me on?"

His breath warmed on her cheek, but he still said nothing, although when she kissed back to his mouth, he returned it eagerly, the slide of his tongue against hers erotic enough to make her moan.

He wanted her—that much was clear, but for a brief moment doubt flickered inside her. Was she doing this right? He wasn't the only one who needed some kind of signal of being on the right track. She wanted to fire him up, to make him lose the careful control he was obviously trying to keep.

She slid a hand between them, and began to stroke her clit. "Mmm," she murmured against his lips, nibbling them with her teeth before sitting back to give her hand more access. "That's nice."

She met his gaze, and her breath caught in her throat at the look in his eyes. Before she could prepare herself, he caught her around the waist and expertly—very expertly, she noticed—flipped her onto her back on the sofa, still inside her.

"Fuck, you're hot," he said, the first words to leave his lips for ages.

"Melting," she said with a groan, half-embarrassed to be so covered in sweat, but loving every minute of it.

He caught her hands and pinned them above her head. He gave a long, slow thrust, their bodies sliding together. When he moved back, his skin peeled from hers with a sticky slurp.

"Oh yeah," he said.

She flexed her hands in his, her heart racing at his sudden, sure confidence. Something she'd done had apparently flipped a switch inside him.

Pushing forward again, he paused and released one of her hands, gently eased her knees up, then recaptured her hand. Circling his hips, he buried himself deep.

"Ohhh…" She closed her eyes for a moment, tremors rippling through her. "Are you trying to spear me to the sofa?"

He tipped his head to the side. "Does it hurt?"

"No."

"Good." He bent and closed his mouth over her nipple, sucked first one, then the other, and thrust again.

"Charlie…" She was beginning to spiral out of control. The humid air, the lashing rain, the wine threading through her system, the taste of chocolate and salt in her mouth, Charlie's deep voice and his wild eyes, all conspired to send her senses spinning.

He dipped his head to her breasts again and then, to her shock, licked up between them.

"Don't!" she squealed. "I'm all sweaty!"

He kissed her. "Why do you think I did it? You did it to me."

"That was different. You're gorgeous."

Her comment made him smile with obvious pleasure. "And you're beautiful. It's pheromones, baby. You're driving me wild."

He certainly looked it. His long hair hung in wet strands and a hint of bristle darkened his jaw. She wasn't sure how to cope with this passionate, sexy guy who'd completely surprised her with the way he'd suddenly switched to being in command.

She had to be careful not to make the mistake of thinking that this man was shy and weak. He might be wary of showing his emotions, but once he knew what he wanted, he clearly wasn't going to hold back.

Lightning suddenly flashed, flooding the room with brilliant white before plunging them into semi-darkness, followed immediately by the loudest crash of thunder she'd ever heard. She jumped violently, and must have tightened around him because he gave a long groan and began to thrust with earnest.

She was losing herself, completely under his power, as if he held the remote control to all her feelings and sensations. Releasing her hands, he shifted up on the sofa an inch or two, still inside her, and slid a hand beneath her butt, tilting her hips up. This time, every thrust he gave ground right against her clit.

Tremors of pleasure ran through her, and she placed her hands on his chest, then slid them around to his back, loving the way his muscles rippled beneath her fingers. Deep inside, everything began to tighten, and she bit her lip. "Oh, I think I'm going to…"

He immediately shifted back an inch and slowed his thrusts, relieving the pressure on her clit. "Slowly," he scolded. "Right to the edge, remember?"

"Oh… Charlie." The tremors died away, and she pouted.

He chuckled and kissed her, taking the time to nibble her lips, to dip his tongue into her mouth, to kiss her as if his life depended on it and he couldn't bear to tear his lips from hers.

Ophelia relaxed her thighs and opened up to him, aware that he was controlling his own desire so he could intensify hers. Once again, her muscles began to tighten, and Charlie must have felt it because he stopped moving, observing her face with his grave brown eyes.

"Tease," she said, panting.

"I want it to be good for you," he said, giving a slow thrust before pausing again.

"It's already good, Charlie." She felt dizzy with desire, knowing just a touch more sensation would tip her over the edge.

"The best, then." He kissed her. "I want to be the best you've ever had." His voice held a surprising hint of fierce possession, and the look in his eyes gave her no doubt he meant what he said. "I'm going to make you come now," he told her, sliding his hand up her damp skin to her breast, "and I'm going to watch you and drink in every second of your pleasure, knowing I gave it to you." He brushed his thumb across her nipple and thrust again.

"Charlie…" Any further attempt at speech halted as her muscles tightened at his demand. The orgasm was fierce and powerful, and she was only vaguely aware that he'd stopped moving as she clenched around him. She knew he was watching her, though, and even though she closed her eyes and turned her head to the side, she could feel his eyes burning into her like lasers.

The pulses finally died away, and her eyelids fluttered open.

He kissed her nose. "You have no idea how many times I've fantasized about that."

Hot and flustered, she decided to divert his attention and slid her hands beneath the waistband of his jeans and onto his butt. "And now it's my turn to watch."

He began to move again, kissing up to her ear. "You're very wet."

"Jeez. Have I not blushed enough this evening?"

"I'm a scientist. Making observations is what I do." Although his speech was calm and clear, his breathing had turned ragged. He wasn't as in control as he looked.

Remembering how he'd enjoyed going deep, Ophelia tilted her hips up and wrapped her legs as high around his back as she could manage. He pushed forward, and his eyelids lowered blissfully as he sank into her.

Lightning flashed again, and thunder rolled around them. Charlie traced light fingers up her arm, looking at where the half light outside shone through the rivulets of rain on the windows to cast patterns across their skin.

"Beautiful," he said, obviously fascinated.

Ophelia had to swallow down a sudden burst of emotion, shocked to feel tears pricking her eyes at his reverence.

"You'll make me cry again," she whispered.

"Aw." He kissed her, still moving inside her. "Sorry. But you are. How does it feel to make a man's dream come true?"

She sniffed, her bottom lip trembling. "You say such nice things."

"If you were mine, *bella*, you'd have to get used to that."

"*Bella?*" She let him kiss her, then asked, "Do you speak Italian?"

"*Si. Vuoi essere la mia ragazza?*"

"What does that mean?"

He lowered down onto his elbows and kissed her again. "Would you like to be my girlfriend?"

She gave a soft laugh, moving to meet each thrust of his hips. "It sounds much more romantic in Italian."

"*Mi rendi felice.* You make me happy."

"*Grazie,*" she said, the only Italian she knew.

"*Voglio stare con te per sempre. Sei l'amore della mia vita. Mi vuoi sposare?*"

She looked up into his smiling eyes. "What does that mean?"

He shook his head and kissed her, his thrusts turning more urgent. Letting it go, she slid her hands up his back and lightly scored her nails down his wet skin. Opening her mouth to his hot kiss, she let him ride her until his body stiffened and he shuddered, spilling into her.

"Fuck," he said, and groaned as his hips jerked, his fingers tightening where he'd gripped her thigh.

"Mmm…" Ophelia clenched her internal muscles, enjoying the ripples of an after-orgasm, and loving being able to watch him the same way he'd watched her. He was right—there was something wonderful about knowing she was the cause of his pleasure.

His eyelids fluttered open. "*Sono in paradiso*," he said, and bent his head to kiss her.

Chapter Sixteen

"Do you speak any other languages?"

They lay facing each other on the sofa. Charlie knew he should suggest moving to the bedroom, but he'd never felt so content, lying there in the warm with his skin sticking to Ophelia's, and he wanted to prolong the moment as long as he could.

He lifted a strand of her hair where it had stuck to her cheek and tucked it behind her ear. "French, German, Spanish, Maori, Latin, and I can swear in Finnish and Polish."

She lifted up onto an elbow to stare at him. "Seriously?"

"Oh, and I knew a few choice phrases in Russian, too."

"You speak Latin?"

"Yep. *Apudne te vel me?*"

"What does that mean?"

"Your place or mine?"

She laughed. "Where did you learn it—in a Roman brothel?"

"Sorry, you want something more romantic?" He thought about it. "'*Omnia vincit amor; et nos cedamus amori.*' That means 'Love conquers all things; let us too surrender to love.'"

"That's nice."

"It's by Virgil. The Roman poet, not the puppet from Thunderbirds."

She chuckled, then leaned forward to press her lips to his. "I don't know why women aren't clambering over each other to get to you, Charlie King. You're warm, gorgeous, and funny."

"I'm glad you think so." He rested a hand on her hip and trailed his fingers up her ribs. "That was nice."

"And that was the understatement of the year. You're surprisingly flash when you get going."

"Flash?"

"Confident. Once you relax." She circled a finger through his chest hair. "I like that."

He looked into her eyes as she lifted her gaze to his, and he gave a small nod. He was happy to take the initiative if he knew he wasn't going to offend her.

Her lips curved up, and she lifted her hand to cup his face. "I love your eyes," she whispered. "They're so expressive. I can see your thoughts whirring away behind them. I love that you're so clever. All those languages! How on earth do you remember them all?"

"I find learning them easy. It's all about patterns of speech, and that's quite mathematical in a way. I like patterns—it's why I like music. And it's why I find natural talent so fascinating, because people create beautiful things without considering those patterns. I can see them, but I have to look for them, analyze them, you know?" He blew out a breath. "I'm not making myself very clear."

"I understand. You remind me of Data from *Star Trek Next Generation*."

"Star Trek? Is that the one with William Shatner?"

"Kind of—it's a follow-up series, similar premise. Data is a robot who wants to be a human. He plays music beautifully, but only because he follows the sheet music. He can't create it himself. And he really wants a sense of humor, but can't get the subtlety of it."

"So… you're saying I'm like a robot?"

She laughed. "Not at all—you have a great sense of humor. But I do think your minds are similar. You operate on a different level to normal people, Charlie. You have to admit that."

"I suppose. Having never been any different, it's difficult to understand how everyone else thinks."

Her brow furrowed. "I hope I didn't upset you by saying that. I really didn't mean you're like a robot."

"I know." He kissed her nose. "You couldn't upset me if you tried. I know what I'm like, and what people think of me. I'm amazed that you can see anything human in me at all." He was joking, but to his alarm, she looked genuinely upset by the comment.

"Oh Charlie, don't say that. I think you have the biggest heart of any man I've ever known." She wrapped her arms around his neck. "I've never met anyone like you."

He felt an unusual surge of emotion. No woman had ever said anything like that to him before. "Are you trying to make me cry?"

She gave a little laugh and shook her head, pressing her face into his neck. "No. I just hate to think your ex called you cold and unfeeling. I want to punch her."

"I'd be interested to see you two wrestle. I'd be happy to supply the custard."

That made her laugh. She moved back, although she stayed close enough to keep their bodies pressed together.

"Lisette would have said I use humor to avoid intimacy," Charlie said. "She would have yelled at me when I said that."

"But that in itself tells me something about you. It's ridiculous to force someone into talking about emotions when they are either uncomfortable or unable to voice what they're feeling."

"I think she just thought I was trying to be smart because I didn't want to let her in. That's not the case."

"I know."

"I'm not scared of intimacy. I just don't know how to handle it."

"Charlie, I get it." Ophelia kissed him. "I get you. Don't worry."

I get you. He didn't think he'd ever felt so happy, and for a brief moment he actually felt tears prick his eyes, something that hadn't happened for... well, he couldn't remember the last time he'd cried.

"I—" What he was about to say was interrupted by the jangle of Ophelia's phone.

"Shit." She glanced at the table where she'd left it and hesitated.

"Go on," he said, aware she'd be worried about Summer. "I'll pour us another glass of wine."

"Okay." She rose from the sofa, walked over to the phone, and answered it. "Hello?" Lowering her gaze, she turned away and crossed to look out of the window at the rain. "Yes. What do you want?"

So it was Dillon, then. Charlie pulled on his boxer-briefs and went into the kitchen to retrieve the wine from the fridge. As he poured two glasses, he wondered whether he should go into the bedroom to give her some privacy. He glanced at her, though, saw her stony face and stiff posture, and decided maybe she'd prefer him to stay for moral support. If she wanted to talk to Dillon on her own, she could leave the room, so he leaned against the kitchen counter with his wine and sipped it while he watched her.

"I put them in her bag," Ophelia said, her voice low. "In the zipped bit at the front." She waited a moment, then ran a hand through her hair. "Of course you can go in and get them." Another pause. "You know why. Stop being an ass and just go and look."

Covering the phone with a hand, she turned toward Charlie with an apologetic look. "I'm really sorry about this."

"It's okay. What's up?"

"Dillon's saying he can't find Summer's Creon tablets. It's bullshit—I know I put them in the front of her bag. He rang to ask permission to go into the house." She rolled her eyes.

"Why ask permission now?" Charlie said, thinking of how Dillon had let himself in before.

"I asked him for his key back. He refused. Now he's trying to make the point that he needs a key in case of emergencies like this. He doesn't, of course, he's being an ass because I'm here with you." She banged on the window and turned away.

Charlie watched her pace angrily up and down while she waited for Dillon to come back to the phone. She seemed unbothered by the fact that she was naked, and he thought how beautiful she looked, her skin still warm and glistening from their lovemaking, her hair ruffled and her lips slightly puffy from their kisses.

"Well?" she snapped into the phone. She stopped walking and put her free hand on her hip. "That's because they're in her bag. They are! Dillon! Stop being a fucking dick." She was so angry, she was almost in tears. "I know you've got them, and I'm not flying all the way back to Auckland only to have you tell me you've 'found' them."

Surely Dillon wasn't going to force her to go back? Charlie put down his wine before he'd had too much to drink to enable him to drive her back to the airport.

"Of course I care." Her voice had turned husky. "Summer will always come first, but that's not what this is about, is it?" She pressed her fingers to her lips.

Charlie walked out of the kitchen and crossed the room to stand beside her.

"Hold on," she whispered into the phone, and lowered it.

"Do you want to go back?" he asked her.

She shook her head.

Charlie cupped her cheek. "Are you sure? Because I'll take you back to the airport now if you want."

"I don't. I mean it, Charlie. I'm having such a great time, and Dillon's making this about Summer, but it isn't. This is what he does, though—he knows how to manipulate me and turn everything around to make me feel guilty. I hate him for that." She stopped and swallowed, but her eyes were hard.

Charlie held out his hand. She stared at it for a moment. Then, slowly, she passed him the phone.

He held it up to his ear. "Dillon? Charlie King here."

"Fuck off," Dillon said. "Put Ophelia back on."

"I will, in a moment. First, though, I understand you've lost Summer's Creons."

"I haven't lost them," Dillon snapped. "Ophelia didn't put them in the bag."

"Regardless," Charlie said, "how about I telephone Summer's doctor and ask him to leave a prescription at the front desk?"

Dillon was silent for a moment. "It's out of hours," he said eventually.

"The front desk is open twenty-four-seven."

"But our chemist will be shut," Dillon said.

"The pharmacy in the hospital won't be. I can call them myself and get them to make the prescription up. Unless you find the pills in Summer's bag in the meantime, of course."

Once again, Dillon fell quiet.

"I'll let you think about it," Charlie said. "I'll hand you back to Ophelia now."

He passed a frozen Ophelia the phone and walked out of the room.

The rain had eased a little, and he switched on the lamp in the bedroom and pulled the curtains, then went into the bathroom. His skin felt sticky, so he put the shower on, let it heat up, took off his underwear, and stepped into the cubicle.

The warm water slid down his body, but it was difficult to relax his tense muscles and stop his stomach churning. Had he done the wrong thing by intervening? Ophelia had handed him the phone, but it might have been an automatic reaction. Had he made her angry by talking to Dillon?

Not knowing how to handle his uncertainty, he recited the Periodic Table in his head to calm himself down.

Hydrogen, Helium, Lithium, Beryllium…

His brain continued to move on though, even as he listed the elements. Had he ruined everything? He couldn't stop his mind playing back the previous scene. He closed his eyes, letting the warm water cascade over his face and down his chest. Maybe she resented him trying to come to the rescue. It wasn't as if he'd felt she'd needed rescuing, just that he wanted to help, and he could see how Dillon used their daughter to continually reinforce the link between them, and also as a tool to manipulate Ophelia and play on her guilt.

Calcium, Scandium, Titanium, Vanadium...

What would he do if she stormed in now and told him he was out of order? Or that she'd decided her first loyalties lay with her husband and daughter, and she'd called a taxi and was leaving straight away? He sank his hands into his hair, blowing out a shaky breath. He'd been stupid to get involved with her so soon. He should have told her he would wait until her divorce had come through, until she'd definitely put Dillon behind her.

Rhodium, Palladium, Silver...

And then he thought of how he'd made her come, the way she'd looked when pleasure had swept over her, and how much he'd enjoyed making love to her. He couldn't have lost her before they'd even started, surely?

Chapter Seventeen

After Charlie's words to him, Dillon gave up any pretense of needing Summer's pills and demanded Ophelia come home. Then he begged. Then he cried. "We need you," he said. "*I* need you."

She leaned her forehead on the glass and closed her eyes. She supposed she should have been touched, but she was tired—of his over-emotion, his manipulation, and his emotional blackmail. She loved Summer, but she wanted a couple of days to herself—was that such a terrible thing? Two days with Charlie, who was so easy, so calm.

She loved the way he thought before he acted. She adored how he was so difficult to offend. Being with Dillon was like living with a hedgehog, where every little word and gesture stuck to his prickles. Charlie was the complete opposite, as if he was made of polished wood and everything just slid right off.

It was so nice to be with someone who didn't pick up on every little slip and store it up to turn it into a weapon that could be used against her. Beneath it all, Dillon was a good man, but he exhausted her. He took everything and gave nothing, and she wanted more.

She inhaled deeply. "I'm staying, Dillon. I'm sorry—I know it's not what you want, but I need this. Please try and be happy for me."

"I can't," he gasped. "I fucking hate it."

"I know."

"I want to kill him."

She swallowed hard. He didn't mean it—he was hurting, and there was no point in developing it into an argument. She thought of what Charlie would say, how he would keep calm and refuse to bring his emotions into it.

"Go and be with Summer," she said. "You're her father, and she needs you to be there for her. I'll see you on Sunday."

A long silence ensued. Ophelia watched the rain sliding down the windows, gradually easing. Lightning still flashed, but it was off in the distance. She fingered a sparkly bauble on the Christmas tree, turning it in her fingers.

"Okay," he said eventually. "Don't be late. I have an appointment at one."

"I won't. I'll speak to you later. Thank you, Dillon."

She hung up.

Leaning against the glass, she stayed there for a minute or two, fighting tears, struggling against the weight of the guilt and the fear that she was doing the wrong thing.

Then she thought of Charlie. She took a deep breath and blew it out slowly, remembering his tender kisses, his softly spoken Italian words, his reverent touch.

Did she feel like this because it was new and shiny like the bauble on the tree? Would it tarnish over time until she felt the same way about him that she felt about Dillon? She couldn't know, but she was certain that Charlie would never try to manipulate her the same way her ex was. If Charlie was unsure, he would step back and try to evaluate the problem, not charge into it headlong and attempt to batter it down.

She thought of the way he'd gently taken the phone from her and completely disarmed Dillon with his calm, sensible suggestion. Why hadn't she thought of saying something like that?

Because Dillon knew exactly which buttons to press to involve her emotions. He knew how to make her feel guilty.

Kate, who was a psychologist, had told her in the past, "You have to move out of reaction and into observation." Ophelia knew she was just feeding Dillon's bad habit. She had to learn not to react to his jibes and taunts, and instead see them for what they were—fear and embarrassment that his marriage had broken up and that he was partly to blame. He did love her, but she was certain that, even more importantly, he didn't want to admit to the world he'd failed at something.

Pushing off the glass, she walked across the room and down the hall. She heard water running—Charlie was in the shower. He must have thought she was so weak, she mused sadly. And yet he hadn't scolded her for not standing up to Dillon, or accused her of still loving him. Instead, he'd gently tried to help, and had then left her to deal with it the way she wanted.

Did he want to be alone? She opened the bathroom door. The room was full of steam, but she could see him in the shower cubicle, tall and tanned through the glass, his head dipped, the water running over him.

Hoping she wasn't making the wrong decision, she walked into the room and opened the cubicle door. Charlie jumped, obviously lost in thought, but before he could say anything she joined him in the cubicle and closed the door.

He wiped his face and turned toward her. She placed her palms on his chest, pushed him back against the tiles, and lifted up onto her toes to kiss him.

He inhaled sharply, and for a brief moment she thought he was going to pull away. Then his hands grazed down her back to her hips to pull her close to him, his kiss turning hungry, demanding.

Relief flooding her, she lifted her arms around his neck and threaded her hands through his hair. "I'm sorry," she murmured against his mouth, trying hard to hold back her tears.

He lifted his head and looked into her eyes. "Are you staying?"

"Yes."

"You're sure? Don't do it for me. I mean, I want you to stay, but I want you to want to stay… "

She pressed a finger against his lips. "I'm not doing it for you, Charlie. I'm doing it for me. I want to be with you. I'm having such a good time. I love Summer, and of course if she was truly in trouble I'd go home, but she's not. And right now, at this moment, I need this. I need you."

A smile spread slowly across his face.

"You should smile more," she whispered. "It suits you." And she touched her lips to his again.

*

Charlie let her kiss him, filled with warmth. The water cascaded over them, sliding down Ophelia's silky skin and turning it to marble. He stroked up her back to her shoulders, and underneath to her breasts, her nipples tightening as he brushed his thumbs across them.

She murmured her approval, her tongue sliding against his in an erotic dance. He sighed, shivering when she scraped her nails against his scalp and clenched her hands in his hair.

Too soon, she moved back, but it was only to pick up the shower puff. She squeezed some gel onto it, then placed it on his chest and began to wash him.

Charlie leaned back against the cool tiles and let her, sensing that she wanted to do this for him as some kind of thank you for speaking to Dillon. Sucking her bottom lip, she cleaned across his shoulders, then down his arms, taking her time and admiring him as she went.

"You're very muscular," she said as she washed over his biceps. "Is that from the swimming?"

He nodded, feeling oddly shy under her perusal. In his experience, lovemaking consisted of the guy concentrating on the girl for ninety-nine percent of the time, and it was strange—and not unpleasant—to be the subject of admiration for once.

The fingers of her other hand followed the puff, exploring the curves of his muscles. She spread bubbles down his chest, tracing his pecs and abs, then lingered on his nipples, running a finger lightly around them. He raised an eyebrow, and she giggled and circled a finger in the air. "Turn around."

He did so, leaning his hands on the tiles, and she sighed as she washed across his shoulders and down his back.

"You have a gorgeous body," she said, somewhat breathlessly. He closed his eyes, enjoying the slide of the puff and her hands over his hips and down his thighs, then back up again, over his butt. "Such a tight ass," she whispered, squeezing the muscles with a hand. "Mmm."

He glanced over his shoulder, an inch away from blushing. "Enjoying yourself down there?"

"I am." She kissed his back. "You're a fine figure of a man, Charlie King."

"Well, thank you."

"Turn around."

He did so, blowing out a breath when she glanced down and her eyes widened.

"I've just been stroked by a gorgeous, naked woman," he said. "Are you surprised?"

"Already?" She took his erection in her hand and stroked him. "Are you insatiable, Charlie?"

"When you're around, yes." He closed his eyes again as she continued to stroke him, her hand warm and firm. "Ophelia…"

"Ssh." She kissed his lips, then his neck and chest, and then to his shock she kissed slowly down, sinking onto her knees before him.

He watched as she stroked him several more times, then finally revealed the tip of his erection and closed her lips over it.

"Holy fuck." The sensation of being enclosed in the warm cavern of her mouth was amazing.

Turning a little so the water fell onto his back and not onto her face, he leaned one hand on the glass wall and slid the other into her hair, holding the strands back so he could watch her. Her cheeks flushed pink, but she didn't stop, sliding her lips down his shaft until the tip touched the back of her throat.

"Jesus." He closed his eyes and concentrated on the sensations she was arousing in him for a while, enjoying the heat and wetness of her mouth, the slight rasp of her tongue, the way he seemed to swell when she sucked.

Then his eyes fluttered open, and he watched her lick up his shaft and over the head, then tease it with the tip of her tongue, making him groan.

She murmured something, closed her mouth over the end again, and started to slide her lips up and down rhythmically while her hand continued to stroke him. Charlie felt transported away, aroused by the warm water running down his back, and loving her gentle but sure touch. She tapped the inside of his leg and he widened his stance a little, then swore softly as she slid a hand beneath him and cupped his balls. Her fingers played over the sensitive skin behind them, and then she squeezed and massaged them tenderly as she continued to arouse him with her mouth.

He lasted as long as he could, but it was never going to take long for her to tease him to a climax, and it was only minutes before his breath was coming in pants and everything began to tighten deep inside.

He clenched his hand in her hair and tugged gently. "Honey, I'm going to come."

In answer, she just slid her lips further down, taking him deep, and he groaned and let go. Heat rushed up from his balls and his body pulsed, jet after jet of fluid entering her mouth. She drank it all down, the contraction of her throat only seeming to intensify the exquisite feeling.

He finished with a gasp, his hand tightening to a fist on the glass. "Holy fucking hell."

She slid her mouth off him and rose to her feet, licking her lips. "Language."

He met her gaze, speechless, and then they both started to laugh. "Come here," he said, pulling her into his arms. "You beautiful woman."

"You're so big," she complained, sliding her arms around him. "My jaw aches now."

He closed his eyes. "For God's sake… You'll make me blush."

She chuckled and kissed his chest. "Mmm. That was nice." She lifted her head and touched her lips to his. "Wasn't it?"

Opening his eyes again, he looked deeply into her green ones. He didn't know where to start with putting his feelings for her into words. He was absolutely crazy about this girl, completely lost, and he didn't know what to do—whether he should tell her everything in his heart, or whether that would frighten her off and put pressure on her.

So, as usual, he said nothing, just wrapped his arms around her and held her tightly, and hoped his actions really were worth a thousand words.

Chapter Eighteen

Ophelia closed her eyes and lifted her face to the cool sea breeze.

She stood at the bow of the *Tangaroa*, the boat belonging to Charlie's friend, Niall. They'd boarded just after ten a.m. on Saturday morning, and were heading out into the Bay of Islands toward the famous Hole in the Rock. Niall had promised they'd almost certainly see dolphins on the way, and Ophelia was excited at the prospect, although even if they didn't, she knew she'd still have had a wonderful time.

As they'd boarded, Ophelia had asked where the other passengers were. Niall had just grinned. Charlie had then admitted to her that Niall had offered to give him two free tickets on one of his standard cruises, but he'd paid for the whole boat for the trip so they had it to themselves. It was the first time he'd done anything like that with his money, and Niall had laughed at the bemused look on her face.

Her heart felt lighter than it had for years, due in no small measure to the man standing by her side, leaning on the rail. Charlie had awoken her that morning by disappearing under the covers to kiss down her body, and he'd made her come with his tongue before sliding inside her and making slow, gentle love to her as the sun came up. She defied anyone to find a better way of being woken in the morning.

She was growing used to his quiet manner. She'd come to terms with the fact that any lack of conversation on his part meant that he was uncertain how to reply and was therefore remaining silent until he worked out what to say. Unlike most people, he really did think before he spoke, and far from his lack of expression meaning a lack of feeling, she'd realized he kept his thoughts and emotions carefully guarded on purpose. He'd been badly hurt in the past, she thought, maybe when he was a child or a teenager, or maybe in love. At some point, he'd said what was on his mind and had been punished for it without understanding why. And since then, he'd been determined not to make the mistake again.

The thought of someone calling him cold and unfeeling gave her a physical pain in her chest. She could only imagine how much that had hurt him, although he made a joke about it now. He'd learned to use humor to cover his uncertainty, and although it obviously worked most of the time, she was beginning to read behind it, to see how he used it as a screen to hide his real feelings.

He was an enigma, and she liked that. He fascinated her, and she wanted to get to know him better, so that eventually he didn't feel the need to keep his guard up. She wanted him to trust her, but of course that was something that would only grow over time.

Opening her eyes, she glanced across at him. As usual, he wore one of his many All Blacks rugby tops, the skintight fabric clinging to his impressive biceps and muscular chest. She made a mental note to try to get him in the water at some point—she'd love to see him swim and knew those powerful arms meant he must be talented in the pool.

When he'd first told her he wore the same style black top every day, she'd briefly wondered whether in his absentmindedness he was one of those guys who forgot to wash, but she couldn't have been more wrong. He'd showered again that morning, and when she asked him why because they'd showered the night before, he'd told her he showered twice a day as well as after swimming because he discovered that body washes with essential oils helped him concentrate. He'd been perfectly serious, and she'd hidden a smile, loving his eccentricities, especially when they made him smell divine.

The wind lifted his long hair, and she could see he was lost in thought behind his sunglasses, studying the open sea, probably thinking about salt-to-water ratios and how he could use that information in one of his inventions. She smiled and slid her arm around his waist. He looked down at her, lifted an arm around her shoulders, and kissed her as she rose up to offer her lips to him.

"Salty," he said, licking his lips when she pulled away.

"You're thinking about using that in one of your inventions, aren't you?" she teased.

"I was, actually."

"Do you ever give your brain a day off?"

"Nope. I get most of my ideas out of the lab. I like wandering in the place you go where you daydream. That's where ideas live, floating in the air like brightly colored balloons."

"That's a lovely image," she said.

"Couldn't have said that before I met you. See what you've done for me?"

She kissed his shoulder, touched by his words. "So what balloon did you catch today?"

He looked back out to sea. "We know that inhaling a mist of hypertonic saline twice a day can help people with CF, but it has a tendency to make the patient's throat sore and it can make their chest tight. I've been thinking about ways to combat that, and maybe build in a saline element to a nebulizer medication."

"What does hypertonic mean?"

"Extra-salty water that's sterile, so there are no germs in it."

She wrapped her arms around him and rested her cheek on his chest. "I love that you're so clever. You make me feel safe."

He kissed the top of her head. "That's a nice thing to say."

"You're like a superhero."

"And I don't even need a cape."

She laughed. "I…" She caught herself just in time. *I love you, Charlie*, she'd been about to say.

Goodness. That wasn't appropriate at all.

"What?" he prompted.

"Nothing." Her cheeks warmed. She had to follow Charlie's example and start thinking before she spoke.

"Get a room, you two."

She turned at the voice behind them, not surprised to see Niall's smiling face. He'd brought them both a takeaway cup of coffee, and she accepted it gratefully, glad of something to distract from her almost faux pas.

"Enjoying the ride?" he asked. Tall—although nowhere near as tall as Charlie—and with dark blond hair, Niall was a typical Kiwi guy, tanned and outdoorsy, down-to-earth, trustworthy, and likeable.

"It's lovely," Ophelia said. "I haven't been out on a boat for ages. I'd forgotten how liberating it is, and how much I love the sea."

"Liberating is a good word," Niall said. "There's definitely a sense of freedom going out on the ocean. Gives me a chance to escape the missus." His smile told Ophelia he was teasing.

Charlie grinned. "Yeah, right. I've never seen you so happy. How is Genie, anyway?"

Niall slid his hands into the pockets of his jeans and looked almost bashful. "Actually, she's eleven weeks pregnant. We're not announcing it as such because it's still a bit early, but..." His shrug told Ophelia he was eager to share his news.

"Oh, congratulations." She kissed his cheek, and Charlie shook his hand.

"Thanks." He beamed.

"How's she feeling?" Ophelia asked.

He pulled a face. "She's lost ten pounds."

"Morning sickness?"

"Her exact words were 'Morning sickness? All the fucking day sickness it should be called.'"

They all laughed. "Hopefully that will pass," Ophelia said.

"Ah, she's already feeling a bit better."

"How's her knee?" Charlie asked.

"Good. She keeps fit, and she's been doing all her physio exercises, so it's healed well." He glanced behind them. "I'd better get back to the wheel, anyway."

"I hope someone else is steering while you're talking to us," Charlie commented.

Niall raised his eyebrows. "You mean it doesn't drive itself?" Giving him a wry look, he backed away. "Keep an eye out for the dolphins."

Ophelia turned to the view of the ocean and sipped her coffee, leaning against Charlie when he put his arm around her. "What's wrong with Niall's wife's knee?"

"Genie's ex-army," Charlie explained. "Got injured when her truck was blown up in Afghanistan."

"Jesus."

"That's not the worst of it, I'm afraid. Her best friend—Niall's sister—died in the blast."

"Oh. That's awful."

"Yeah. They've had a tough time of it, but they appear to have found consolation in each other."

"That's nice." She rested her head on his shoulder. "Charlie?"

"Yes, sweetheart?"

"Thank you."

"For what?"

"I don't know."

He squeezed her shoulder and kissed the top of her head. "You're welcome."

*

They reached the Hole in the Rock, and Ophelia held her breath while Niall navigated carefully through the narrow tunnel to the other side. Then they began the journey back, diverting slightly when he spotted a pod of dolphins to the north.

Ophelia and Charlie leaned on the edge of the boat and looked down to watch the gray-backed sleek dolphins speed alongside the boat.

"They're so fast," Ophelia said in wonder, her jaw dropping in admiration as one leapt high out of the water, then dived back in to continue swimming at the same pace.

"It's their tails—their flukes," Charlie said. "They're like wings. They generate a lift force that's directed forward on both the upstroke and downstroke. Holy shit!" He stepped back and laughed as a dolphin leapt right over the front of the boat.

Ophelia loved watching them, but she had to admit she found Charlie even more fascinating. She loved his boyish enthusiasm for anything vaguely scientific, and the way his brain never seemed to stop working. She adored his calm and placid manner, but also the way it hid a deep sensuality she sensed she hadn't even come close to exploring.

She'd nearly blurted out that she loved him. How crazy was that? How long had she known him? She made herself take a deep breath. It was just one of those things people said when they got carried away in the moment. There was no such thing as insta-love. Lust, yes, and she was happy to admit she was in lust with Charlie King. Even now, as his fingers trailed up her arm, ripples of desire ran through her, prompting memories of that morning and excitement about what lay before them when they returned to the bach. But it wasn't love, and she'd be foolish to start thinking it was. Just because a man had been vaguely nice to her didn't mean it was going to lead to roses around the door and happy ever after.

Her phone vibrated in her pocket, and her heart sank.

"Excuse me," she said, and turned away. Hoping it was her sister, she pulled out the phone—nope, it was Dillon.

"Hello?" she said, heart racing as she took a few steps away from Charlie.

"Ophelia? Where have you been? I've been ringing you for an hour."

"I'm out at sea and there hasn't been a reception," she said. "What's up?"

"Um... nothing really. I wanted to apologize for yesterday."

She wrapped her free arm around herself, hunching her shoulders. She didn't want this, not today when she was having such a nice time. Dillon confused her, muddied her thoughts and emotions, like mixing together different color Play Doh until it made a murky gray-brown. "It's okay."

"It's not. I shouldn't have done that. I was jealous, and I saw red for a while. I'm really sorry. Now I've calmed down, I can see what an idiot I've been."

She scratched at a mark on the railing. "It's all right. This is difficult for both of us. Don't worry about it."

"Forgive me?"

Irritation flared inside her, along with a bout of tiredness. He always did this—turned nice after an argument. She never knew whether it was genuine or not. "Yes, Dillon, I forgive you. How's Summer?"

"She's great. We've been swimming this morning, and now we're watching *Frozen* for the umpteenth time." He laughed.

Ophelia smiled reluctantly. The three of them had gone to the cinema to see it when it first came out. Dillon had always been very good with their daughter, and had never complained when they wanted to do girly things.

"I miss you, babe," he said.

"Don't call me babe," she whispered.

"Sorry. It's automatic. I do miss you though."

She gritted her teeth. "It's strange how you've been more attentive since you found out I was going out with Charlie. Dog in the manger comes to mind."

"That's not fair." His voice turned sharp. "I've just been trying to give you some space so you can realize what a good thing we have."

"Had."

"No, have. We're still married, and we will work this out."

Cold filtered through her. "We're separated, Dillon. That's not going to change."

"We'll see."

Her hand tightened on the rail. "No. We're done. You have to accept that."

"I don't. And I'm going to prove to you that we're right for each other. We promised to love each other forever, remember? I know you still love me, deep down."

Her throat tightened with frustration.

"Goodbye, Dillon," she said. After ending the call, she held the button at the top and turned off the phone.

Chapter Nineteen

Charlie had been watching her while she talked.

She was the most beautiful thing he'd ever seen. Today she wore a pair of very sexy denim shorts and a gray T-shirt that clung to her curves, with a short black jacket she'd zipped up against the cool sea air. She'd pulled her hair back in a scrunchie, but the wind had tugged several strands free, and they danced around her rosy cheeks, held back by the sunglasses she'd lifted on top of her head.

He'd tried to analyze why she captivated him but had failed, and it puzzled him. Although he thought her stunning, in essence she wasn't really different to any other young woman of her age—no taller, slimmer, cleverer... She was just a pretty girl with a bright smile and attractive green eyes.

And yet she was so much more than that. From the first moment he'd seen her, he'd been unable to take his eyes off her. He felt as if their connection went deeper than physical attraction, although that didn't make sense scientifically. But he was crazy about her, and he already knew he was interested in more than a casual relationship.

As he watched her slide her phone into her pocket, though, he could see that Dillon had gotten to her, again, and his heart sank. Her ex was determined to make this as difficult as possible, playing on Ophelia's kind nature and in-built loyalty until she was so mixed up she didn't know what she wanted.

She turned to look at him, saw him watching her, and walked slowly over, her hands in her pockets.

"They say dolphins are getting smarter and smarter," he said. "I swear I just saw one doing a Sudoku."

She met his gaze, her lips curving up, and then she moved close to him and rested her cheek on his chest.

He wrapped his arms around her and hugged her.

"You're so easy," she said.

"Yep. Sleep with anything in a skirt, me."

She laughed. "I meant easy to be with. I can't tell you how different I feel with you. With Dillon I always have to watch what I say. I'm constantly worried I'm going to make him jealous or angry. He's clever, but in a different way to you—every time he says something, I have to dig around like an archaeologist to find the real meaning beneath it. He forces me to be someone I don't want to be. But with you, I feel like I can be myself."

"I feel the same, funnily enough. I've grown used to watching what I say in case I put my foot in it, but I feel with you that you're not going to jump down my throat if it comes out wrong."

"It's nice." She relaxed against him, resting her hand on his chest. "I'm sorry, Charlie. I'm high maintenance, I know. New relationships should be all about laughter and light, not doom and gloom. You shouldn't have to put up with this."

"I don't care," he said, his voice sounding fierce, which surprised him. "I want you, and I'm here for you. I know it's not easy, but if you want to be with me, we'll get through it together."

She moved back and looked up at him. Without saying anything, he lowered his lips and kissed her. He poured as much passion into the kiss as he felt appropriate considering they weren't alone, and she rewarded him with a sexy sigh that turned into a moan as he cupped her head and held her there for a few more seconds.

When he finally moved back, his heart was thudding, and it took all the restraint he possessed not to slide his hands beneath her jacket and push her up against the railings.

"You still want to stay?" he said.

She moistened her lips and nodded. Her eyelids had lowered to half-mast and her gaze was fixed on his mouth as if she, too, was having trouble not continuing with their kiss. "I want you too," she whispered. "I want you to kiss me and make love to me until I forget everything else. Everything in my life seems muddled and murky, but you're like a bright coin at the bottom of the well. I want you so bad it hurts."

He tightened his fingers on her hips and looked across the Bay. "Not long now. We're nearly home."

*

Even so, it took nearly thirty minutes for the boat to dock, and then they had to say goodbye to Niall, who made them promise they'd join him and Genie at the *Between the Sheets* cocktail bar that evening. They left the boat and went to the car, and Charlie drove them the short distance back to the bach.

On the way, Ophelia didn't say much, and neither did he. Vaguely, he wondered if he had some kind of infection in his blood. He felt hot and edgy—not himself at all. *I want you so bad it hurts.* His head rang with her words. Could she feel the strange atmosphere between them, the passion that seemed to be making the air crackle with electricity, or was it all in his head? He was hard inside his jeans, his body tense with desire. Not unusually, he couldn't think what to say, but this time even his ability to fall back on humor deserted him. All he could think about was getting her naked and sliding inside her, the urge so strong it overrode every other thought in his head.

He pulled up outside the bach and they exited the car, still not saying anything. Charlie's face had felt dry and tight in the fresh sea air, but as they left the air conditioned car, the atmosphere turned hot and sultry. The New Zealand flag above the bach hung limp, and sweat broke out between his shoulder blades.

Again, though, he wondered if it was all in his head. So many times, he'd been certain of something only to discover he'd gotten it completely wrong. People rarely said what they were thinking, and he was expected to read between the lines, which was fine if he could see the lines, but more often than not he was lucky if he could see the page at all, let alone anything written in invisible ink.

He unlocked the sliding doors and pulled them wide open. The north-facing living room had grown hot and stuffy from the sun, and even though the Christmas tree stood right near the doors, the tinsel barely stirred.

He walked across to the kitchen and threw his keys and wallet on the counter, then slid off his sunglasses and laid them there too. He ran his hands through his hair, which was tangled and a little wild from the wind.

Turning back, he stopped as he saw Ophelia standing in the center of the room, her gaze fixed on him. She'd taken off her jacket in the car, and it was obvious to him now that she wasn't wearing a bra— her nipples showed clearly through the thin T-shirt fabric. Her breasts rose and fell quickly, and when she saw his gaze fall on them, she moistened her lips with the tip of her tongue.

The only sound came from their breathing and the distant sweep of the waves up the beach. A bauble slipped on the tree, adding a brief jingle to the air that faded away quickly. Outside, the sun glittered on the ocean, a natural Christmas decoration, lending a touch of sparkle to the afternoon.

Ophelia crossed her arms, took the base of her T-shirt in her hands, drew it over her head, and dropped it to the floor. Next, she took off her sandals, then she unzipped her shorts, pushed the denim down her legs, and stepped out of them. Finally, she slid her thumbs beneath the elastic of her panties, slid them down, and stepped out of them too. Pulling the scrunchie out of her hair, she let it fall around her shoulders in glorious brown waves.

Charlie caught his breath. He'd never seen anything so erotic—the sight of a beautiful woman stripping, in broad daylight, in his living room.

Even he couldn't misread that sign.

He strode across the room, cupped her face, and kissed her.

No tentative peck or gentle exploration this time. He kissed her hard, plunging his tongue into her mouth, and she lifted her arms around his neck and returned it with enthusiasm. Her tongue slid against his, and she gave a low purr deep in her throat that superheated his blood and sent it flooding to his groin.

Dropping his hands, he slid them down her back and skimmed her ribcage. Jeez, it was so sexy having her naked in his arms. Her skin felt soft and damp, and he loved the way it looked as if she wore a white bikini, the skin over her breasts and between her legs in the shape of small white triangles.

Turning her, still kissing her, he walked her backward until she bumped against the wall. There he broke contact for a moment to step back and grab a handful of his top, pull it over his head, and drop it to the floor. He unzipped his jeans and removed them, and added his boxers to the pile until they both stood there naked.

"Condom," she instructed, her eyes wide, her pupils dilated as she looked down at his eager erection.

He crossed to his wallet, retrieved a packet, and tore the wrapping off as he walked back to her. In seconds, he'd rolled the condom on, and then he pulled her into his arms.

She rose up to brush her lips against his. "I need you, Charlie," she whispered, her hands tightening on his arms until her nails dug into his skin. "I want to lose myself in you."

A small voice in his head queried whether this was only a temporary refuge from her problems with Dillon, but at that moment he didn't care. So what if it was? He couldn't have refused her for all the tea in China.

Placing his hands on her shoulders, he turned her so she faced away from him, her back against his chest, with her hands on the wall. His erection pressed against her bottom, and he slid his hands around her ribs to cup her breasts.

"I think it's the other way around," he murmured against her ear as he took each nipple between a finger and thumb. "I think I'll be losing myself in you." He squeezed, and she rewarded him with a moan and arched her back to push her breasts into his hands.

He slid a hand down her body between her legs, and slipped his fingers into her folds. As he'd hoped, she was already swollen and wet. Pleasure filled him that he hadn't gotten it wrong, and she felt the same way about him as he did about her.

He drew some of her moisture up to her clit and swirled his finger over it. "You're ready for me," he said, kissing the soft skin behind her ear. "Sweet Ophelia. You know how good that makes me feel?"

She shivered and leaned her head back on his shoulder, catching her bottom lip between her teeth as he continued to stroke her. "Mmm," she said, pushing the soft cheeks of her bottom back against his erection. "I want to feel you inside me."

"Oh, you will, very soon. I'll fill you up, and go deep, the way I like it. And I'll ride you all the way, and watch you come again." She was close—he could tell. His fingers slipped easily into her, while he continued to play with her nipple with the other hand. "I love watching you come," he said, adoring the way her eyelids fluttered closed and her lips parted. "I could watch you again and again. And actually, I think I might. How many orgasms do you think you could manage in one day?"

"Charlie..." She groaned. "Oh..."

He turned her to face him, then glanced to the side. A small bookcase stood against the wall to their right. Leaning down, he swept the magazines and knick-knacks from it onto the floor, then pushed her back against it so she rested on the top. Parting her legs, he blew out a long breath at the sight of her glistening flesh. Positioning the tip of his erection at her entrance, he held her hips and then pushed forward, burying himself inside her.

"Fuck." He closed his eyes.

Ophelia wrapped her legs around his waist, tilting up her hips, and when he pulled back and thrust again, he went deep, as he'd promised.

He'd planned to go slowly, but it was no good. She looked too sexy spread wide for him, her creamy skin glistening in the sunshine, her nipples softening in the warmth and begging for his mouth to close over them and suck. So he did, groaning as the velvet tips puckered in his mouth and she cried out with pleasure. The sultry heat, the smell of the sea and the jasmine growing around the deck, and the sheer sensation of standing there naked in broad daylight and making love to her, all combined to override his best intentions.

He set a fast pace, plunging into her soft flesh, and Ophelia leaned back and let him, pinned between him and the wall. She tipped back her head, closing her eyes, but he said, "Open," and her eyelids fluttered again to reveal her large green eyes, sleepy with desire. He kept his gaze fixed on hers, wanting to make sure she was thinking of him and only him, wanting to banish all thoughts of anyone else from her mind.

"Charlie… " She slipped a hand into his hair and tightened her fingers. "Oh, yeah. Oh, I like this. I like the feel of you inside me. Oh, don't stop."

He loved the way she told him what she was feeling. This woman was going to drive him insane. He pushed his hips forward and paused for a moment. For a few seconds he just enjoyed the sensation of being inside her, of stretching her until he'd filled her to the brim.

"Fuck," she said as he gave a slow rock of his hips, grinding against her. "I can feel you all the way to the top… aaahhh… Charlie… I'm going to…"

He watched, fascinated, as her orgasm claimed her, feeling her muscles clamp around him as pleasure spread across her features and her breath came in short, tight gasps. Jeez, he wanted to do this to her again and again, all day and all night. His own climax had nothing on giving pleasure to this woman.

He held on as long as he could, wanting to concentrate on her, but his traitorous body wouldn't wait, and muscles deep inside contracted and heat rushed through him. He groaned as he came, his hips jerking, and it seemed like hours before the pulses finally stopped and the world stopped spinning.

Chapter Twenty

"I'm shattered," Ophelia said.

They'd managed to make it to the bedroom and had drawn back the covers, but it was far too hot for the duvet, and so they were both lying on the bed naked, letting what little breeze meandered in from the open sliding doors drift across them. He lay on his back, ankles crossed, one arm behind his head and the other around her. She lay on her side facing him with her head on his shoulder.

"Get used to it." Charlie gave her a lazy smack on her rump. "I intend to wear you out on a daily basis."

"Mmm. I'm not going to argue with that." She kissed his shoulder, sleepy and sated. "You're surprisingly bossy."

"Am I?"

She thought about it. "No, not bossy. Sure of yourself, maybe."

"I'm sure of myself. Just not sure about other people."

That summed him up, she thought. He appeared to have plenty of inner confidence, born either from his intellect or his money, or possibly both. She liked that about him. There was nothing sexier than a confident man. His uncertainty where other people were concerned just gave him an interesting edge.

The vivid blue sky sported a couple of fluffy white clouds on the horizon, but otherwise it was bright and clear. The intense atmosphere that had accompanied them back in the car had passed, leaving her feeling warm and fuzzy.

"Thank you," she whispered, not sure how else to express her pleasure at what they'd done, and the way he made her feel.

"You're welcome," he mumbled. "Wake me up before it gets dark."

They actually only dozed for less than an hour. Ophelia stirred to see the sun had passed by them, and the room was now a little cooler, although she felt far from cold.

The man by her side still had his eyes closed, and she took the opportunity to study his features at her leisure, his sculpted lips, straight nose, dark eyebrows, and long hair that had fallen across one eye. The intense brown eyes that always gave her goose bumps were hidden, but she still got a tingle at the thought of the way he looked at her, as if she were something special, some marvelous experiment he'd completed in his lab that had yielded amazing results.

Her gaze slid down his body, over his broad, muscular shoulders and arms, down his chest, and followed the happy trail of hair to his groin.

"Enjoying the view?"

Her gaze snapped back up to his, but his eyes were still closed.

"Didn't know scientists believed in a sixth sense," she said, a little embarrassed at being caught ogling him.

"I can feel your eyes burning into me like lasers," he murmured sleepily.

She chuckled. "Is that a complaint?"

"Not at all. It's very pleasant."

"This feels so decadent," she said, trailing a finger through his chest hair, "lying naked in broad daylight with a gorgeous guy. I'm not used to being so lazy. I feel as if I should be doing something."

"If you get up, I'll only drag you back to bed and tie you to it."

She lifted her head and rested her chin on his chest, studying his face.

He opened one eye. "That was a joke."

"Oh." She wasn't sure whether to be disappointed or relieved. Maybe he wasn't into playful sex. Not that she was particularly kinky, but the notion of trying out a few things with him gave her a sexy tingle. Never mind, she'd question him more about that when she knew him a bit better.

She yawned and settled down beside him. "This is so nice. I wish we could stay here forever, sleeping, waking, making love, walking on the beach, eating chocolate, and starting all over again."

"That's what my heaven would be like." He kissed her hair. "I was thinking…"

"Oh?"

"About Christmas. I wondered whether you and Summer would like to come to Brock's party on Christmas Eve? Erin's boy will be there and I think there will be other kids for Summer to play with. It should be fun."

Ophelia pushed up onto an elbow. Shit, this was awkward. "Oh, Charlie, that's a lovely offer, but I'm really sorry, I've already promised Summer we'll spend it with Dillon."

He surveyed her, his face carefully blank. "Okay."

"I thought it would make it less upsetting for her."

"Of course. That makes perfect sense." He kissed her hair again. "No worries at all." He checked his watch. "Okay, I'm going to take a shower and then we can go out for dinner." He rolled off the bed and walked toward the bathroom.

"Charlie?" Ophelia called out. He stopped and turned. "I'm sorry if I upset you," she whispered.

"All good," he said. He smiled at her, then went into the bathroom and closed the door.

She sat up and wrapped her arms around her knees. He hadn't asked her to shower with him. Even though she'd only known him intimately a few days, she knew him well enough to be certain she'd upset him. Poor Charlie. He'd felt relaxed enough with her to pluck up the courage to ask her to stay for Christmas, and then she'd thrown it back in his face.

Resting her cheek on her knees, she looked out of the window at the ocean. What else could she have done, though? This was the first Christmas she and Dillon had spent as a separated couple, and the first Christmas Summer would be without her father. Ophelia had told Dillon he could stay on Christmas Eve providing he slept in the spare room, so he'd be there first thing for when Summer woke up. At the time it had made sense, but now it felt incredibly awkward having him there overnight when she was dating another man. How was it going to make Charlie feel knowing Dillon was there at night with her? No matter how much she insisted nothing would happen, he was bound to worry.

Her stomach churned uneasily at the thought of Dillon being there. A few weeks ago, it hadn't bothered her, but his behavior had changed since she'd started seeing Charlie, and now that Dillon had told her he was determined he wouldn't let her go, she knew it wasn't beyond the realms of possibility that he'd make a move on her Christmas Eve. If he was aggressive and angry, it wouldn't be so much of a problem, even though the last thing she wanted the night before Christmas was a huge row with him. But with her emotional state the way it was, if he came on all sweetness and light, playing on her guilt, talking about the past, and bringing Summer into the equation, she knew he was going to mix her all up again. She didn't want to get back with him, but she wasn't a hundred percent certain that her resolve was stronger than her guilt.

Then she thought of Charlie again. Gentle, kind Charlie, who didn't deserve to be messed around, who had enough trouble figuring out the right thing to do without her adding to his confusion. Hopefully she hadn't ruined everything.

*

It was Saturday evening, and as they approached the *Between the Sheets* cocktail bar, Ophelia saw it was heaving with people. Although there must have been a lot of locals there, it looked as if everyone was on holiday. Nearly everyone wore shorts and T-shirts, a reggae song filtered out of the open windows and doors, and the smell of barbecued ribs and seafood mingled with the sea, filling her with the sounds and smells of summer.

She'd talked Charlie into taking a taxi so they could both have a drink, and Charlie paid the driver, then took her hand and led her across the road and through the tables and chairs out the front yard into the bar.

She hadn't brought up the issue of Christmas again, not wanting to upset him further, and not knowing how she could comfort him anyway. He didn't appear particularly upset—he'd kissed her when he came out of the shower and they'd talked normally as they got ready to go out, but it was difficult to tell how he was feeling.

Resolving to talk to him later when they returned to the bach, Ophelia decided to try to enjoy the evening. She followed Charlie through the large room, noting the sand-covered floor, the pastel beams and walls, the large black-and-white photographs of surfers caught in mid wave on the walls that were obviously taken by the same guy as the shots in the bach, and the shell-and-driftwood mobiles and table decorations that gave the bar a fun and breezy beach feel.

He took her up to the bar itself and introduced her to the barkeep, a tall guy with a beard and a ready smile who Charlie called Beck.

"What can I get you?" Beck asked, gesturing to the list of cocktails behind his head.

"Ooh, a Singapore Sling please," Ophelia said after studying the ingredients.

"Coming right up."

Charlie ordered an Old Fashioned, and when they were ready, they took their drinks and he led her to a table in the corner. Niall sat there with his arm around a pretty young woman with blonde hair who was obviously his wife, Genie, and beside them were a tall, rough-and-ready sort of guy Niall introduced as Danny, and his girlfriend, Hermione, a pretty girl with long brown hair and an English accent. Ophelia slid onto the bench beside Hermione, and Charlie pulled up a chair opposite her.

He'd told Ophelia that Niall and he had met through their parents some time ago, so she was interested to see him with friends. Dillon had tended to change depending on the company he kept—with his mates he became loud and showed off, with her parents he was the epitome of politeness, with her sister Kate and her husband or Ophelia's own friends he tended to be dry and sarcastic. What would Charlie be like?

It became clear after ten minutes or so that he was probably going to be the same no matter what company he was in. He remained attentive and thoughtful, still thinking before he spoke, but warm and amusing, and clearly the others liked him a lot. He obviously hadn't met Hermione before, and Ophelia watched him talk to her, asking her questions about England, and making her laugh with his attempt at a Cockney accent. He was perhaps a little quieter than normal, and she wondered whether that was just being in company, or due to the conversation they'd had in the bedroom. She caught him looking at her several times throughout the evening, but whenever she met his gaze, he smiled, and he held her hand, so she hoped he wasn't too upset with her.

After a few drinks he disappeared to the Gents', and Ophelia sipped her cocktail, a little shy to be on her own with the group. Not that they weren't nice—Niall and Danny were both lovely, and the girls were incredibly friendly and seemed keen to make her feel welcome.

"Wow," Genie said as Charlie disappeared through the door. "Have you cast a spell on him or something?"

Ophelia raised her eyebrows. "What do you mean?"

"I've never seen him like that."

Heat rose inside her. "Like what?"

"I don't know. Kind of shy and bashful."

"Is he not normally like that then?"

Niall, Genie, and Danny laughed. "No," Niall said wryly.

"He has his head in the clouds half the time," Genie clarified. "But he can't take his eyes off you. It's lovely."

Hermione nudged Ophelia. "You're blushing. Aw."

"I don't know what to say." The thought that they'd noticed him looking at her made her feel gooey inside.

"I'm glad the two of you finally got together," Niall said. He frowned at his wife. "When did he first mention her—six, seven months ago?"

"More than that," Danny said, "it was before I met Hermione."

Ophelia's blush deepened. Charlie had told them about her all that time ago? How strange.

"Ssh, stop talking about him, he's here," Genie said in an exaggerated whisper, and Ophelia glanced over to see Charlie walking toward them.

He sat back in his seat and raised an eyebrow at her. "Are you warm?"

She touched her fingers to her cheeks. "No. They're teasing me."

"We were saying how you can't stop staring at her," Genie said. Ophelia was quickly beginning to understand that the other girl wouldn't say anything behind anyone's back that she wouldn't say to their face.

Charlie shrugged. "That's because she's sexy as hell."

Niall and Danny laughed, the girls giggled, and Ophelia blushed even harder. "Stop it," she scolded. "Change the subject, quick."

To their credit, they did, moving on to talk about Danny and Hermione's trip to the UK that they'd planned for the following year. Ophelia listened, but her gaze kept drifting back to Charlie, who was concentrating on the conversation, his brown eyes fixed on Danny as he relayed what cities they were planning to visit and how he was going to enjoy staying at Hermione's folks' house and having a butler.

It sounded as if Charlie was quieter than usual. Her heart sank a little as she thought that she'd probably upset him deeply when she turned him down. Did he not understand that she had to do what was best for Summer? She'd made the break with Dillon, but it didn't mean she could cut herself off from her ex completely.

If Charlie couldn't understand that, then maybe this wasn't going to work.

Chapter Twenty-One

The rest of the evening passed pleasantly enough, as they ordered a few platters to share and washed them down with alcohol.

Charlie didn't normally drink very much. He enjoyed a cold beer on his deck at night after a swim, but he tended to limit himself to one because he didn't like the feeling of numbness that accompanied more than a single drink. He liked his brain sharp, plus he was aware of how alcohol had a strange effect on the tongue, loosening it until he seemed to have no control over what he was saying, and that was the last thing he wanted.

But tonight, he felt the need for a drink. He had a couple of cocktails because he was in a cocktail bar, but when the guys moved on to whiskey he went with them and indulged in a couple of expensive Scotch single malts.

He only had a couple—he had no intention of passing out when he returned to the bach—but it was enough to wash away the hard knot he'd had in his stomach since his conversation with Ophelia, and he welcomed the mellow relaxedness that gradually overcame him.

In the end, he had a great evening, and he thought Ophelia probably had too. Her face had taken on a general rosy glow rather than the bright blush she'd sported earlier, and although she listened more than she talked, she joined in with the conversation and laughed enough to convince him she'd had a good time.

Eventually, however, when Genie—who wasn't drinking due to the pregnancy nobody was supposed to know about but clearly everyone did—suggested they make a move, the knot returned to Charlie's stomach.

He tried to ignore it, kissed Genie and Hermione on the cheek, shook hands with the guys, and said goodbye to Beck at the bar. The others headed off, Genie telling Danny and Hermione that she'd drop them home, and Charlie took Ophelia's hand and led her outside to wait for the taxi that Beck had called for them.

Over the past few days, summer had descended on the Northland, and although the sun had set, the evening air was warm enough for Charlie not to shiver in his shirt sleeves, although Ophelia pulled a thin jacket over her T-shirt. She wore her short shorts again, though, and he found it difficult not to stare at her slim, shapely legs.

They waited across the road for the taxi, looking out toward the sea. It looked like a dark blue varnished plate, the half-moon lying on the surface like a piece of silver foil.

"Are you okay?" Ophelia spoke softly, her voice almost inaudible over the sound of the waves. "You've been quiet this evening."

He looked down at her. Her green eyes were as dark as forest pools, her face pale. "I'm fine. Did you have a nice evening?"

"Yes, thank you. They're a lovely group of people. Very friendly."

"I'm glad you enjoyed it. It's a nice bar, isn't it?" They were being as polite as strangers, he thought. She thought she'd upset him when she'd turned down his offer to join him for Christmas. That was unfair, and he wanted to explain himself, but he couldn't seem to find the words.

The taxi drew up, and he went to open the door for her, then hesitated. Fuck, this dating game was so difficult. His stomach knotted even harder, and for a brief moment nausea rose in his throat. He shouldn't have drunk so much. He was having trouble thinking clearly.

"Charlie?" She put a hand on his shoulder. "What is it?"

He shook his head and opened the door.

"Thank you," she said, and got in.

He closed the door, walked around to the other side, got in, and gave the driver the directions to the bach.

They traveled in silence. He closed his eyes and leaned his head on the back of the seat until the taxi slowed and stopped. Ophelia offered to pay, so he let her, not knowing what to say, and got out of the car to breathe deeply of the fresh sea air.

Calm down, he scolded himself. He had to get this into perspective or he was going to give himself an ulcer. Nothing terrible had happened. He just had to take this a step at a time, and make decisions as they came up rather than trying to second guess himself all the time.

They went into the bach, and Ophelia excused herself to visit the bathroom. The lights on the Christmas tree glittered in the darkness, and in the reflection of the window he couldn't tell which were lights and which were stars. He told himself to turn on some lamps, make the place welcoming and homely, but his feet refused to move, and in the end he remained at the window, hands in his pockets, looking into the dark night.

Behind him, he heard Ophelia come back into the room and pour herself a drink, presumably water judging by the amount of liquid sloshing into a glass. The fridge closed, and her footsteps echoed across the room until she stood beside him.

"Charlie?" She placed a hand on his arm. "I think we need to talk."

He swallowed. He didn't want to have this conversation, but equally he knew the knot in his stomach wouldn't go away until they did.

"Come on, honey," she said, "sit down with me."

He let her lead him across to the sofa and sat next to her. She curled up on the seat, turning to face him, and sipped her water. Removing his glasses, he massaged the bridge of his nose, suddenly tired.

"We need to talk about our conversation earlier." Ophelia leaned forward to place her glass of water on the coffee table. "You were so kind to invite me and Summer around for Christmas, and I know I hurt your feelings by saying no. But I need you to understand why I said no. It wasn't because I don't want to spend time with you, or because I'm getting back with Dillon."

"Okay."

"I feel I should tell you, though, that I had already said he could stay the night on Christmas Eve. In a spare room, obviously, but Summer wanted him there when she opened her presents in the morning."

The knowledge that Dillon would be in the house after Summer went to bed made unfamiliar anger rise inside him. The man would no doubt make the most of the opportunity. Charlie could envisage them having a drink together, talking about old times, remembering when they'd loved each other, and how much Summer bound them together. Dillon would do his best to win her back, and the worst of it was that Charlie couldn't blame him, because if he was in the same situation he would have done the same. The thought of actually having Ophelia, of being married to her and promising to love her forever, and then being stupid enough to lose her, made him feel physically ill.

"I understand," he said, because he did.

"I'm glad. That doesn't mean you have to like it though." She smiled.

He considered her comment. She understood that it made him angry to think about it? And that was okay?

"I'm kinda regretting asking him," she said. "I didn't think, but I know it's going to be awkward having him there. I might put a lock on my bedroom door." She rolled her eyes and gave him a wry smile.

"I don't blame him for wanting you back," he said. "He must be kicking himself that he lost you."

"He should have thought about that over the last seven years." Her voice had turned hard. "I've given him plenty of chances. It wasn't as if we had one row and I walked out. I've told him on numerous occasions that I don't like the way he speaks to me sometimes, and that I wouldn't put up with his jealousy and possessiveness." She put a hand on Charlie's knee. "And to clarify, it's not the jealousy in itself that I can't cope with, because I think it's natural to be jealous if you love your partner, but the point of a good relationship is that you trust them, you know?"

Charlie nodded slowly. "He didn't trust you?"

"Not at all, and I find that insulting. For example, one day I went out with a couple of friends, and while we were having lunch, one of my friend's brothers walked by. He stopped and joined us at the table. A few days later, Dillon came home one evening in a furious mood because a friend of his had seen us all having lunch and had told him that Harry was there, and I hadn't mentioned it. Dillon took it to mean I was keeping it secret because I had some sort of crush on Harry or something, which is rubbish. But the worst thing was that I purposely hadn't told Dillon because I knew he would make a fuss, and I'm terrible at lying, so of course he discovered that it hadn't just slipped my memory but that I'd kept that detail to myself. It blew up into a big row, and that is one of the main reasons I broke up with him. Does that make sense?"

"Yes, of course."

"I'll never be able to erase my history with Dillon," she said. "For good or bad. I don't regret meeting him because he gave me Summer, and we've had some great times, mainly in the first few years. Of course he'll always be around to play a role in Summer's life. But our marriage is over. Meeting you has confirmed that to me. Being with you makes it easier, because I feel this is what a relationship should be like. I want to explore that with you, and get to know you better."

The knot in Charlie's stomach eased a little, and he nodded.

"How many girlfriends have you had?" she asked.

The question came out of the blue, and his eyebrows rose.

"Sorry," she said, pulling an embarrassed face. "I didn't mean to pry."

"It's not that. Even though you've told me you prefer the honest approach, I'm not sure whether that relates to questions like this." How could he explain that this was the crux of his whole problem?

"I understand," she said. "I think most men struggle with that sort of honesty. I am sorry. I'm curious, that's all—I can't understand why you're still single and yet so good in bed."

"You say the nicest things."

"It's the truth," she said, laughing.

What should he say? "I'm not in double figures. How's that?"

"That's good." She kissed his chest. "Were any of them serious?"

"Some were funnier than others."

She smacked his arm. "You're misunderstanding me on purpose now, and don't say you're not because I can tell by the twinkle in your eye."

He sighed. She obviously wanted him to be honest. "I haven't had a serious relationship, in the sense that I've never lived with anyone."

"Is that by choice, or did you never meet the right woman?"

He studied the ocean, observing how the wave tops seemed painted with silver. "It wasn't a conscious decision. I haven't dated anyone for more than a few months. I've never found anyone willing to put up with me for longer than that."

"Aw, Charlie. Be serious. You haven't met a girl you've wanted to settle down with?"

He said nothing for a moment, trying to consider the best answer, but his brain was too fuzzy so he decided he'd just have to tell the truth. "My life's been too full of work, I suppose. There wasn't space for anything else, and I guess that was evident when I dated."

"And now? Do you want to settle down? Have kids?"

Of course he did. He wanted it more than anything in the world. But the thought of making that kind of commitment scared him, because he had no idea how to go about it. There was no manual for being a husband or a father, no rules he could follow. And without a set of instructions, he couldn't believe he'd ever be able to pluck up the courage to ask a woman to spend the rest of her life with him.

Chapter Twenty-Two

Ophelia waited for Charlie to answer. A long silence ensued during which he studied the ceiling as if it had a complex mathematical theory written on it.

Maybe he wasn't interested in anything long term. Just because he'd told others he liked her months ago didn't mean he wanted more than to get into her knickers. The thought made her a little panicky. She hadn't expected him to propose on the first date, but she had thought sex would lead to something more. Perhaps sleeping with him so early on hadn't been such a good idea.

"Charlie?" she prompted.

"I'm thinking."

She nibbled her bottom lip. "It's okay, you don't have to answer," she said, although she desperately wanted him to.

His arm lay along the back of the sofa, and he moved his hand to pick up a strand of her hair. Absently, he wound it around a finger. "I don't know."

"A long term relationship doesn't appeal to you?"

He turned his head to look at her, and she was relieved to see his eyes were warm. "It definitely appeals to me. I'd like to be comfortable enough with someone to feel I could share my life with them without having to watch what I say all the time. But I don't know that I'm good enough."

She frowned. "What do you mean? Of course you're good enough."

"I meant good enough at relationships. Men joke that the manual for understanding women is ten feet thick. Well it has to be at least double that for me."

To her surprise, his eyes flickered with fear. "You're scared," she said.

"Terrified. I wouldn't know where to start to make it work. I'd be terrible at it."

It almost made her want to cry. "Of course you wouldn't." She moved a little closer to him and kissed his shoulder.

He looked back out at the ocean. "I would. I've watched Brock with Fleur and Matt with a hundred girlfriends. There's a secret code that other men seem to be born understanding. They instinctively know the right thing to say. What to do on a first date, a third date, a fifth. When it's appropriate to suggest sex and when it isn't. Even stupid things like how to work out what a girl really wants for her birthday when she tells you not to bother with a gift."

It was just beginning to dawn on her how hard he found the social interactions that most people took for granted. "It must be difficult," she said carefully.

"It's got harder, not easier, as I've gotten older. Brock, Matt, and I were brought up to be gentlemen—it was the most important thing my parents felt the need to teach us. But last year a girlfriend told me I was being sexist when I held the door open for her, as if I was implying she couldn't open the door for herself. Another girl got offended when I offered to pay for dinner. One woman actually shouted at me when I stood up to give her my seat on a train, telling everyone in the carriage that I was the perfect example of the sort of man who thought that women weren't equal to them in every way."

She remembered how he'd hesitated when he'd gone to open the taxi door for her. "Oh, Charlie..."

"I respect women," he said. "Especially in the bedroom. But apparently even that can lead to trouble." He gave a long, gloomy sigh.

Ophelia reached out, cupped his cheek, and brushed her thumb against his stubble. Outside, she could just hear the swoosh of waves on the beach. The only light came from the silver moon and the white Christmas lights on the tree, and the two of them looked as if they were actors in a black-and-white movie, cast into a monochrome world of light and shadows.

She was so glad she'd started this conversation. Clearly, Charlie found it difficult to talk about certain things, but it was important to her that he felt comfortable saying whatever was on his mind. She liked him so much, and it touched her deeply that he'd suffered in the past because women had misunderstood him, and hadn't been patient enough to get to the bottom of any issues they'd had.

Something had obviously happened that had upset him enough to make him wary of committing himself to a long-term relationship, and she wanted to understand it so she could help him if she could.

"Was it Lisette?" She knew he'd not dated for a while, and he'd hinted that his relationship with Lisette had ended badly.

"Yes," he said.

"What happened?"

He said nothing.

She continued to stroke his cheek. "Come on, tell me." She tipped her head to the side. "Did she ask you to do something you were uncomfortable with?"

He looked at her again. "Sort of."

"It's okay, Charlie, you can tell me. Everyone likes different things in bed and that's why it's important to talk. If there are things you don't like doing, I'd much rather know."

"It's not quite that easy." He blew out a breath. "My parents drummed into the three of us when we were teenagers that when we're with a girl no means no, and I wouldn't dream of flouting that rule. Respecting the girl has always been top of my list of bedroom rules."

"So what went wrong?"

He sighed. "I like sex."

"I'm glad to hear it."

"I don't think I'm bad at it."

"You're fantastic in bed, Charlie."

He didn't seem to have heard her. "Lisette and I were okay for a few months. I'm happy to... experiment in the bedroom, and she kept pushing me to try different things, but one night she started to talk about other... stuff."

"Like what?"

"Things she wanted me to do to her."

Ophelia slipped her hand to the nape of his neck and stroked it. "Can you tell me what kind of things?"

He leaned his head back and stared at the ceiling again. "She wanted me to tie her up. To hurt her. She told me she had a rape fantasy and she wanted me to force myself on her." He ran a hand through his hair, taking a shivery breath. "I didn't get it then, and I still don't."

Ophelia closed her eyes momentarily. "Oh, sweetheart..."

"I couldn't do it," he said miserably. "Where's the line between play and reality? I wouldn't be able to tell the difference between when no meant don't stop, and no meant no. I'd be terrified I'd get it wrong."

Now she understood why he was worried she'd misunderstood his comment about tying her up earlier in the day. His fear went much deeper than concern about upsetting his partner. It must be confusing for men in general, she thought, because men's and women's roles had changed so much in the past few decades. But it was obviously even more difficult for Charlie, who struggled to read body language and to make sense of social interaction.

"Did you try to explain?" she asked him. "To tell her why you felt uneasy?"

"Of course. It just seemed to make her angry though. She called me a wimp and said I wasn't man enough for her." For the first time since Olivia had known him, his expression flickered with anger.

"I'm sorry." She kissed his face. "You deserve so much better than that."

"I felt such an idiot." Now he looked upset. "I decided it was easier not to date than to put myself through that again. And I didn't, until you came along."

She cuddled up to him and rested her cheek on his shoulder. "I'm so glad you had the courage to ask me out."

"Did I do the right thing, telling you?" His voice was hoarse with emotion. "I don't want you to feel sorry for me. I'm not trying to blackmail you into staying with me. I can take rejection."

In answer, she lifted her lips to his and kissed him.

For a few moments he just let her, his body stiff and resisting. Then, when she didn't stop, his hand slid into her hair, his body relaxed, and he kissed her properly, long and slow.

"Thank you," he said when she eventually moved back.

She remained in the circle of his arms, though, wanting to reassure him. "Okay, let's get a few things sorted. For a start, I can tell you straight up that I have no rape fantasies whatsoever."

He nodded, looking relieved. "Okay."

"I'm not experienced in any of this, Charlie. I've only had the one partner and he was hardly adventurous." Dillon hadn't minded her wearing sexy underwear, but he hadn't been a fan of extended foreplay, and sex with him had always been about mutually satisfying physical needs rather than spending hours in titillation. "But I do read some racy romance," she continued. "Enough to know that if Lisette wanted to encourage you to do some of the things she liked, she should have suggested you use a safeword."

"Safeword?"

"A word you'd agreed between you that meant stop, so there was no confusion. We'll make one now. Let's say ours is... lightning. That means if we're making love and I decide I don't like something and I want you to stop, I'll say the word lightning, and you'll know I'm not playing. Okay?"

He nodded slowly. "Okay."

"It doesn't mean we have to do anything you don't want to do. It doesn't mean I'll ever use it. And it doesn't mean that if I do use it, it's all gone horribly wrong and we're over. It just so you know that you don't have to worry you're reading the signs wrong. Does that make sense?"

"Yes." He stroked her hair. "I can't believe you're being so good about this."

"Look, relationships are incredibly tricky. I understand why you feel at sea. That's why it's important for us to talk. And in the bedroom, it's especially important. You can ask me anything you like."

He twisted a strand of her hair around his finger. "Why would a woman fantasize about being taken by force? I don't understand that."

She thought about it. "Well, I can't answer for other women of course. I can only guess. And my guess would be that it's not about the horrific reality of being brutally raped by a stranger, an act which involves no consideration for the woman and is a violation. It's a fantasy—it's about being wanted by someone you love, so much so that he won't take no for an answer."

His frown remained in place.

She tried again. "Everyone wants to be desired. It's the biggest turn on there is. Knowing that another person whom you find attractive is watching you, thinking about having sex with you, to the point of being out of control with desire."

"I suppose." He still looked doubtful.

It still didn't make sense to him. Maybe she was coming at it the wrong way. She had to think like him, she realized. Scientifically, not emotionally. "It's also about giving up control," she said slowly. "Outside of the bedroom, the roles of men and women are changing, and have been for a while. Women no longer consider themselves subservient to men—we think ourselves equal. We take charge of our own lives, and we no longer expect men to tell us what to do. In its basic form, though, sex is animalistic, isn't it? We revert to our baser instincts. If you watch any nature program, you'll see the female being taken by the male and having little say in the matter. Maybe that's inbuilt in us, I don't know, and that desire to be conquered comes out during sex, which is why women—even strong, independent ones who'd normally punch a guy if he bossed them around in the office—like the man taking charge in the bedroom."

His eyes had grown warm again. "I like your scientific approach."

"Does it make more sense now?"

"Actually, yes." He stroked her neck. "Do you?"

"What? Like the man to take charge in the bedroom?" She thought about. "Sometimes. I quite like reversing the role too. It's exciting, knowing you have power over someone else's desire. But yes, sometimes it's nice for the man to take control. Like I said, there's something primal about it. Confidence is always sexy. I do think it was unfair of Lisette to push you right to the end of the scale immediately, though. Delving into extremes can be scary if you don't take baby steps first. Do you like role playing?"

"Not sure. Never done it. Wouldn't know where to start."

"Perhaps that's something we could try."

"I'm not a great actor."

She giggled. "I doubt I'd win any Oscars either, but that doesn't matter, you know? It's about having fun, and finding out about each other. If you try something and you're not keen, well, you don't have to do it again, but you might have a go at something and discover you love it."

"Maybe some examples would help me understand," he said.

Her lips twitched. "Warming up to the idea, are you?"

"You make a convincing case." His hand slid down her back, and his body had relaxed.

She ran a finger around the neckline of his shirt. "I'm happy to discuss options. Like I said, I'm hardly experienced, but I'm very open to ideas. If it's just me and you in the room, I can't think of anything I wouldn't want to try."

His gaze fixed on hers. Heat spread through her at his amused interest. "Nothing at all?" he said, skimming his hand over her hips.

"No." She moistened her lips. "I want to know what you like and don't like. And I want you to feel safe enough to experiment with me. I can't deny it—the thought of a slightly kinky Charlie turns me on."

To her pleasure, instead of him looking wary, his lips curved up a little. "Does it now?"

"It does. I think it would be fun to talk about things we could try."

"Define kinky," he said, turning on the sofa a little to face her.

Hmm, he was interested. Her notion of a safeword had worked.

She nibbled her bottom lip. "I suppose it means different things to different people. What positions do you like?"

"I've always preferred face to face so I can make sure the woman's enjoying it," he said, with a tad of wryness in his voice.

"But now we have a safeword?"

He thought about it, and his lips curved a little more.

"Maybe toys?" she suggested.

"I'm guessing you're not talking about Lego and Play Doh."

"No." She wasn't going to let him cover his awkwardness with humor this time. "I'm talking about a vibrator. Don't you think that would be fun? They're just like body massagers. We could tease each other with it. Maybe insert it in some fun places." She lifted her eyebrows.

"Places?" He emphasized the plural.

"Mmm. Maybe. Don't you think that would be fun? To tease each other?" She leaned forward and touched her lips to his, just a brush, sending her tingling all over. "What about you?" she asked. "What would you like to try?"

Chapter Twenty-Three

Charlie's head was spinning. This was by far the most erotic moment of his entire life.

He would never have been able to explain to Ophelia how different her approach was to Lisette's. He'd been attracted to Lisette because she was confident and sexy. She'd obviously been experienced sexually, but he hadn't minded that, and he'd been happy for her to take the initiative sometimes, and to do things like dress up in pretty underwear. But the night she'd broached the subject of rough sex had been horrific.

She'd obviously played out the fantasy with other partners and had thought all men would find it a turn on. His complete bafflement had thrown her. Instead of taking Ophelia's approach, and discussing it with him so he understood more about what she wanted, she'd turned on him, told him he was a freak, and had thrown insults at him until he was so bewildered he'd gotten completely tongue tied and she'd walked out.

In contrast, Ophelia's frank discussion, her attempt to scientifically analyze the reasons behind the fantasy, her gentle encouragement, and her obvious desire for him, all combined to help him understand that he wasn't a freak. He wasn't weird because supposedly he didn't like what other men liked. In fact, the notion of trying out a few things Ophelia had suggested made blood rush to his groin. She made him feel normal. No, more than that—she made him feel special and sexy, and that was a gift more precious than gold.

He was so crazy about this girl. He wanted to show her.

What about you? she'd asked. *What would you like to try?*

"Everything," he said, his voice little more than a whisper. "I could spend every day of the next ten years in bed with you and not get bored. It could be like a scientific experiment."

"Oh?" She shivered, and his gaze dropped to her nipples, which had tightened and showed through her T-shirt. "Tell me," she whispered. "Tell me what you're thinking. I want to know."

His courage was growing now he understood the game. The notion of a safeword was such a simple idea that he couldn't believe he hadn't thought of it before. He knew Ophelia would never have to use it—in spite of what she'd said, he would never want to reach the point where he wasn't sure if she was enjoying herself. But the idea that he didn't have to guess anymore, that one simple word would unambiguously tell him she wanted him to stop, was like the sun coming through the clouds to banish all the shadows.

If it's just me and you in the room, I can't think of anything I wouldn't want to try, she'd said. Now he realized that was what he'd wanted all these years. Someone who wanted to play, to help him discover the depths of sexuality he'd read existed but that he'd never really experienced. But in a safe way. A way that contained only pleasure, not pain or fear.

"I'd like to test your limits." He pulled her against him so she half lay on him, her soft body molding to his. "Find out how much pleasure you can handle. Discover what you like, what turns you on." He traced down her spine with a finger and decided the best thing to do was to speak from the heart. "I'd like to explore every inch of your body, slowly, with my mouth and fingers, and maybe other things."

"Other things?"

"To give you different sensations. Soft, hot, wet, cold. Feathers. Ice. Whatever I can think of." He could try different textures too, velvet, brushes, metal, smooth, rough. He liked that idea. It was like a scientific experiment.

She looked as if she was having trouble breathing out. "My mouth's gone dry," she said.

He lifted his other hand to brush his thumb across her bottom lip. "You like the sound of that?"

"Yes," she whispered.

"Then… maybe I will tie you up," he said, warming to the notion. "Have you at my mercy."

"Oh…" She opened her mouth, closed her lips around his thumb, and sucked gently, her wide green eyes staring into his.

Heat flooded him. He shifted so she was fully on top of him, and nestled his erection into the softness of her mound. He knew he'd hit the right spot when she murmured around his thumb, and her hips began to rock against his. Her short shorts exposed her pale thighs, and he ran his free hand up the outside of one, reveling in the feel of the silky skin.

"I'll tie your hands above your head," he said huskily, "and your ankles to the corners of the bed, so you're spread wide for me." Fuck, that was a hot idea.

She shivered, lacing her tongue across his thumb.

"Maybe I will use a vibrator," he said. "I could tease your nipples with it before lowering it between your legs." He kissed her top lip above where she was sucking him.

She closed her eyes. Removing his thumb from her mouth, he slid his hands down her body to tighten on the plump muscles of her bottom. "Then I'll concentrate here," he said, holding her as he thrust up, stroking his erection against her clit. "Do you think you'd like that? Tiny vibrations drawing you nearer the edge every second, until you're gasping for release?"

"Mm," she murmured, lips parting as he kissed her.

He teased her tongue with his while he lifted his hands to her breasts, which sat in his palms like soft, ripe fruit. He squeezed her nipples gently, and apparently that was enough to tip her over the edge. She rocked her hips a last time, then shuddered, and she gasped repeatedly against his lips as her orgasm claimed her.

Charlie watched in delight, enjoying her pleasure, loving that he'd given it to her.

When she finally opened her eyes, her cheeks flushed, and she lowered her forehead onto his shoulder with an embarrassed laugh.

"I'm sorry," she mumbled.

"Don't be." He stroked her hair. "That was lovely."

She nuzzled his neck. "See what you do to me? All that sexy talk got me hot under the collar."

He wrapped his arms around her, inhaling the scent of her hair, the sensation of her soft body against his. Then he shifted to the edge of the seat and stood, bringing her with him in his arms.

"Ooh!" She wrapped her arms around his neck. "You're so strong."

"I don't know how you make me feel like a sexy Superman," he said as he carried her through to the bedroom, "but don't stop."

She smiled and kissed him, and he sighed, then lowered her feet to the floor so she slid down him. She moved back and took off her T-shirt, undid her shorts, and slipped those and her panties off with them. He did the same, tugging off his top and dropping his jeans and boxers on the pile of clothes, and together they climbed onto the bed and slid under the duvet.

They hadn't pulled the curtains, and outside the moon glittered silver on the ocean, a heavenly Christmas decoration.

Without further ado, Ophelia took a condom from the bedside table, took off the wrapper, and rolled it onto him. Then, pushing him onto his back, she climbed astride him.

Maneuvering herself so the tip of his erection parted her folds, she pushed down, and he slid inside her with a groan.

For a moment, they closed their eyes and just enjoyed being together. Charlie stretched out beneath her, lifted his arms above his head, and concentrated on the sensation of being inside her. She was so tight, and as she moved her hips and ensured he was coated with her moisture, he knew he'd filled her entirely, right to the top, a notion that made him give a happy sigh.

He opened his eyes to see her watching him, a small, sexy smile on her face as she rocked her hips.

"That feels fucking amazing," he said.

She leaned forward to kiss him. "Good." Her tongue played with his for a while, and he closed his eyes again, feeling her soft breasts on his chest, her nipples grazing through his chest hair, and her muscles tightening around him as she moved with slow, regular rocks of her pelvis.

Pushing herself upright, she continued to move, watching his face while she did so. "You look as if you're enjoying this," she said, running her hands down the muscles of his arms.

"I am. I like this position. You look fantastic. A feast for the eyes."

She smiled. "You too. You have a wonderful body. A perfect example of manhood." She traced the muscles of his shoulders and chest with her fingers, and he lay there and let her, enjoying her admiration.

"I mean it," he murmured. "You make me feel so good. I don't know how you do it. Everything you've said to me this evening has made me feel like I'm a better person."

"I just tell it like it is," she said, but he knew she was being modest.

"Thank you, anyway." He lowered his arms and placed his hands on her waist, skimmed them up to her breasts, and cupped them.

"You're welcome. If it helped give you a little confidence, I consider it a job well done."

He moved his arms around her, held her tightly, and flipped her onto her back.

"Ooh!" She looked up at him, eyes wide. "Gosh that's such a smooth move."

"Years of practice with a pillow."

She laughed, and he covered her smiling mouth with his and thrust a few times while he kissed her. He understood what she'd said about the animalistic nature of sex. Watching her take her pleasure from him was fantastic, but being in control of the action gave him a kind of smug satisfaction he'd tended to feel guilty about before. Now, though, it was as if she'd given him permission to enjoy that control, and as he looked into her eyes, he felt a thrill deep inside at the idea of spending his life exploring sex with this woman again and again, until he knew her body as well as his own.

Carefully holding the condom, he withdrew.

She pouted, and he bent and kissed her nose.

"Turn over," he whispered.

Her green eyes studied him, and a slow smile spread across her face. Rolling onto her front, she made herself comfortable, pulling down a pillow to hug, then looking over her shoulder at him expectantly.

Kneeling between her legs, he pushed them wide, exposing her glistening flesh to his gaze. She buried her face in the pillow, and he heard her give a soft moan as he stroked his hands over the swell of her bottom, then slipped his fingers down into her folds. She was swollen and wet, and he dipped his fingers inside her to coat them with her moisture, then moved them down to find her clit. He circled a finger over the tiny button, and she moaned again, so he did it for a while, until her breathing turned ragged and he knew she wasn't far from climaxing.

Pressing his erection between her legs, he slid down into her folds, and pushed home.

In the past, he'd preferred to face his partners during sex so he could read on their faces when he did something they liked. The girl's pleasure had always been the most important factor, with his own enjoyment a definite second, and he'd never had any complaints until he'd met Lisette.

But Ophelia's explanation of how the female desired to be conquered made sense, and this time he concentrated on being in control. He set the pace, and he let his base desire to claim her take him over, losing himself in the exquisite sensation of plunging into her slick flesh.

"Yes," she said, lifting a hand to grab his hair and yank his head down for a kiss. "Oh God, yes, Charlie, harder."

So he let himself be spirited away by the soft body beneath him, and he was only half aware when she cried out and clamped around him. Still he thrust, until his own climax swept over him with the heat and strength of a forest fire. He exclaimed and shuddered into her, feeling at that moment as if it was his birthday and Christmas Day all rolled into one. She was all he wanted, all he'd ever want, and he was never, ever going to let her go.

Chapter Twenty-Four

As the car threaded through the busy Auckland streets to Dillon's house, Ophelia's heart sank.

She'd had such a lovely weekend. Sure, she was looking forward to seeing Summer again, but being back in Auckland made the magic of the past few days dissipate like mist in the morning sun. Although it had never really vanished, the reality of her life, of having to deal with Dillon and the end of her marriage, returned to hover over her as oppressive and ominous as a coming storm.

Next to her in the back of the car, Charlie squeezed her hand. She turned her gaze from the view of houses and shops to look at him, and a warm glow spread through her as he winked at her.

Their talk the night before appeared to have lifted a weight from his shoulders. After they'd made love, they'd spent several hours talking until late in the night, about all sorts of things, but mainly about the complexities of relationships both with a partner and with other people in general. Charlie had talked more about Lisette and his previous girlfriends, as well as some of the issues he'd had growing up, giving her a greater understanding of his past. He'd encouraged Ophelia to be open about her marriage too, obviously wanting to understand what had gone wrong. In the beginning, she'd struggled with a feeling of disloyalty to Dillon, but once she realized that Charlie wasn't storing up details to use as ammunition in an argument but that he was genuinely interested, she relaxed and was able to discuss the problems they'd had.

Oddly, in spite of his problems with communication, Charlie had proved more understanding than anyone else she'd talked to about the failure of her marriage, even her sister Kate, in whom she confided everything. Kate reacted from the heart, usually with outrage at the way Dillon treated her, and tended to tell Ophelia what she thought she wanted to hear or what would make her feel better. That was great, but it didn't always help her make the best decisions.

Maybe it was Charlie's nonjudgmental nature, or the way he approached everything scientifically with his need to analyze, but everything he'd said had seemed to make sense. She'd been impressed that he hadn't kept trying push his own views on her. Dillon would have done. He'd have said she was better off out of the marriage and given her a hundred reasons why. But when she admitted to Charlie that she felt a lot of guilt where Summer was concerned, he'd told her he understood, and that obviously her daughter's first loyalty would always be to her father.

Then he'd gone on to talk about the bigger picture, and he'd asked her what lessons he thought Summer should learn from her parents' marriage. Was it more important she learn duty and responsibility? Charlie had said his mother had told him and his brothers that no relationship was perfect, and it took hard work and compromise to make a marriage look effortless. Staying with Dillon, and maybe putting her own desires to one side for a few years at least, would teach Summer that marriage was about commitment and loyalty, which were no small things.

As soon as he'd said that, though, Ophelia had started to cry. Because she didn't want Summer to think marriage was all about duty and loyalty. Yes, it was about those things, but more important than that, marriage was about love, trust, and respect. She knew Dillon loved her in his way, but he didn't always respect her, and he certainly didn't trust her.

And she no longer loved him. At least not in the way she should. They would always be bound together by the past, but she didn't feel the deep devotion toward him that she felt she should toward her husband. She didn't desire him anymore, and he'd hurt her too much too often for her to keep brushing it aside.

Charlie had hugged her and just let her cry, and she'd lain there with her head on his ribs and her tears trickling into his chest hair, wishing it was two years later, her divorce was final, and her relationship with Charlie had become solid and permanent. Because it was too new at the moment to let any decisions she made be based on how she felt for him. She couldn't tell herself she was choosing Charlie over Dillon because this relationship with Charlie might not work out, and where would she be then? No, she had to keep the two things separate—put her marriage behind her once and for all, and let her relationship with Charlie evolve at its own pace without using it as a lifeboat to keep her afloat every time she felt as if she was drowning.

Luckily, Charlie made it easy. He hadn't pushed her to explain her tears; he'd just held her until she'd fallen asleep. And then, in the night, he'd awoken her with gentle kisses and light strokes on her skin, and he'd made love to her so tenderly that she'd almost cried again. Without smothering her, he made her feel as if he worshipped her, something that she'd never had from Dillon, and she discovered she rather liked it. She was far from perfect, but Charlie made her feel as if she was. And that, if nothing else, was enough to convince her she was doing the right thing.

"All right?" Charlie asked.

She nodded. "Thank you for a lovely weekend. I had such a great time."

"Me too." He glanced at Lee, sitting in the driver's seat, and then back at her. The twinkle in his eye told her he would have elaborated if they'd been alone.

"I'm sorry we had to rush back. It would have been lovely to stay for lunch." Ophelia checked her watch for the umpteenth time. They should have had plenty of time to get from the airport to Dillon's house, but an accident on the state highway had stopped the traffic and made them late. It was one-fifteen, and she knew Dillon was going to blow a fuse because she'd made him miss his appointment. She wasn't scared of him, but even so her palms were sweating at the anticipation of the meltdown she was sure he was going to have.

Charlie watched her wipe her hands nervously on her jeans. "That would have been nice, but it's only fair that you stick to a schedule when you share custody."

She gave him a shaky smile. "I only wish Dillon was so understanding."

"I'm sure he'll be fine. It's not your fault the traffic's so bad."

Ophelia didn't reply, knowing it wouldn't matter to her ex.

When they finally pulled up outside his house, though, and Ophelia saw Dillon waiting at the door, her nerves vanished when she saw worry and not anger reflected on his features. "Shit." She picked up her handbag, her heart pounding. "Something's wrong."

She got out of the car and ran up the path, conscious that Charlie had come with her, even though she'd been planning to say goodbye to him in the car, as Dillon had been going to take her and Summer home.

"What's up?" she asked as she approached.

"Summer's not well." To her surprise, Dillon didn't say anything about Charlie being with her, although he didn't acknowledge his presence. "Last night she started coughing and this morning she has a temperature. It happened really quickly. I was just thinking about taking her to the doctor's but I didn't want to miss you. I couldn't reach you on the phone." Worry lines creased his forehead.

Ophelia went cold. She'd turned off her phone the day before, and she'd forgotten to turn it back on.

Swallowing hard, she went into the small house, then paused as she realized Charlie had remained on the doorstep. "Is it okay if he comes in?" she asked Dillon. "He is a doctor."

"Sure," Dillon said, which told her how worried he was about their daughter.

She led the way through to the bedroom where Summer stayed. As soon as she saw her, Ophelia could see how poorly she was. Summer's face was as white as the sheet she lay beneath. She looked asleep, although as Ophelia sat on the bed, her eyes opened. As soon as she saw her mother, Summer burst into tears.

"Hey, poppet." Ophelia gathered her into her arms. "It's okay, Mummy's here now." She rubbed her back and pulled her onto her lap. Summer was hot even though she only wore a thin pair of pajamas and Dillon had opened the window wide.

Summer coughed, the horrid deep bark that usually meant she had a chest infection, then sobbed some more. Ophelia was vaguely aware of the two men talking softly behind her, but she tried not to worry about that and concentrated instead on Summer. "How are you feeling, sweetie?"

"My chest hurts. And my throat's sore." She rubbed her nose and then sneezed.

"Sounds like you've got a nasty cold there." Charlie came forward and dropped to his haunches before her. Summer curled up on Ophelia's lap.

"Charlie's a doctor, remember?" Ophelia said softly. "Like Dr. Brock."

Summer gave a little nod.

Charlie showed her a thermometer that Dillon must have given him. "How about we take your temperature?"

She didn't answer, but she didn't pull away when he leaned forward and placed the tip in her ear. After a few seconds, it beeped. "One-oh-four," he read.

"It was one-oh-three an hour ago," Dillon said. "I gave her some paracetamol too."

Ophelia's heart raced—she knew that was high. She watched Charlie take Summer's pulse, then observe her breathing. The girl's chest rose and fell quickly, and it seemed to Ophelia that Summer was struggling to get air into her lungs.

"You put her on the neb thirty minutes ago?" Charlie said to Dillon.

"Yes, but it didn't seem to do anything." Dillon ran a hand through his hair. "She seemed fine yesterday. A bit of a cold, that's all."

"Okay." Charlie smiled at Summer, then pushed himself up. "Obviously I don't have my stethoscope, but I suspect because of the swiftness it came on that she has bacterial pneumonia. One-oh-four is high but not dangerous—however, because she's so young and because of her CF, I think it's probably best if we get her to the hospital. I'll ring Brock and ask him to come in and see her."

"It's his weekend off, isn't it?" Ophelia remembered Charlie telling her that Brock had Erin and her son staying with him for the night.

"Yes, but I know he'd want to see Summer." Charlie smiled at them. "Please try not to worry. Summer's going to be fine. This is precautionary, and I don't think we need to ring for an ambulance if you're happy to take Summer in your car."

Dillon nodded, obviously relieved. "Sure."

"I'll meet you there," Charlie said, and walked to the door.

Ophelia ran to catch up with him. He paused and smiled at her again. She hadn't really comprehended until that point that even though he worked in research, he'd trained as a doctor. Suddenly his calm, reassuring manner and gentle personality made sense.

"Are you sure…" She felt awkward about asking him to go to the hospital, and even more awkward about going with Dillon and not him.

"Of course. I'll see you there," he said. He cupped her cheek and brushed her cheekbone with his thumb. Then he walked out.

Dillon was already packing Summer's things into a bag. Ophelia let him and took Summer to the bathroom, braided her hair back to keep her cool, and sponged her face. By the time she'd finished, Dillon was ready, and they left the house.

Ophelia clipped Summer into her car seat. The girl was having trouble keeping her eyes open, and that didn't seem right either. "I'll sit beside her," she told Dillon, who just nodded and got in the front.

"Are you okay?" Ophelia asked him as he drove away. He'd hardly said anything since she arrived.

"Worried," he said. His eyes met hers in the rearview mirror, and then he looked away.

"I'm sorry," Ophelia whispered, unable to help herself.

"For what?"

"Not being here. And for turning off my phone."

"It's okay."

She looked out of the window. It wasn't her fault. Summer hadn't fallen ill because Ophelia was with Charlie, and if she'd turned on her phone it wouldn't have made Summer better.

It didn't help, though. Her stomach clenched into a knot, and she felt nauseous with guilt and worry. It would have been better if Dillon had yelled at her because she'd have been forced to defend herself, but his reassurance only made it worse.

"Did you have a nice time?" he asked.

"Don't," she said, biting her lip hard.

"I'm not having a go. I'm genuinely glad it went well for you."

"That's what I meant," she said hoarsely. She couldn't bear it if he was nice. "Don't."

He didn't say anything else.

She looked down at Summer, who was dozing off again, and tried not to cry. Poor Summer. She didn't deserve this. Why were some children born perfectly healthy, and some born with diseases like this? It was so unfair.

Chapter Twenty-Five

To Ophelia's relief, Charlie was waiting for them in the Emergency Department when they arrived, and he admitted Summer himself and made sure she was comfortable before carrying out some basic tests and filling in her chart. By the time Brock turned up—with a twinkle in his eye that suggested he and Erin had enjoyed their weekend together—Charlie was able to give him a rundown on Summer's condition.

Ophelia listened to the two brothers discussing her daughter calmly and knowledgeably, and bit her bottom lip hard to stop it trembling. Between the two of them, they would make Summer better. There was no need to get emotional.

Charlie finished his summary, and Brock nodded and turned to talk to Summer.

"I'll leave you in Dr. King's capable hands," Charlie said, turning to Ophelia and Dillon. "I'm sure she'll make a speedy recovery and be running around in no time."

"Thanks." Dillon held out his hand. "I appreciate what you've done for my little girl."

"You're welcome." Charlie shook his hand.

Ophelia watched them, her cheeks heating. Dillon was being ultra-nice. She couldn't tell whether he was genuinely touched by Charlie's help or if it was all an act to prove to her how nice he could be as part of his plot to get her back.

Then she felt terrible. Talk about have a huge ego—when would she realize she wasn't the center of the universe? Dillon might be many things, but he wasn't evil. The man's daughter was in hospital, and his expression held nothing but genuine relief and pleasure that Charlie had been able to help her.

Charlie turned to her. "Will you call me later and let me know how she is?"

"Of course." She glanced at Brock, who was studiously concentrating on Summer, although she thought he was probably listening with interest to their conversation. Then she looked at Dillon. He met her gaze, then looked down at his daughter.

Ophelia swallowed hard, caught Charlie's hand, and led him out into the corridor.

"Please don't feel you have to go," she said.

"Brock's her doctor, and Dillon's her dad. I don't want to step on any toes." He smiled. "It's okay." His eyes behind his glasses shone with gentle humor.

It wasn't okay, because it made her feel like crap that he felt he had no place by her side. She liked him being with her. He was so calm and in control, and he just made her feel better.

But he was right. In spite of the fact that he'd shaken Charlie's hand, Dillon wouldn't want him there, and there was nothing more Charlie could do for Summer.

"Okay," Ophelia said. Her throat tightened. "But I don't want you to go."

That made him smile. She looked up into his eyes, warmth flooding her at the thought of making love with him, and her lips parted a little at the hope that he might kiss her.

But he didn't. His gaze flicked behind her, then came back to hers. "Ring me later," he said. And then he turned and walked away.

Ophelia had to catch her breath and fight not to let the tears fall. It took every bone in her body not to yell after him to stay. Instead, she watched him walk down the corridor until he disappeared around the corner. Then she turned to the room.

She wasn't surprised to see Dillon watching her. No doubt that was why Charlie hadn't kissed her goodbye.

She walked back into the room and stood at the foot of the bed. Summer looked as if she'd dozed off again. Brock was in the process of giving some directions to a nurse, but as Ophelia walked in he stopped and started talking to her and Dillon.

"We're going to put her on IV antibiotics and Prednisone, step up her use of the nebulizer and give her regular physio, and monitor her closely over the rest of the day," he began. Then he stopped and sympathy crossed his face as he saw Ophelia fighting with her emotion. "Aw," he said.

That touch of sympathy pushed her over the edge, and she burst into tears.

There was nothing she could do about it, even though she could have died from embarrassment over crying in front of Brock and the nurse.

"Sorry," she squeaked, covering her face with a hand.

"It's all right, you've been through a lot," Dillon said. He pushed a tissue into her hand and put his arms around her. "Come here."

She stood stiffly in his arms, trying hard to control her tears, although they refused to stop. It didn't help when Dillon stroked her back and attempted to murmur consoling words in her ear. What was Brock going to think? She felt hot and angry and embarrassed and miserable, conscious of Brock and the nurse talking in low voices. She didn't want Dillon, she wanted Charlie, and the last thing she needed right now was for Charlie's brother to think there was still something between her and Dillon.

Then she felt upset because she should be thinking about Summer and not herself, and that just made her cry more.

"She'll be okay," Dillon was saying. "Our little girl's strong like her mum. She's going to be fine."

Our little girl. The words rang in her head. She should have trusted her instincts. This was all for show, to remind her that Summer tied them together.

Dillon kissed her cheek. "Come on babe," he murmured.

"Stop it." She put her hand on his chest and pushed hard. He stumbled back, and anger flashed briefly across his face before he smothered it with innocence. She was right. Dillon loved his daughter and he was worried about her, but he hadn't stopped being his usual manipulative, clever self. Unfortunately, it just served to make her sadder.

Brock had looked up at her as she'd pushed Dillon. Now he was frowning as if he didn't know what to say. Highly embarrassed and upset, she turned away and walked out of the room.

A little down the corridor was a small empty waiting room with seats and a vending machine selling cold drinks. Ophelia sat there, head in hands, and tried to compose herself.

"Are you okay?"

She looked up at the sound of Brock's voice and blew her nose. "Yeah. I'm so sorry."

He waved a hand. "We see it all the time. All the worry leads to heightened emotions. It's perfectly normal." He sat beside her and leaned forward with his elbows on his knees. "I'm sure Summer's going to be fine. You did the right thing bringing her in. We'll monitor her closely and give her all the medication she needs, and I'm sure she'll be right as rain in days. You know what kids are like."

Ophelia wiped her cheeks. "Thanks. And don't get me wrong, I'm sick with worry about her. But that's not really why I'm crying. I'm crying because this situation with Dillon is making me so fucking miserable, and then I feel guilty because I'm thinking about my personal life instead of my daughter."

He sighed. "I can't imagine how difficult this is for you. Try not to be too hard on yourself. Looking after a child with a condition like CF is extremely draining. It's not surprising you're feeling overwhelmed by everything."

"I feel so selfish. Obviously Summer wants her daddy with her, but I just want him to go away." A wave of longing swept over her, strong enough to make her give a shivery sigh. "I miss Charlie, Brock. I miss him so much." More tears flowed down her cheeks, and she stifled a sob.

"Ah, come on, he'd hate to think he was the cause of your tears."

"He's really not. He makes me happy, but I feel so guilty that he has to put up with all of this. It's not fair on him."

"Goodness, what is it with mothers and guilt?" Brock's wry voice held more than a hint of humor. "They say it comes with the milk."

She gave a small laugh. It was true that she'd been worse since she'd had Summer.

"Look," he said, "Charlie's a grown up, and he understands what a difficult situation you're in. He wouldn't be hanging around if he wasn't in it for the long haul."

"I just feel so bad for him. I felt awful when he walked out today. It was like I was saying he had no part in my life."

"He knows that's not the case."

"I know, but I still felt terrible. He deserves better. And I wonder if it would be easier to cope with Dillon if we hadn't hooked up." It wasn't until the words had left her mouth that she realized what she'd said.

Brock's brown eyes, so like his brother's, observed her levelly. "Are you trying to say you want to stop dating him?"

She wiped her face again. "No. Yes. I don't know. I feel so confused. I'm crazy about him, Brock, but my feelings are just muddying the water, and I wonder if things would be clearer if I finish off one chapter of my life before I started the next, you know?"

Brock examined his hands for a moment. Then he said, "You want my advice?"

"Please."

"Just slow down. You don't have to make any decisions right now. Summer's not well, and it's Christmas time, and that always makes family situations more complicated. Charlie told me you're spending Christmas Eve and Christmas Day with Dillon and Summer, so you'll probably be seeing less of him anyway. Why not wait until the New Year and then see how you feel?"

She nodded slowly. "That's probably good advice. I'll do my best. It's not my natural way. I like things to be sorted, to be clear cut. But you're right. There's no point in rushing to make decisions when I can't see the road ahead."

He pushed himself to his feet. "Okay. We'll get Summer transferred to the ward and have a bed made up for you for tonight—I'm guessing you'll stay?"

"Probably, yes."

"And we'll see how she is in the morning. Any worries, though, you can get a nurse to call me, or you can call me yourself. You still have my number?"

"Yes." She knew it off by heart.

"I'll be in first thing in the morning to check on her." He smiled and walked to the door.

"Brock?"

He stopped and turned. "Yes?"

"Did you have a nice weekend with Erin?"

He grinned. "Yeah. We took Ryan, her boy, to the zoo, and then she spent the night at my apartment."

"I'm so pleased for you. You deserve it."

He shrugged. "She has her problems too. Love's never easy, but we three Kings are very determined men." He winked and walked away.

His words had an ominous ring to them. Dillon and Charlie were both determined, but whereas Dillon's sly deviousness irritated her and had even begun to make her skin crawl, Charlie's quiet, resolute patience just sent a shiver down her spine.

It would probably be the wisest course of action to end their relationship now. She should tell the tall, handsome doctor that she was going to finish what she had with Dillon and cleanse her life of all the hurt, fear, and worry before she started a relationship with him.

She should. But she wouldn't. Because she was beginning to realize that she didn't want to be apart from him, and the absolute last thing she wanted was to tell him it was over.

Chapter Twenty-Six

The next few days were long and arduous.

Ophelia hated it when Summer was in hospital. She thought she would have gotten used to it by now considering the amount of time Summer spent there, but even though the doctors and nurses were wonderful and she couldn't have asked for better care for her daughter, she still hated every minute.

Summer slept for most of Sunday, and the hours passed slowly, made worse because Dillon was also there. Ophelia knew he deserved to be by his daughter's side as much as she did, and she wouldn't have minded if he'd kept himself to himself and concentrated on Summer. But every chance he got he spent talking to Ophelia, about the past, about how much he loved her, playing on her emotions until she wanted to either scream or sob or throw things at him.

To her relief, he did go home that night, leaving her alone. As she curled up on the rollaway bed, she felt so tired that she thought she'd fall straight asleep. But the regular visits of the nurses, the half-light, and the occasional crying child further down the ward conspired to keep her awake.

Turning on her side, she thought about Charlie, and her eyes pricked with tears. She missed him so much. Closing her eyes, she imagined his arms around her, his mouth on hers, his young, strong body beneath her fingertips. In spite of her tiredness, she hungered for him. More than anything, she wanted to lose herself in him, let him spirit her away to that wonderful place where all she thought about was pleasure, and where for a short while she felt as if she could conquer the world.

If only she'd met him years ago, before her life had become so complicated. But then of course she wouldn't have Summer, and she couldn't imagine her life without her daughter.

Lying in the semi-dark, exhausted with worry, it was difficult to believe she hadn't screwed up her life. Summer's condition wasn't her fault, and yet it was hard to convince herself that she hadn't done something wrong during her pregnancy to cause it. Maybe that small piece of soft cheese she'd snuck one day or the half a glass of wine on her birthday that had seemed so innocuous at the time had done some irreparable damage.

She'd failed Summer as a mother, and she'd failed Dillon as a wife. He wasn't a bad man. There were many worse husbands out there. No marriage was perfect, and all relationships took effort to make them work. Instead of repairing the vase, she'd just dumped it in the bin, making herself, Dillon, and Summer miserable in the process.

Why had she been so selfish? She sat up and put her head in her hands. She'd ditched her seven-year relationship because she'd wanted more. But what if there wasn't any more? What if all relationships were like a piece of silver that gradually tarnished over the years? She could start dating Charlie, but what if the same thing happened a few years down the line? Would she dump him too and start looking for someone else?

Tears ran down her face and leaked through her fingers. Why did everything she touch turn to salvage? Maybe she should just get on the earliest plane out of Auckland and never come back. Summer would live with Dillon, and both he and Charlie would soon forget about her. Maybe the plane would crash, and then she wouldn't have to worry anymore—there would just be the deep, dark stillness of the ocean, and blessed peace.

After a few minutes of quiet sobbing, the dark cloud that had hung over her lifted a little. Irritated with herself for subsiding into self-pity, she fumbled in her pockets for a tissue, found one, and did her best to mop her face.

Her phone lay on the window sill, and she picked it up and swiped the screen, then brought up her contacts.

Her gaze fell on Charlie's name, a couple of entries above Dillon's.

She stared at the two names for a long time, debating which to call.

Then, slowly, she put the phone down. She was tired, exhausted from the worry of looking after a sick child. She shouldn't make any decisions in this sort of state.

Leaning forward, she studied her daughter's face. It was pale, but with maybe a little more color than she'd had when they'd brought her in. Her breath was even and sounded less labored than before, too. She was on the mend.

Lying back down, Ophelia curled on her side and closed her eyes. It was a long while before sleep claimed her, though.

*

Monday was much of the same. Summer slept for most of it, although by the evening she was feeling hungry, which Ophelia knew was always a good sign.

The following morning, Summer felt better, although then she turned grouchy because she was stuck in bed, and it became a matter of entertaining her all day and trying to keep her still so she didn't pull out her drip. The Ward Seven toys clipped to the equipment helped comfort her, but it still took hours of card playing, story reading, and jigsaw puzzle solving to keep her amused.

Dillon had to work, but he came when he could, and to be fair he was invaluable, spending hours with their daughter so Ophelia could take a break.

She rang Charlie a few times, when Dillon left the hospital. Charlie always seemed pleased to hear from her and was happy to chat, but he didn't offer to come and see her, and Ophelia didn't ask him, aware of his comment about not wanting to step on any toes. She promised she'd call him once she was home, and he said that would be fine and he looked forward to it.

It was all very formal and polite, and she hated every minute of it, but she kept remembering Brock's words about taking things slow, so she kept her thoughts to herself and tried to be patient.

The rest of Tuesday and the following morning passed at a snail's pace, and she was immensely relieved when on Wednesday lunchtime Brock did his rounds and announced that Summer was well enough to be discharged.

By the time they'd sorted out the paperwork, received new medication, met with the physio, and Summer was up and dressed, it was late afternoon. Dillon left work as soon as he could and drove them home. Ophelia didn't say much, exhausted from lack of sleep, almost nodding off as he negotiated the busy streets.

"You look shattered," he said when they finally drew up. "How about I come in and look after Summer for a while so you can catch up with your sleep?"

Ophelia hesitated, but Summer said, "Yes Daddy! We can watch *Frozen*."

He stifled a groan. "Whatever you want, sweetheart."

Ophelia would have protested, but she was so tired that the notion of a few hours' uninterrupted sleep made her say, "Sure, that would be lovely."

They got out of the car and Ophelia went to get Summer's stuff out. To her surprise, Dillon lifted out a night bag. "I packed it just in case," he said innocently, taking Summer's hand and leading her to the door.

Ophelia walked slowly up the path, unease bubbling in her stomach, but her eyelids drooped, and she pushed away her misgivings. Dillon was Summer's dad, and Ophelia knew that when she was tired she had the tendency to overreact. It was the day before Christmas Eve and Summer was clearly happy to have her father there, so what was she complaining about?

They went in, and Summer immediately ran over to put the DVD on. "Go on," Dillon said to Ophelia. "Go to bed. I'll give her a bath and do her physio, then put her to bed."

"I'll only have a nap," Ophelia protested, but he just waved his hand. "It doesn't matter if you sleep all night. I'll be here if our daughter wants anything."

Our daughter. Ophelia met his calm gaze. His words were like the surface of the sea—they always had a riptide running beneath them, waiting to pull her under. But then again, he was right—Summer was their daughter, and nothing would ever change that.

Saying nothing, she kissed Summer goodnight and gave her a big hug, then went into her room.

After shutting the door, she leaned against it for a while. It was a three-bedroomed house, so Dillon could sleep in the spare bedroom, which was always made up in case any of Summer's friends came to stay.

She studied her own bed. It was a king, far too big for her alone. She and Dillon had conceived their daughter in this bed. Made love countless times.

They'd also argued here. Shared harsh and bitter words. Some of the things he'd said came back to haunt her, ringing around her head, names he'd called her, spiteful things he'd accused her of to back up his argument. She'd cried so many times in this room. It carried more sad memories for her than happy ones.

Grabbing the chair in front of her dressing table, she moved it beneath the door handle.

Then she felt foolish and put the chair back. Biting her lip, she lay on the bed, fully dressed. Briefly, she wished she'd thought to bring her phone in with her so she could ring Charlie, but she didn't want to go back out into the living room.

Sighing, she closed her eyes.

*

In what felt like four minutes but must have been more like four hours, she opened her eyes to find the room dark.

Pushing herself up, she frowned, disorientated. Was it still Wednesday? Of course it was. She got up and looked out of the window. Further along, the deck was covered in jewels of light from the Christmas tree that Dillon must have switched on. It was evening, probably around nine, as the sun had already set.

She opened the door and padded down the corridor. Stopping outside Summer's door, she looked inside. Her daughter lay asleep, her chest rising and falling easily, her cheeks flushed with a healthy pink.

Ophelia walked past the bathroom, noting the damp towel on the rail and the smell of bubble bath in the air. Dillon was a good father, and cared deeply for their daughter. She couldn't fault him on that.

Continuing on, she walked into the living room. It was dark, lit only by the Christmas tree. Dillon sat on the deck, on the swing seat where she'd sat with Charlie what seemed a lifetime ago, sipping a beer.

Where had he gotten the beer? Ophelia didn't drink it and only bought wine. He must have brought it with him.

Frowning, she crossed the room and walked out onto the deck. He looked up as she appeared, tucking something down beside the cushion. A smile spread across his face. It didn't reach his eyes, though—or was she imagining it?

"Babe! You're awake." He patted the seat. "Come and sit down."

Chapter Twenty-Seven

"You've made yourself comfortable," she said, somewhat irritably. He looked puzzled, and she suddenly felt mean. "Sorry." She rubbed her face and then went to sit beside him. "Summer looks better."

"Yeah. I gave her a bath and she ate six fish fingers in a sandwich and a bowl of ice-cream." He grinned. "Good to see her on the mend."

Ophelia nodded, trying to ignore the uneasiness she felt at the thought of him cooking in their kitchen, making himself at home. "Thanks for looking after her. I was really tired."

"Of course. She's my girl. As are you." He smiled and curled a strand of her hair around his finger.

Charlie had done the same, not that long ago, and suddenly she didn't want Dillon touching her. She pushed his hand away. "Please, don't."

He let the strand of hair drop and rolled his eyes. "What, can't I even be nice now? Jesus."

She swallowed hard. How did he always turn everything she said to make it seem as if she was being mean? "You can be nice. Just... don't touch me."

"For God's sake. I've touched every inch of you, Ophelia, with my hands and my mouth. I know you inside and out. Why the sudden coyness?"

Her cheeks burned at his words. "Because I don't belong to you." She didn't want to think about Dillon's mouth or fingers on her most intimate areas. It made her feel queasy. "I'm not yours anymore."

"But you'll let him touch you." His anger flared as quickly as if someone had struck a match inside him.

"Don't be like that. Why can't you be pleased for me? He's nice, Dillon. He treats me well. He's even running a research project for CF—he wants to help Summer."

"I don't give a fuck. I don't want him anywhere near my daughter."

Her jaw dropped. "My God, can you hear how selfish that sounds?"

"Can you blame me? You're the love of my life."

"Then you should have treated me like it," she snapped.

They glared at each other for a moment.

"I guess I asked for that," he said eventually, glowering.

She sighed. "You said you were genuinely glad for me."

"I lied." Hurt replaced his anger in milliseconds. She'd never known anyone with moods as mercurial as Dillon's, and it had always unsettled her. He ran a hand through his hair. "You don't seem to have any idea how difficult it is watching you with someone else. I hate that you're cheating on me."

"I'm not," she said, exasperated, and hating that he made her feel as if she was. "We're separated."

"Just saying the words doesn't make it so."

"We don't live together, Dillon. Our marriage is over."

"Not for me," he said stubbornly. "I've been faithful to you, and patient. I understood that you needed some time to yourself, but I've waited for you."

"I didn't ask you to."

"I know, but I love you, and I don't want to break up."

"It's too late," she said, desperate now. "What we had—it's gone."

"Don't say that." He looked distraught. "Please, give me one more chance."

"I can't."

"I know you want to. I can see it in your eyes. You still love me."

"I don't, Dillon," she said, only realizing as she said it that it really was true. "I don't love you anymore."

The truth must have shown on her face because panic flared in his eyes. "What about Summer?" he whispered. "Are you really going to do this to her? At Christmas?"

"I'm not 'doing' anything to anyone. It'll be even worse for her if we stay together, with you always shouting and me always in tears."

"I swear I won't shout anymore. I promise, I'll never make you cry again."

"You can't promise something like that," she said, near to tears at that moment. "You've said it before and it worked for a few weeks and then we sank back into the pit. Don't you remember how miserable we were last summer? I'm tired of it. I've had enough."

"But I—" He stopped as the muffled sound of a ringtone rang out.

Ophelia met his gaze, going cold. "That's my phone." Now she knew what he'd stuffed down the side of the seat cushion when she walked out. "Give it back."

He took it out, but instead of handing it to her, he read the screen and then ended the call.

"Dillon!" She stared at him, outraged. "How dare you!" It had almost certainly been Charlie.

"I don't want you talking to him," Dillon said, confirming her guess as he gestured at her angrily with the phone. "I don't want him anywhere near you."

"That's not your decision to make." Now she was getting frightened. How was she going to stop this?

"We're not divorced yet." He faced her, eyes blazing, suddenly aggressive and full of confidence. "You still bear my name, and I don't want you seeing that guy."

"I can see whomever I want."

He ignored her. "And I don't want him seeing my daughter, buying her Christmas presents. That's my job."

She opened her mouth to reply, then realized why he'd said that. Charlie had texted her earlier in the day to say he had a present for Summer. "Have you been reading my texts?" Damn it, Kate had told her she needed to lock her phone, but she was too impatient to put a code in every time she wanted to use it.

"*Ciao bella*," he said, mocking her. "Fucking prick. Thinks he's superior because he knows a few foreign words."

"Stop it. He's not like that."

"And look at you," he snarled, "all doe-eyed over this guy. What is it, his money? I didn't think you'd be so shallow."

"I don't give a shit about his money. He's nice to me."

"What are you talking about? Do you really want a namby-pamby wuss?" He laughed. "I know you better than that. I know you like it rough. You're a dirty girl, deep down."

"Shut up. You don't get to talk to me like that anymore."

He leaned forward. "I know you."

"No, Dillon, you knew me, or you thought you did. I'm not the same person I was."

He looked upset then. "Do you love him?"

"We've only been going out a few weeks. It's too early for that."

"Then why are you prepared to throw away our marriage for this guy?"

She thought about Charlie, about the way he held her, the look in his eyes. The way he made her feel.

She might not have known him long, but the promise of what could be lay before her like a glittering present on Christmas Eve. Love didn't come with a guarantee, and she wouldn't be able to foresee whether eventually the relationship would end up the way her marriage with Dillon had. But like the parcel, it held the promise of something beautiful. And at the moment, that was enough.

She held out her hand. "Give me my phone."

"Not until you tell me you're not seeing him again."

She stood up, shaking with anger. "Give me my phone."

He stood too. "No."

"Give me my fucking phone!" she yelled.

"No!" He pulled his arm back and threw it. Mouth open, she watched it fly across the lawn to meet the wall, where it splintered into a dozen pieces.

They both stared at it. Then they looked at each other.

"I'm sorry," he whispered. Then, a bit louder, "I'm really sorry. I lost my temper, and I shouldn't have. Please…"

"That's it," she said. Her anger had turned to white hot steel. When she'd asked him to move out six months ago, she'd spent ages explaining and pleading and consoling. This time, she made the demand with confidence. "We're done."

"Ophelia…"

"You can keep the key to the house in case you need to come in for Summer, but I forbid you to enter without my express permission, and if you do, I'll call the police." Her voice was icy cold, even to her ears. "As soon as possible after Christmas I'll be seeing a lawyer to draw up a legal document defining your visiting hours for Summer."

He went white. "Please…"

"You won't be staying here ever again. I want you to go. You can come back Christmas morning at seven o'clock to watch Summer open her presents, but you'll go before lunch."

"But… Christmas Eve… it's family time."

"You should have thought of that before."

"Can't I come over, please…"

"Brock King is having a party and Charlie has invited me and Summer, and we're going to go."

His eyes filled with furious tears. "Ophelia, please… It's Christmas…"

At any other time, she would have caved. But she'd seen it all before. The pleading, the tears, the begging for forgiveness. He would never change. The vase was broken, but it was in so many pieces she would never be able to put it back together. It was sad, and it made her want to cry, but their marriage was over.

"I'm tired and I want to go to bed now," she said. "Please go."

"Babe, please…"

"Now, Dillon."

Tears ran down his face. "I love you," he whispered.

She thought of Charlie. He hadn't said he loved her yet because it was far too early for that, but he acted as if he did, and that was what she wanted—to be treated right. "You think you do, but love isn't cruel or manipulative."

He moved toward her. "Come on, babe. I'll make it right." He tried to take her in his arms.

She held out a warning hand. "Dillon…"

He grabbed her and crammed his lips to hers. His mouth was wet from his tears, bruising hers, his fingers pressing into her scalp. She put her hands on his chest and tore her mouth from his. "Stop it!"

She turned to walk away, but Dillon pushed her. She fell against the wall, banged her forehead, and cried out.

Immediately, he stepped back. He'd never hurt her before, not physically, and when she turned to look at him, pressing her fingers to her forehead, she could see on his face his shock at what he'd done.

"I'm sorry." He pressed the back of his hand to his mouth. Then, without another word, he turned and walked away.

Breathing heavily, she waited until she heard the front door shut, then went into the living room. He'd gone.

Shakily, she walked over to the settee and sat. For a brief moment, she thought she was going to be sick, but the nausea welled up, then faded away.

Reaching across, she picked up the landline phone receiver that lay on the coffee table. She looked at it for a moment. All her contacts had been on her mobile, and she couldn't remember Charlie's number. He'd given her a card, but she'd thrown it away after she'd programmed the number in. She did, however, know Brock's number off by heart.

She dialed it and waited for him to answer.

"Brock King."

"Brock." Her voice came out as a squeak, and she cleared her throat. "Brock, it's Ophelia Clark." She made a mental note to go back to using her maiden name. She didn't want Dillon's surname attached to hers anymore.

"Ophelia, I was just talking to Charlie about you. Is Summer okay?"

"She's fine, she's doing well."

"Good. What can I do for you?"

"I need to get hold of Charlie but I don't have my mobile and I can't remember his number."

"Sure. I can give it to you."

"Actually, could you do me a favor and ring him for me?"

"Of course."

"Can you... can you ask him if he'll come around?" If she rang him and spoke to him now, she knew she'd break down, and she didn't want that.

"Yes, sure," he said cautiously. "Are you all right?"

"Not really. There's something I need and I wonder if either you or Charlie could help." She told him what she wanted.

"What's happened?" Brock demanded, his voice hard. "Are you hurt?"

"No," she said, although her head was stinging where she'd banged it. "Just shaken up a bit."

"Do you want me to ring the police?"

"No, it's okay, it's all over. But I'd love to see Charlie."

"Of course. I'll ring him now. You know where I am if you need anything else."

"Thanks, Brock."

"No worries." He hung up.

She put the phone on the table and sat there for a moment. Then she got up and walked through to Summer's room.

Her daughter was still asleep. Ophelia leaned on the doorjamb tiredly and watched her for a while, calmed by Summer's gentle breathing, the peace and quiet of the room.

Eventually, she turned around and went back into the living room.

She was still trembling, not from the cold because it was a lovely evening, warm and humid, but from the memory of what had happened, the feel of Dillon's mouth on hers. Dashing her hand across her lips, she filled the kettle with water, looking out of the window as it boiled, lost in thought. When it switched off, she made a plunger of coffee and poured herself a mug. Then she went into the living room and sat to drink it, comforted by the warmth of the cup and the rich taste, while the lights on the tree twinkled in the darkness.

It was only about another five minutes before she heard a car pull up outside. Placing the cup on the table, she stood and waited. Sure enough, a soft knock sounded on the door. She crossed and opened it a crack, her heart flooding with relief to see Charlie's tall form.

She stepped back to let him in, and closed the door behind him.

He stared at her for a long moment. Then, without saying anything, he put down the bag he was carrying, took her hand, and led her into the kitchen. Taking a piece of kitchen towel, he moistened it under the tap and touched it to her forehead. To her shock, it came away red.

Still saying nothing, he cleansed the graze carefully. Then he finally said, "Plasters?" She gestured to the drawer, and he opened it and took one out. Dabbing the graze with a dry piece of tissue, he applied the plaster, pressing it gently to her skin.

He put the wrapper in the bin. "Are you hurt anywhere else?"

"No."

"Are you sure?"

"Just my pride. I feel like an idiot. I can't believe it took me this long to realize what I wanted."

He surveyed her face. "And what do you want?"

"You." She slid her arms around his waist and pressed her cheek to his chest.

Chapter Twenty-Eight

Ophelia bit her lip hard, determined not to cry as Charlie put his arms around her and held her tight.

"Ssh, it's all right," he murmured, stroking her back and kissing her hair. "Everything's going to be okay."

Strangely, it felt like it now he'd arrived.

She moved back, trying to stop shaking, and failing. "Did Brock mention to you about the chain?"

He slid his backpack off his shoulder, unzipped it, and brought out the security chain she'd requested, as well as a small electric drill and a screwdriver.

"Wow," she said, impressed. She hadn't thought he'd be into practical things at all. "Where did you get all that at this time of night?"

"I have my contacts. Well, Brock does. He knows someone who knows someone who was willing to open up his hardware shop for a generous fee."

"I guess money had its uses at times."

"Absolutely." He gestured to the door. "Do you want me to do it now?"

"Yes please, if that's okay."

He was surprisingly efficient. Ophelia watched him drill the holes and screw the security chain onto the door, silent as he concentrated, a slight frown on his brow.

It only took him five minutes. When it was done, he popped the button of the chain into the sliding channel and showed her how the door would only open an inch. "Okay?"

"That's great, thank you." She felt a swell of relief at the knowledge that she could put it on at night. She wouldn't have to worry that Dillon would creep into the house after dark. She was sure he wouldn't, but she knew she'd have nightmares about waking up and finding him standing by the bed.

She watched Charlie place the drill and screwdriver back in his bag.

"Do you have a dustpan and brush?" he asked, looking at the sawdust on the carpet.

"I'll do it tomorrow." She was still trembling. Wrapping her arms around her waist, she asked him, "Do you want a drink?"

His gaze dropped to her stiff posture, then came back to her face. "A glass of wine would be nice."

She poured them both a glass, took a large mouthful, and led the way out onto the deck.

He sat beside her on the swing seat, and they looked out across the garden. It was growing late, but the air was warm and humid indoors, and the air out here was cool. The citronella candles kept the insects away, and the Christmas lights made it feel as if they were in a grotto, covered in colored jewels.

She liked the house, and the thought of selling up and moving had made her sad, but she no longer felt that way. It was tainted now, and all she could think of was being somewhere else and making a fresh start.

It was too soon to move in with Charlie—they'd only been dating for a few weeks, but for the first time she wondered whether he would be interested in it in the future. There was no rush, though. She was content to let things proceed at their own pace.

She curled up by his side and nudged him. He removed his glasses and placed them on the table, then lifted his arm around her.

"I can't believe it's Christmas Eve tomorrow," he said, pushing with his feet to make the swing seat rock a little. "It kind of snuck up on me a bit."

"I know what you mean. Luckily I bought most of Summer's presents a while ago." She rested her head on his shoulder. He'd been for a swim, and then he'd had a shower. His skin smelled faintly of chlorine, topped with a nice body wash, and his hair was still damp around his ears.

He sipped his wine, and she saw him glance across to his left, at the scattered bits of metal and plastic on the floor. Her phone, broken into pieces. She'd forgotten to pick them up. In Charlie's position, Dillon would have exclaimed and sworn, demanded to know what was going on. Strutted around like a gorilla marking out its territory.

Charlie stiffened, but he just stroked her hair. "How's Summer?" he asked.

"She's fine, on the mend. Luckily she didn't wake up." Ophelia took a large swallow of wine.

He kissed her hair. "Do you want to tell me what happened?"

"I don't know. I think it'll make me cry."

"I don't mind. You don't have to talk, but if you want to, I'm here. Whatever will make you feel better."

She leaned her head on the back of the seat and looked up at him. She didn't want to go into detail about her argument with Dillon, but there was something she felt she needed to get off her chest.

"The last few days, with Summer in hospital, I kept feeling guilty, that my first priority should be to keep me, her, and Dillon together as a family. That it was the 'right' thing to do. That otherwise I was giving up a seven-year marriage for a relationship that has no guarantee of working out. I've known you less than two weeks. It's hardly a solid foundation for the future."

He sipped his wine and nodded, his expression turning blank, telling her he was thinking furiously. "True."

She looked up at the canopy above their heads. "But all I kept thinking about was you. I've missed you so much. Even before Dillon came around tonight, I knew that I couldn't stop seeing you. I know I've seemed a bit mixed up, but I've lived apart from him for six months and things haven't been good between us for a year or two, so this isn't a rebound thing for me. I'm not scared of living alone, and you're not the first port in a storm because I need a man. It's important to me that you understand that." She looked back at him.

A gorgeous smile spread across his face. "That's good to know."

She stared into his eyes. "I know we've not been going out for long, and I must seem like high maintenance at the moment. I don't want to go all intense on you and frighten you off." She nibbled her bottom lip, not sure how much to say.

His gaze dropped to her lips. Then he bent his head and kissed her.

His mouth moved across hers, slow and sensual. Then he lifted his head. "I love you," he said.

Her eyes widened, and her heart stopped beating. "Oh."

He shrugged. "I know that love is something that's supposed to develop over time, so maybe that's not what I'm feeling, I don't know, I'm not very experienced at this. All I know is that I can't stop thinking about you. I don't want to be apart from you. I want to be with you all the time. I want to kiss you and make love to you, and I don't want any other man to touch you." He brushed the plaster on her forehead. "Matt would find this extremely funny, but I'm trying very hard not to go medieval on Dillon's ass."

That made her laugh. She loved that he was upset, but that he was able to control his emotion. "I'd like to see that."

"At the moment, nothing would make me happier than to take out this anger I feel on him. I'm suppressing it because you don't belong to me and you're not my property, and I know you can fight your own battles—you don't need me sweeping in on my charger to rescue you. But he's hurt you, physically and emotionally, and the strength of the rage I feel about that tells me how powerful my feelings for you are."

She caught her breath, bent forward to place her wine glass on the table, then leaned back and lifted a hand to his face. "I love you too."

He stared at her. "Really?"

"Really. Like you say, I suppose it's far too soon to say it, but I don't care. I love the way you look at me, and I like kissing you and going to bed with you, but most all I like the way you make me feel good about myself. Does that make sense?"

"It does. More than you could imagine."

She thought he was probably referring to how Lisette had made him feel. They'd both suffered at the hands of other people. It was wonderful to be with someone who understood how she felt.

She stroked his cheek. "I told Dillon I don't want to see him tomorrow. I'd like to come to the party with you, if that's okay."

"With Summer?"

"Yes."

"I'd love that."

She nodded, relieved. "I told Dillon he can come around on Christmas morning to watch Summer open her presents, but I want him to go after that. He won't be on his own—he has a big family and he can go around his parents' house for Christmas dinner, but I don't want to spend the day with him."

"Do you think Summer will mind?"

"I don't know. Tomorrow I'm going to have a chat to her about everything—something I should have done a few weeks ago. It's possible she'll be upset, but I think she understands what's going on. She knows Dillon makes me unhappy."

She paused and looked out across the garden. "Something struck me earlier this evening. We always feel we have to say that our kids are the most important things in our lives. And of course in many ways they are. If we were on a sinking ship and there was space for only one person on a raft, I'd gladly die for her. I wouldn't think twice about it. And I want her to be happy. But I don't think any person should sacrifice their own happiness for another's. At least, I don't think a person should knowingly make him or herself unhappy for another person. Dillon and I have lived apart for six months, and I don't think Summer has suffered because of it. She still gets to see her father regularly, and sometimes I think she gets a better deal because I think he makes a special effort when she stays with him."

"I can see that," Charlie said, although she only half heard him.

"I've spent most of the last six years worrying about her," she continued, somewhat fiercely. "Terrified every little cold will lead to a chest infection. Going to the hospital, seeing specialists. Working out what pills she has to take, doing physio several times a day, reading about the condition, speaking to other parents on the Three Wise Men forums. My life has revolved around her. And that's okay—I'll do whatever's necessary to keep her well, and I'm glad to do it."

"Of course."

"But I promised myself when Summer was diagnosed with CF that I wouldn't make her life about her condition. I feel that's giving in to it, you know? If we do that, it wins. I'm not going to treat her as if she's weak because she has CF. If she wasn't ill, I know I wouldn't have had the moral dilemma I've been struggling with over the past year over whether to leave Dillon. I'm not saying other single mothers have it easy, of course I'm not. I'm sure many of them feel guilty because their kids don't see their fathers as much as they would if they were at home. But I know her CF has been a factor in my indecision, and I'm done with that. She's not weak, and she's not a victim because she has CF. She'll cope with our separation the way every other child has to when their parents break up."

She looked up at Charlie and blinked to re-focus on him. "Sorry, that was a bit of a speech."

"It's okay. I understand. It must have been hard for you. I wish I could help." He took a deep breath. "I'll do my best with the research. We're looking into gene therapy, and I think we're on to something. I didn't want to say because I don't want to get anyone's hopes up, and you seemed concerned that it would be a factor in our relationship. But I'm excited about this new research, and I think we might be close to a breakthrough."

Wonder swelled inside her. "That's wonderful news."

"I want to make her better. And I want to make you happy. I'd do anything for you, do you know that?"

A tear spilled down her cheek. She brushed it away. "Would you kiss me?"

He smiled. "That I think I can manage."

Chapter Twenty-Nine

Charlie pressed his lips to Ophelia's again, making sure to keep the kiss soft and gentle.

How strange, he thought as he closed his eyes and lost himself in the soft press of her mouth against his. They'd sat on the swing seat together like this the evening after he'd taken them to Rainbow's End, but it felt as if everything had changed since then, even though it had only been ten days.

Why did he feel so different? He'd been thrilled to take Ophelia out, but they hadn't slept together then, and she'd been like one of the stars in the night sky twinkling above his head, something to be admired from afar.

Now, though, as his eyes flickered open and he saw the plaster on her forehead, he felt a fierce protectiveness, an unfamiliar anger to think that another man had done this to her.

He said nothing, though, and contented himself with kissing her. He was sure she wouldn't want him to carry out a testosterone-fueled declaration of his territory. Dillon had frightened her, and she wanted to feel comforted and safe. So he sealed his anger away into a box to deal with later.

It hadn't gone, though. It had far from gone. Its ferocity surprised him, and made him realize, with some relief, that he wasn't the weak, gutless freak Lisette had accused him of being. A strong reaction was the product of a strong emotion, and it was only now that he understood how powerful his feelings for Ophelia were.

But it was easy to lose himself in the kiss. She felt small and soft in his arms, and he had to fight the urge to crush her to him and slide his hands over her body, to assess her curves and weigh her breasts in his palms. But he didn't—he just kissed her, sedate and gentle, and contented himself with the touch of her lips, the innocent exchange of affection that had grown between them and maybe surprised them both.

It was easier to show her how he felt than tell her, because his heart burgeoned with feelings that refused to form themselves into words. *I love you* didn't come near to expressing it, and he felt that somehow it was inadequate to just say it anyway. Dillon had said it to her—had even promised he'd love her and take care of her forever in front of their family and God, and yet he'd broken that promise, so what did the words actually mean?

Instead, it was better to show her. He appreciated her fear of the unknown, and that love didn't come with a guarantee, but he already knew he would worship this woman and treat her like a princess until she tired of him, and hopefully it would be a very long time before that happened.

So they kissed for a while, stopping every now again to take a sip of wine, to exchange quiet words, or just to look at each other and enjoy the peace of the evening and the pleasure of each other's company. He leaned his head on his hand and traced a finger across her eyebrows and down her nose, learning every dip and curve of her face, every freckle. He studied her eyes, realizing that they weren't one solid color but instead were a light green around the pupil, surrounded by a ring of forest green and another even darker shade around the edge.

"You make me blush the way you look at me," she whispered, touching her hand to where her cheeks had turned pink.

He tipped his head to the side. "How do I look at you?"

"Like you can see through my clothes. Like you want to touch me." She moistened her lips with the tip of her tongue. "Be inside me."

Something was happening between them, subtle and gradual, the way that stars were appearing in the darkening sky. Charlie could feel the hairs rising across his body, the increase in his heart rate, the way their bodies were communicating without words. He'd thought she wouldn't want this tonight, but he sensed now that she needed comfort, and maybe she wanted to prove to herself that she'd put Dillon behind her, and was ready to move on.

"You want me to stop?" he murmured, desire spiraling inside him at the realization that she might want more than just kisses.

She gave a tiny shake of her head. He held her gaze for a moment, thinking about where this was leading, that before long he would be holding her, touching her; he would slide his hands up her silky thighs, slip his fingers into her moist folds, and caress her until her breaths came in gasps and he brought her to a climax. He knew his thoughts were showing in his eyes, and he watched her pupils dilate as she registered that he was hoping for the same outcome she was.

Still, he kept it slow and gentle. He kissed her again, now enjoying the anticipation of what was to come. Her hand rose to his cheek, cool against his skin, her fingers sliding into his hair. He shivered when she clenched her fingers and scraped her nails along his scalp, and her lips curved under his, enjoying the effect she had on him. He smiled back, wanting to please her, to erase all bad memories from her mind until all she could think about was him.

She rose up, and he helped her straddle his lap, waiting for her to settle so he could tighten his arms around her and kiss her properly. She opened her mouth to him willingly, her tongue sliding against his, and he relaxed back into the cushions of the swing seat and just enjoyed the sensation of having her on top of him, in his arms, her soft body molding to his.

"Take off your shirt," she said, pulling at the material of the All Blacks top. He did so, tugging it over his head, and she let it fall to the floor before placing her hands on his chest and stroking them over his shoulders. "You have an amazing body, and an amazing mind," she murmured, bending to kiss him again. "I love you, Charlie King."

He sighed a sigh of pure happiness and slipped his hands beneath her T-shirt. "I love you too." He stroked up her back, around her ribs, and cupped her breasts in her lacy bra, enjoying their weight in his palms. Although the garden wasn't overlooked by neighbors, he wasn't sure whether she'd want him to strip her naked, and anyway there was something sensual about making love fully clothed.

He took her bra strap in his fingers and released the clasp, then watched with amusement as she did the fascinating girly trick of retrieving each strap and sliding them over her hands before reaching under her top to remove the item and throw it onto the ground.

"So sexy," he murmured, moving his hands underneath the T-shirt again and enjoying the unrestricted access to her breasts. Her nipples had peaked in the cool air, or maybe from anticipation of his touch, and he brushed his thumbs across them, then took them between his fingers and thumbs and squeezed gently.

She exhaled with a moan, her lips parting beneath his, so he did it again, giving small, tender tugs on the tips until they hardened and lengthened in his fingers. When he couldn't wait anymore, he lifted her T-shirt and bent his head, taking a nipple in his mouth. He explored it with his tongue, running it around the edge, then teasing the end with his lips before sucking again.

Ophelia tipped back her head and rocked her hips, arousing herself against his erection, and while he continued to suck, he dropped his hands to her thighs and slid them up under her short skirt and onto her bottom. She wore a tiny pair of panties that seemed all straps and hardly any material, and he groaned when his hands met bare skin.

"I can't take any more," she whispered, and moved back to fumble at his jeans. He let her, breathing heavily, watching as she popped the button, slid down the zip, and released the erection barely contained in his boxers that was all too eager to break free. Without further ado, she moved aside the thin strap of her panties, and he pulled down his boxers, shifted until he parted her folds, and pushed down.

He tightened his fingers on her hips and closed his eyes, reveling in the sensation of being encased in her wet heat. "Fuck," he said, struggling to keep his self-control.

"Whatever you say, Charlie." She kissed him and began to move, her voice holding amusement as she rocked her hips, sliding him in and out of her.

He let her ride him, pushing the swing seat in time with her thrusts and enjoying the feeling of moving with her. God, he wished he could do this with her all day and all night. He never wanted this feeling of blissful sensuality to stop. He wanted to please this woman over and over again until she couldn't live without him.

They kissed for ages, rocking slowly, their hands stroking over each other's bodies, filling the air with their sighs and the slick sound of him moving inside her. But he couldn't last forever. As her breaths started to come in pants, heat built and muscles started to tense inside him.

"Come for me," she whispered, tightening her fingers in his hair and holding his head as she kissed him deeply.

He wanted to wait for her, because he was a gentleman and that was the polite thing to do, but after her words, as her thrusts became more urgent and her tongue delved into his mouth, heat rushed through him and he gave in and let his climax take him. He was vaguely aware of her watching him, her hands caressing his face, and then her thrusts intensified and she came too. She clamped around him, the tight pulses of her internal muscles squeezing him and extending the after-ripples of his orgasm until they were both gasping, and she fell forward onto his chest with deep, ragged breaths.

"Jesus." He wrapped his arms around her, leaned his head back, and closed his eyes. "You'll be the death of me, woman."

She gave a little chuckle, but didn't move, snuggling into his embrace and placing tiny kisses on his chest. "Thank you."

"Oh, you are more than welcome."

"I mean it, Charlie. Thank you for coming over. For looking after me. For loving me."

He kissed the top of her head. "Any time. I'm yours now. I'm here for you. I'll always be here for you. Everything else is just the little details."

She pushed up and kissed him, then sighed and lifted up. Only then did they both realize they hadn't used a condom.

"Oh. Shit. Sorry. Hold on." She stared into his eyes for a moment, her hand over her mouth, then got up and walked away, into the living room.

Charlie stared across the garden, mentally scolding himself. *What the hell, dude?* He surveyed his crotch with exasperation, too sticky to tuck himself back into his boxers. He'd never had sex without a condom. It had been drilled into him since he was a teenager by both his parents and sex ed classes at school.

He was just about to get up when she reappeared with a box of tissues. "Here."

"Thanks."

"I'm so sorry." She sat beside him on the swing seat and curled her legs under her.

He cleaned himself up and then zipped his jeans. "Me too. I've never forgotten before."

"It happens," she said. Something in her voice made him look up at her. She flicked her eyebrows and her lips twisted as if she was saying *Been there, done that.* For the first time, he wondered whether she'd fallen pregnant with Summer by mistake. Maybe that was why she'd gotten married. If that was the case, he was sure the last thing she'd want would be another unplanned pregnancy.

She looked into his eyes, her own apologetic and ashamed. He'd never understood before he met Ophelia how a human's basic animal urges lay so near to the surface of their civilized selves. He could have made her pregnant tonight. He knew he should have felt guilt and panic, but to his surprise, he felt only pleasure. How fucking prehistoric of him. And yet he couldn't stop his lips from curving up.

Her eyes widened and she blinked several times. "I... ah... I guess there's always the Morning-After Pill," she said.

He shrugged, and continued to smile.

"Oh," she said, flushing.

With that one little word, Charlie felt their relationship finally shift from a temporary fling to something more. If she got pregnant, it wouldn't matter. They were together now, and although it would take months, if not years, to really get to know each other, they'd hopped onto the carriage, and they could just wait for the train to take them to their destination.

He lifted his arm, and she nestled up against him again. He tightened his arm around her, and lifted her chin to study her face.

"Mine," he said, and raised his eyebrows, asking her if she understood that he was referring to her.

She nodded and smiled. "Yours."

With a satisfied sigh, he leaned his head on the back of the swing seat, and let the evening breeze cool his warm skin.

Chapter Thirty

Dillon opened his eyes slowly. Someone was banging on the front door.

"Go away," he moaned, falling back onto the couch. His hand hit an almost empty bottle of whisky standing on the floor and knocked it over. He didn't bother picking it up. He'd been drinking since he got home after leaving Ophelia. He wasn't in the mood for entertaining.

The banging didn't stop, though, and it was making his head worse, so in the end he pushed himself off the sofa, staggered to the door, and wrenched it open.

He blinked at the figure leaning against the post outside, not recognizing him at first. Then his vision cleared. It was the fucking bastard who'd stolen his wife.

"You." Rage flooded him. He'd spent the past few hours cursing this guy, blaming him for everything that had gone wrong with his life. The chance to do something about it made him swell with glee.

He lurched forward to grab the guy around the neck. Charlie sidestepped neatly, though, and Dillon crashed into the doorpost, blinking and confused. He turned with a roar and bulldozed forward, but again, Charlie was waiting for him, and a simple step backward was all it took to disorient a bewildered Dillon. He tripped up the step, stumbled forward, and fell onto the living room carpet.

Charlie walked in and dropped to his haunches beside him. Dillon went to get up, but Charlie put a hand on his chest, and Dillon gave in and flopped back onto the floor.

Charlie leaned forward. He wasn't wearing his glasses, Dillon realized, which was why he hadn't recognized him.

"Are you sober enough to understand what I'm saying?"

Dillon belched, then coughed. "Fuck off."

"Good. Now, unfortunately I promised your daughter I wouldn't hit you, otherwise I'd have smashed your face into the wall. I might not have made that promise to her had I known what you'd do to her mother, though."

Dillon's eyes widened at the thought of Summer finding out he'd hurt Ophelia. "Don't tell her," he blurted out.

Charlie studied him coolly for a while. Then eventually he said, "I won't. I'll leave it up to Ophelia to decide whether Summer should know. But I will say this. You know I'm a scientist, right? That I work at the hospital?"

"Is that supposed to impress me?"

Charlie leaned closer. "Have you heard of the drug Tetrodotoxin?"

Dillon frowned.

"I'll take that as a no," Charlie said. "When injected, it makes the recipient appear dead. You would remain conscious but be completely paralyzed. If I hear that you've touched Ophelia again... If you even look at her in a way that offends her... I'll use it on you and tell the hospital you gave your body to medical research."

Dillon stared at him. If Charlie had threatened to beat him up, he would have laughed. If he'd said he'd call the police, he would have told him to fucking do it then.

But the guy's calm, cool declaration filled his veins with ice.

Charlie raised an eyebrow. "Is that clear?"

Dillon gave a short nod.

Charlie pushed himself up, then looked down at him for a moment. His pitying look hurt more than a punch would have. Dillon closed his eyes.

"I feel sorry for you," Charlie said. "You took her for granted, and now you've lost her. That can't be easy to live with. But you've still got your little girl. Clean up your act, man. Don't let Summer see you like this."

He walked out and closed the door behind him.

Dillon went limp, too tired and dispirited to even get up off the floor. Tears filled his eyes as he thought of Summer. "You're the best daddy in the world," she'd told him at the weekend. And look at him now. Blind drunk, having assaulted his wife, the beautiful Ophelia, who'd never done anything wrong except put up with him for far too long.

He put his arm over his face and wept.

*

Ophelia hadn't asked Charlie to stay, uncomfortable about sharing the bed she'd slept in with Dillon, and he hadn't mentioned it either, so she suspected he'd understood why. He'd just given her a parting kiss and promised to pick her up at five on Christmas Eve ready for the party.

After he'd gone, and she'd slid the chain across the door, she went to bed, thinking she'd crash straight out. But in the end she spent an hour or so lying awake thinking about how things had changed, and how she felt so different from only a day ago, when her loyalties had still felt torn in two. Now it all seemed so clear. How strange that things could turn so quickly.

She would need to have a conversation with Summer, she knew that. She planned out a few things to say, although she'd have to play it by ear depending on Summer's reaction.

Finally, as sleep began to claim her, she rested a hand on her stomach and thought about the look on Charlie's face when it had sunk in that they hadn't used a condom. She'd felt mortified, because although generally it was considered the guy's duty to supply them, she'd always told herself it was her responsibility to safeguard against disease and pregnancy. She would have hated him to think she was either lazy about that sort of thing, or that she'd done it on purpose.

She'd been totally unprepared for the slow smile that had spread across his face, and the shrug that accompanied her announcement that she could using the Morning-After Pill. The thought of her being pregnant hadn't scared him. He really did love her, she realized.

Mine. The thought of his possessive declaration gave her a shiver. He was gentle, kind, and considerate, but he was still a man. She'd seen the dangerous glimmer in his eye when he'd looked at the plaster on her forehead. His passive manner hid a deep passion she was only just beginning to uncover, and the thought excited her and brought tears to her eyes at the same time.

She probably wasn't pregnant, but the knowledge that it didn't scare her either told her more about how she felt about Charlie than anything else.

A smile on her lips, she let sleep claim her.

*

The next morning, as they ate their breakfast on the deck, Ophelia finally had the talk with Summer that she knew she should have had six months ago.

When Dillon had moved out, she'd told Summer they were having some time apart, playing down the break-up to try to save Summer from being too upset. In retrospect it was possible that had been the wrong thing to do, but it was too late for regrets, and all she could do now was be honest.

"I want to talk to you about tonight," she said to Summer.

"Can I stay up late?" Summer asked.

"You certainly can because we've had a change of plans. We're going to a party!"

Summer's eyes widened and she paused with her spoonful of cereal halfway to her mouth. "What kind of party?"

"At Dr. Brock's house. It's a grown up party, but there will be other children there."

Summer jumped up and down in her seat. "Can I wear my princess dress?"

Ophelia frowned. "It's got ketchup stains on it." She should have thought about that and washed it.

"Please, Mummy."

"I'll take a look at it and see if I can get the stain out."

Summer clapped her hands and then shoveled another spoonful of cereal into her mouth. "Will Charlie be there?"

"Yes. He's picking us up at five o'clock."

Summer chewed thoughtfully. "Is Daddy coming?"

Ophelia took a deep breath. "No. We won't see Daddy tonight. He'll come early tomorrow to see you open your presents." She picked up the other half of her toast, then put it down again. "There's something I need to tell you, sweetie."

Fishing out a cereal hoop with her spoon, Summer said, "Are you and Daddy getting a divorce?"

Ophelia stared at her. "Oh. Well. Um, yes. Yes, we are."

Summer ate the hoop. "Fliss said you were." Fliss, or Felicity, was her best friend at school, and her parents were divorced. Obviously the two of them had been talking.

Summer fished out another hoop with her finger. "Has Charlie asked you if you want to be his girlfriend? He said he wanted to be your boyfriend."

Ophelia smiled at the thought of Charlie asking her out like a sixteen-year-old. "He has, yes. And use your spoon, not your fingers."

"What did you say?"

"I said yes. Do you mind?"

Summer stirred her cereal and shook her head. "Charlie said people change."

"That's right. It's sort of sad, but that's what happens."

"Don't you love Daddy anymore?"

Ophelia swallowed hard. "He'll always have a special place in my heart because he gave me you. But no, honey. I don't love him in that way anymore."

"I still love him."

"Of course you do, and he loves you very much."

"Will I still see him?"

"Of course! The same as now, every other weekend and sometimes in the week if you're doing something special."

Summer ate her cereal. "Will you marry Charlie?"

"I don't know yet. We haven't been going out long, and it takes time to decide something like that."

"Will he live here with us?"

"No, I don't think so. I'm afraid we'll have to sell this house. Half of it belongs to Daddy, you see, and he should have that money so he can buy himself a nice house of his own."

"Will Daddy marry someone else?"

Once, the thought had been painful. Now, Ophelia just wanted him to be happy. "Maybe."

"Where will we live if we sell the house?"

"I don't know yet. We'll find somewhere else."

"With Charlie?"

"I'm not sure. He does have a swimming pool."

"Ooh." Summer's eyes lit up. "I could swim every day!"

"You could. Would you like that?"

"Yes!"

Ophelia smiled. "When the house is sold, maybe we'll ask him." Somehow, she thought Charlie wouldn't mind the idea.

Summer finished her cereal, pushed her bowl away, and picked up her orange juice. "Charlie said I was pretty."

"Of course he did. You're gorgeous. Do you like him?"

"Yes. He's funny." She scratched her nose. "He's not my daddy, though."

"No. He'll never be your daddy. He just wants to be your friend."

"Will his other brother be there tonight? The one who writes the Ward Seven books?"

"Matt? Yes, I think so."

Summer's jaw dropped. "Fliss is going to be so jealous!"

"We'll take a couple of your books and ask him to sign them if you like. You can give one to Fliss."

"Yes!" Summer bounced and finished off her orange juice. "Can I go and choose the books now?"

"Go on then." Smiling, Ophelia watched her run off.

She blew out a long sigh of relief. That had gone better than she'd hoped. Maybe she had done it the right way. Summer had grown used to her father not being around, so maybe the notion of a divorce wasn't as shocking as it might have been six months ago.

A fantail hopped onto the railing around the deck, fanning out its tail and jumping about before flying off to the jacaranda tree. Ophelia closed her eyes, enjoying the warmth of the sunshine on her face. She'd been dreading Christmas, but all of a sudden it seemed filled with promise.

She wasn't yet certain what the future held, but she wasn't going to worry about it. It was important that she concentrate on living in the moment, she decided. Tonight, she was seeing Charlie, and although she was certain the situation with Dillon still needed some sorting out, she was confident things would get better. Dillon ran on emotions, reacting instantly to everything, but he wasn't completely unstable, and she suspected that once he'd given it some thought, he wouldn't be so difficult to deal with.

Instead of worrying about the future, she was going to concentrate on creating herself an ideal present.

She rested her hand on her stomach and smiled.

Chapter Thirty-One

"Charlie!"

He shut the car door and smiled at the sight of Summer jumping up and down in the doorway. "Hey," he said with a wave.

"It's Christmas Eve!" She clenched her hands to her mouth, and he laughed.

He opened the passenger door and retrieved a bag from the seat. "I know. I'm so excited."

"Santa's coming! With Rudolph!"

"In seven hours," he said. "I think I'm going to explode."

Summer thought that was hysterically funny. He grinned, shut the door, and walked up the path to her. "How are you, princess?"

"Fine, thank you," she said, suddenly the epitome of politeness. She scratched her head. "What are you wearing?"

He looked down at himself. "It's called a DJ."

"DJ?"

"A dinner jacket. Or a tuxedo."

"You look like James Bond. Except you're wearing glasses. And your hair is too long."

"And scruffy," he agreed. "Do you like it? The suit, I mean."

Summer shrugged. "I think Mummy will."

"Mummy will what?" Ophelia appeared behind her and stared at him. "Holy shit."

"Mummy!"

Ophelia clapped a hand over her mouth. "Sorry." Her eyes had nearly fallen out of her head. "Jesus. Look at you."

"What?" He began to have doubts that he'd done the right thing.

She beckoned him inside and closed the door behind him, then gestured at what she was wearing. It was a pretty, deep blue summer dress that reached to just above her knees and clung to all her curves. "I thought it was smart casual tonight."

"It is. I thought I ought to wear something other than an All Blacks shirt, and this is the only other thing I had in the wardrobe."

"I feel distinctly under-dressed."

"I can go home and change."

"No, no…" She walked up to him and ran his lapels through her fingers. When she looked up at her, her eyes had turned sultry. "No, you look perfectly acceptable."

Summer rolled her eyes. "Told you she'd like it." She wandered off.

Charlie dropped the bag he'd been holding and rested his hands on Ophelia's hips, liking how thin the fabric was. "So I meet with your approval?" he murmured.

"Oh yes." She reached up and touched her lips to his. "Definitely."

It was a demure kiss but it had his heart pounding in seconds. More importantly than that, though, was the fact that she'd kissed him with Summer in the room.

"You've spoken to her?" he whispered.

"Mm. It went very well. She accepts we can be boyfriend and girlfriend."

"Oh, I see." He nuzzled her ear. "Is that before or after we pass notes in English Lit?"

She laughed. "I know. It does sound a bit silly."

"Not at all. I like the idea of being your boyfriend." He kissed behind her ear, and she shivered. "Mm," he said, conscious that her nipples had peaked against his chest. "Do that again."

"Stop snogging," Summer said from beside them. "I want to go to the party."

Charlie moved back reluctantly. "I see you're wearing your princess dress."

"It has a stain on it." Summer pointed it out to him. "I think it's ketchup."

"Looks like it," he agreed. "I guess this came at the right time then." He picked up the bag, took out a present, and handed it to her.

Summer stared at it. "Ooh. Shall I put it under the tree?"

"Normally I'd say yes, but this is a special occasion, so I think you should open it tonight."

The little girl looked up at her mother, who nodded, throwing him a curious look.

Summer tore off the wrapping paper to reveal a pile of shining white fabric. Holding it at the top, she let it unfurl.

It was a long party dress, similar to the one she was wearing but much higher quality. And this one had small red flowers sewn onto the skirt, very similar to Princess Sapphire's. "Sixty-five roses," he pointed out. "So only you can wear it."

Summer's jaw dropped. Her gaze met a speechless Ophelia's before returning to the dress.

Then, to his surprise, Summer burst into tears.

"Okay," he said, "not quite the reaction I was expecting."

"Oh, Charlie." Ophelia's eyes glistened. "It's beautiful." She took it carefully out of Summer's hands and knelt to wrap her other arm around her daughter. "Do you like it?" she whispered, rubbing Summer's back.

Summer buried her face in her mother's neck and nodded.

Ophelia looked up at him and winked. "She's just a bit overcome. She'll be all right in a minute."

"Oh. Okay. Good." He gave a sigh of relief.

Ophelia studied the dress behind Summer's back. "It's absolutely gorgeous. Where did you get it?"

"I had it made. I hope that was okay, me getting her a present. I don't want to step on any toes."

"It's fine, Charlie. You're a lovely man. We don't deserve you."

"Aw." He adjusted his glasses. "It's the least I can do."

It didn't take long for Summer to recover, and within seconds she'd taken off her old dress and put on the new one over her T-shirt and shorts. It was a tiny bit too big, "But that's okay," Ophelia said, "it means she'll be able to wear it for longer. Tonight, we'll put a couple of safety pins in the back. Come on."

*

By five thirty they were in the car, and by six they'd arrived at Brock's apartment on the waterfront. Charlie parked in the underground car park, and they made their way to the elevator.

"Is he in the penthouse?" Ophelia asked suspiciously when they entered the elevator and he punched in a code.

"Yeah. It's pretty impressive."

"Oh dear." Ophelia smoothed down her dress.

"You both look amazing," he reassured her, smiling at Summer, who was admiring herself in the mirrored wall.

"So do you." Ophelia turned to him and placed a hand on his chest. "Thank you."

"What for?"

"Everything. For being you. I'm crazy about you. Do you know that?"

He felt a sudden surge of emotion. "I'm crazy about you too."

"Merry Christmas."

"Merry Christmas." He touched his lips to hers.

The lift pinged and the doors slid open. Charlie took her hand. "Come on. Let's have some fun."

"You're early," Brock said as they walked out.

"It's six o'clock," Charlie protested.

"You're supposed to be fashionably late."

"I'm not fashionably anything," Charlie said.

"Good point." Brock grinned and gave him a manly bear hug, then turned to Ophelia. "Hey, good to see you." Charlie saw his brother's gaze flick to the slight graze on her forehead, but he didn't say anything. "How are you?"

"Good, thank you."

"I'm glad you could come. And Summer! Wow, look at your dress. You look like a princess."

Summer jumped up and down. "Charlie bought it for me."

"It's lovely." Brock gave his brother an approving glance. Then he turned and held out his hand to bring forward the blonde woman who'd been waiting quietly by his side, carrying a small boy on her hip. "This is Erin, and this is Ryan. Erin, this is Charlie, Ophelia, and Summer."

They all made their introductions, and then wandered into the living room, where Summer immediately took charge of Ryan and began to boss him about.

Erin grinned at Ophelia. "That'll keep him occupied. Shall I show you around?"

"Sure." Ophelia gave Charlie a parting smile, and the two women wandered off.

The guys watched them go. Then they looked at each other and gave wry smiles.

"Beer?" Brock asked.

"Please."

Brock gestured at one of the waiters, who brought over an ice-cold bottle, and then the two of them walked out onto the deck overlooking the City of Sails.

"Nice tux," Brock said, amused.

"Don't start."

Brock grinned. "How did last night go?"

"Good. I put the chain up."

"I saw her forehead."

"Yeah." Charlie's smile faded. "Bastard."

"Was she okay?"

"Yeah. In a way it was a good thing, brought things to a head, you know?"

"Do you think he'll make trouble?"

Charlie sipped his beer. "Nah." His gaze met Brock's and he couldn't stop his lips curving up.

Brock raised his eyebrows. "What did you do?"

"Roughed him up a bit."

"Seriously?"

"Nah. I threatened to give him Tetrodotoxin and hand him to medical research."

Brock snorted. "He fell for that?"

"I meant it."

Brock gave him an appraising look, and then nodded. "Yeah. Fair enough."

They turned and sipped their beers as they watched the two girls making their way slowly back through the apartment, talking as they walked.

"They seem to have hit it off," Charlie said.

"Yeah." Brock cleared his throat, and then he slid his hand into the pocket of his jeans. He nudged Charlie and pulled a small velvet-covered box an inch out of his pocket to show him.

"Holy fuck." Charlie stared. "You're going to propose?"

Brock shrugged and slid the box back in. "If I find the right moment. Didn't quite have enough time."

"Do you think she'll say yes?"

Brock's gaze caressed Erin, his lips curving up as she laughed in response to something Ophelia had said. "We'll have to wait and see." His smile suggested he was hopeful of a positive outcome.

He looked back at Charlie. "How about you? Going to pop the question? In English this time?"

"Technically, she's still married, and will be for a while," Charlie reminded him. "Plus it's only been a few weeks. I don't want to scare her off."

"I saw how she looked at you. There's no way she'd say no."

Charlie trusted his brother's compass more than his own, and the notion that Brock thought Ophelia felt that way about him gave him an internal glow, but he just gave a dismissive shrug. "You've been speaking to Erin for a year online, don't forget. Before two weeks ago, Ophelia and I had only discussed muffins."

Brock laughed. "I guess. I think you've caught yourself a fine one there, though."

Charlie watched Ophelia glance over at him and then blush. He smiled. "Yeah, me too."

Brock nudged his arm. "Come on. Seems a shame to leave two such beautiful women alone."

*

Within an hour, most of the guests had turned up, and the party was in full swing. Christmas anthems had several people up dancing, and the waiters weaved through the room constantly refilling trays of food and drink that rapidly emptied.

Ophelia stood by the window, looking down at where the lights from nearby restaurants and clubs glittered on the water. Her heart felt lighter than it had for a long time. Summer was playing a game with the other children in the living room, showing off in her new dress. Charlie had only just left Ophelia's side, having spent the previous hour glued to her as he introduced her to his friends and family.

"Need another drink?"

She turned to find Brock smiling at her.

"Charlie's gone to get me one. This is a great party."

"It seems to be going well."

She glanced around. "I haven't seen Matt yet."

"He's always late. Artistic temperament."

She laughed. "Summer was looking forward to seeing him."

"Oh, he'll be here. He won't pass up the opportunity to brag about his books." Brock grinned.

Ophelia smiled at him. He was very like Charlie in some ways, and totally different to him in others. He was lovely, handsome, responsible, and hardworking, but he didn't make her bell ring the same way his brother did.

She looked across at Charlie, who had been captured on the way back by a relative, some maiden aunt who Brock had felt pressured to invite. To his credit, Charlie was giving the old lady his full attention, but as she watched, she saw his gaze slide over to her and his lips curve up before he returned his gaze to the aunt.

He looked gorgeous in the tux. Unfortunately, he wasn't coming home with her so she wasn't going to have the opportunity to have sex with him while he was wearing it. She made a mental note to ask him to bring it with him next time Summer was staying with Dillon.

"I'm glad he's found you," Brock said. She looked up at him. He was smiling.

"Me too."

"He hasn't found it easy. I must admit at one point I thought he might have seen his days out as a bachelor."

She realized Brock was referring to Charlie's Aspergic tendencies. "I like the way he says what he's thinking. He's transparent, and that appeals to me."

"I can see that."

"I'm pretty crazy about him," she said. "And I think he likes me too."

"Likes you?" Brock chuckled. "Ask him to translate what he told you in Italian."

Ophelia blinked at him, confused. "What?"

"When you went away to the Bay. He told me what he said to you in Italian. Ask him to translate it."

Ophelia thought back to the first time they'd made love on the sofa. He'd started talking in Italian. He'd told her *You make me happy*, and then he'd said a long sentence but had shaken his head when she'd asked what it meant. Why had he told Brock?

"Ask him," Brock murmured as Charlie walked up.

"Sorry. Got waylaid." Charlie gave her the glass of wine and bent to kiss her cheek.

She looked at Brock, who winked at her. She gave a little shake of her head. She'd ask him later, when they were on their own, in case it was embarrassing.

"What are you two talking about?" Charlie asked suspiciously.

"Nothing." Ophelia slipped her arm around him. "Just how lovely you are."

"I sincerely doubt that." He kissed her forehead, touching his lips to the graze there. "But thanks anyway."

Brock wandered off, and Ophelia cuddled up to Charlie and rested her cheek on his chest.

"Thank you for that gorgeous dress you got for Summer," she said.

"I'm glad she liked it."

"It was really thoughtful, Charlie. So special."

"I hope Dillon won't mind when he sees it."

"He'll be okay. I got a text from him earlier." She'd bought herself a new mobile and had texted Dillon to tell him, and he'd sent her a message back. "It just said 'Sorry,' but he always was a man of few words. It's a good sign. And don't worry about the present. He's got Summer a trampoline for Christmas."

"That'll be great for her CF," Charlie said.

"Yeah. She'll love it. She's having a great time."

"So am I." He turned her to face him and kissed her properly, only lifting his head when a cheer sounded from the corner of the room. "It sounds as if Matt's finally arrived," he said. "Come on, I want to show him that for once I've got the prettiest girl in the room."

She laughed and took his hand as he held it out, and let him lead her across the room as the song *All I Want for Christmas is You* rang out through the speakers.

*

Continue the story of the Three Wise Men in Matt and Georgia's story, *A Secret Parcel (Three Wise Men Book 3)*.

Sneak Peek at Chapter One of A Secret Parcel

Even with her eyes closed, and without him saying a word, Georgia knew that the person who'd just walked into her office was Matt King.

She was sitting on the sofa under the window, cross-legged, her hands resting palms up on her knees. Everyone at the office knew not to disturb her when she was meditating, so when she'd first heard the approaching footsteps she'd kept her eyes closed and hoped they'd go away.

Then the footsteps paused, and her nostrils filled with the distinctive smell of his aftershave.

She inhaled, her trained nose separating the notes of myrrh, cardamom, warm amber, and bergamot. In her relaxed state, she observed the way her heart rate increased and heat spread through her at the thought of seeing him again. Hmm, that was interesting. She'd thought she was over her schoolgirl-style crush. Apparently, that wasn't the case.

She kept her cool though, and just said, "Matt King," before opening her eyes.

He was leaning against the doorjamb, hands in the pockets of his jeans. He was a fine figure of a man, she thought, tall without being lanky, slender and yet muscular, with short sexy hair and an irreverent, 'I don't give a shit' air about him that drew the attention of most women he met. Today, he wore a pair of tight jeans and an open-necked blue shirt, with his usual surfer's necklace around his throat. He looked gorgeous, and he smelled even better.

She'd never tell him that, though. Instead, she scowled at him, irritated that he'd interrupted her quiet time. "Go away. I'm busy."

He remained where he was, oblivious to her glare. "How did you know it was me?"

"I would have known it was you from a mile away. You smell like a tart's boudoir."

He grinned. "Boudoir? Been reading the Marquis de Sade, have we?"

That made her laugh. She couldn't stay cross at him for long. "Come in." She shifted into the corner of the sofa to make room for him.

He pushed off the doorjamb and walked in, passing through the golden bars of sunlight that lay across the tiles of the second-floor office. It was a beautiful, early summer day in the Bay of Islands. Through the open window, the sounds of people having lunch at the café down the road filtered through—light conversation, the clatter of cutlery against plates, and the higher ting of spoons stirring lattes in glasses, accompanied by faint jazz music from the shop further down that sold musical instruments, CDs, and second-hand vinyl.

Matt sat next to her, a piece of summer himself with his tanned skin that brought with it images of surfers riding the waves and beach cricket on Christmas Day. "What were you doing?" he asked.

"Meditating. Until you ruined my concentration."

"Meditating?" He gave her an amused, quizzical look.

She turned to face him, still cross-legged. "What's so funny about that?"

"You can be so flaky sometimes."

"Meditation isn't flaky. It's an effective treatment for stress, worry, addiction, and lack of focus. It gives peace of mind and wellbeing. It can even help creativity. You should try it."

"Maybe I will." He sighed. "I could do with some inspiration."

"Oh? Lost your muse?"

"A bit." He glanced out of the window.

She studied him for a moment, admiring his strong profile, his straight nose, the slight stubble on his cheeks and chin. He'd acted the playboy for so long that sometimes she forgot he was a genius.

Matt was the author of *The Toys from Ward Seven*, a series of children's picture books. The books themselves were adored by children across both New Zealand and Australia, but it was the fact that characters from the books had been used to decorate medical equipment for children that had led to an increase in the popularity of the tales. Matt and his two brothers owned the company that produced the equipment, and Georgia ran the Northland office of the charity part of their business, We Three Kings. She helped to make the wishes of sick kids come true, as well as liaising between the charity and the local hospitals.

Matt was a talented artist and a great writer. She didn't like his admission that he'd lost his muse.

"What are you working on at the moment?" she asked. "The Squish the Possum book?" He'd told her about his new character the previous week.

"That's almost done. The Ward Seven books aren't the problem."

"So what is the problem?"

He hesitated, still looking off into the distance, and she felt certain he was about to confide in her. But the moment passed, and he blinked and turned his gaze back to her, his ready smile reappearing. "Nothing. Doesn't matter."

She felt a little hurt that he hadn't told her. "Matt..."

"Those jeans are exceptionally tight." He glanced at her thighs. "Are they spray-painted on?"

She gave him an exasperated look. "What are you doing here, exactly?"

"I missed you."

The previous weekend, it had been his turn to visit Whangarei Hospital dressed as Ward Seven's Dixon the Dog to hand out presents to the sick kids with her. His brother, Brock, had swapped with him at the last minute because he'd wanted to meet a parent he'd been in contact with online for a while.

"Brock and Erin seemed to hit it off," Georgia said. "I'm pretty sure he pulled."

"He did." He blew out a breath. "He's offered to take her to a hotel at the weekend for her birthday. Fucking idiot. She's going to think he's expecting sex."

"I'm sure he'll be hoping for it," she remarked wryly.

"Well, he says he's not, but that's not the point, is it? Even if he was, he doesn't have to be so obvious about it. He should have just bought her chocolates and taken her out to dinner."

She shrugged. "Some women prefer the direct approach. She's been single for a while, according to Brock. Perhaps she's desperate for sex."

Matt raised his eyebrows. "Speaking from experience, are we?"

Oh yes. Georgia hadn't had sex for so long, she was worried it would close up down there the same way a person's pierced ears did if they didn't wear earrings.

"Let's just say I sympathize with her predicament," she said.

His eyes took on a hot, interested look. "The direct approach, huh?"

Since she'd joined the company a year ago, Matt had asked her out approximately once a week, every week, without fail. The last time had been the previous Friday, when he'd suggested she go with him to the party Brock was having on Christmas Eve. She'd said no, but it hadn't been easy. He was so tempting, like a slightly warm chocolate truffle she knew would melt in her mouth.

She had no doubt he knew his way around the bedroom. Over the past year, he'd dated—and dumped—four women. And those were the ones she knew of.

She'd spoken to one of them, Tina, or Taylor, or Trinny, something like that, after bumping into her while shopping in Kerikeri. She'd asked her how Matt was, only to be met with a snort.

"We broke up," Tina, or Taylor, had said.

"Oh. Sorry to hear that." Georgia had managed to hold back the question for about five seconds before it had burst out. "Why?"

Taylor, or Trinny, had shrugged. "This and that. It was never going to be a long term thing. He's too secretive and private. He doesn't let anyone in. To be honest, I'm relieved. The guy's insatiable. I mean, I like sex, but not *every* day." She'd rolled her eyes and walked off.

And you're complaining about that? Georgia had wanted to yell after her. She got all hot under the collar every time she thought about those words.

The guy's insatiable.

Georgia liked sex. And she hadn't had any for a really long time. The notion of dating this guy, this knowing, confident, slightly arrogant, gorgeous man, and letting him do unimaginable things to her as often as he wanted, made her feel slightly faint.

But even though it had been hard sometimes to turn him down, she'd managed to fight the urge to say yes to his requests. He still flirted with her all the time, still asked her out repeatedly, and she flirted back, a little, but she'd managed to keep him at arm's length, and because of it, they'd grown to be good friends.

Now, though, his lips had curved up in such a sexy smile that it took every ounce of willpower she possessed not to let her tongue roll out onto the carpet like a cartoon character's.

He rested his arm along the back of the sofa, not quite touching her, and yet she could feel the heat from his body, smell his glorious aftershave. They flirted a lot, but this was the closest she'd been to him.

She could see small details she'd missed from a distance. The way the sleeves of his shirt stretched across impressive biceps. A small, well-faded scar on his chin, probably caused by falling off a skateboard or playing rugby as a child. The interesting mix of green and brown in his warm, hazel eyes.

In the past, he'd always teased her as if he fully expected her to say no. This time, however, his gaze caressed her lips before returning to her eyes, holding sexy interest. This man really wanted her.

Holy moly.

The direct approach, huh? he'd asked her.

"Don't get any ideas," she warned.

He grinned. "I'm full of ideas when you're around. It's my creative brain."

She gave a long sigh, wishing she could just lean forward and press her lips to his. "Why did you come here today, Matt?"

"I have a proposal."

"Before we've even dated?"

He gave her a wry look. "Not that sort of proposal. A business one. It's the New Zealand Children's Book Awards on Friday. I wondered if you'd like to go with me?"

She stared at him in surprise. "They're in Wellington, aren't they?"

"Yeah."

"Isn't it black tie?"

"Yep."

Suppressing her shock—and more than a little pleasure—that he'd asked her, she raised an eyebrow. "Do you even own a suit?" She'd never seen him in anything but jeans.

He grinned. "It's your chance to see me do my James Bond impression."

She could think of worse ways to spend a Friday night. "You're shortlisted for the Picture Book Award, aren't you?"

"Yeah." He ran a hand through his hair.

"Aw." Warmth spread through her. "You're nervous."

"It's a big award. Of course I'm nervous."

She tipped her head to the side, amused and surprised. "I didn't think you had nerves."

"Of course I have nerves. Charlie's the robot in the family. Although apparently he's asked Ophelia out on a date this evening, so even he seems to be growing emotions."

Georgia knew he was teasing—the King brothers were tight, and only they were allowed to mock each other. She liked Charlie, the scientist of the trio of geniuses, who always looked slightly puzzled and seemed to spend most of his time staring into space, lost in thought as he worked on his next amazing invention.

"Oh," she said with interest, "so he finally got around to asking her out?"

"Yeah. He's taking her to McDonald's."

They both laughed. "He's such a sweetie," Georgia said. "So... both Brock and Charlie are getting into the dating game, eh? Are you going to join their ranks?"

"When you say yes," he retorted.

"I don't want to go on a date with you, Matt."

He pouted. She reached out and flipped his bottom lip with the tip of a finger.

He rolled his eyes. "This isn't a date. It's a business proposal, like I said. I don't want to go alone."

"But why me? You must know a hundred other girls you could have asked."

He shrugged. "I don't want just any old girl. I want you." He met her gaze. He looked completely serious.

"Why? Is this just another ploy to get in my knickers?"

"It wasn't, but tell me I'm in with a chance and I'll make a concerted effort."

"Matt..."

He shifted on the sofa. "I want someone I feel comfortable with. A friend."

"Can't you take Charlie?"

A look of impatience crossed his face. "A female friend."

"Come on, you must have other female friends."

"Not really."

They studied each other for a moment.

"Oh," she said. "I see. Every woman you've ever met is an ex."

He tipped his head from side to side. "Not every woman..."

But she could see she'd gotten it right. When he met a girl he liked, he slept with her, and then he broke up with her. And then, presumably, they refused to talk to him again. So he didn't have any friends who were girls.

"Am I the only woman in the world who's ever said no to you?" she asked curiously.

He didn't say anything, but she could see from his expression that she was right again.

Her heart sank a little. The only reason he wanted her was because he couldn't have her. It was hardly a revelation, but she was surprised at how much it hurt.

Thank God she'd had the sense to say no to him, and she was going to continue to say no. If she slept with him, she had no doubt it would be fantastic. But then he'd dump her, and that would be it. She'd be alone again, and she'd lose his friendship. And that would break her heart.

Newsletter

If you'd like to be informed when my next book is available,
you can sign up for my mailing list on my website,
http://www.serenitywoodsromance.com

About the Author

Serenity Woods lives in the sub-tropical Northland of New Zealand with her wonderful husband and gorgeous teenage son. She writes hot and sultry contemporary romances and would much rather immerse herself in reading or writing romance than do the dusting and ironing, which is why it's not a great idea to pop round if you have any allergies.

Website: http://www.serenitywoodsromance.com
Facebook: http://www.facebook.com/serenitywoodsromance
Twitter: https://twitter.com/Serenity_Woods

Printed in Great Britain
by Amazon

60544702R00129